First Time

His eyes were on her face, his hands on her hair, sliding his fingers through its silken mass. He took her wineglass and set it beside his own on the coffee table while she watched, everything drumming inside. Suddenly they were on their knees before the dancing fire, eyes locked as he cupped her face in his hands, drawing her forward to his mouth. He unzipped her dress and she pushed his sweater up to bare his chest, to stroke him. And she closed her eyes so that she could feel herself swimming in this unbelievable pleasure. . . .

Gillian had known so many men, and now it seemed she had never known a man before. She had known so many nights of lovemaking, and now she felt like a virgin in this man's hands. Never before had she known so wild an ecstasy . . . never before had she been so afraid of her own passion. . . .

Gifts of Love

SIGNET Big Bestsellers

If you wish to order these titles, please see the coupon in the back of this book.

Gifts
of Love

by Charlotte Vale Allen

A SIGNET BOOK

NEW AMERICAN LIBRARY

TIMES MIRROR

SIGNET TRADEMARK REG. U.S. PAT. OFF. AND FOREIGN COUNTRIES
REGISTERED TRADEMARK—MARCA REGISTRADA
HECHO EN CHICAGO, U.S.A.

SIGNET, SIGNET CLASSICS, MENTOR, PLUME AND MERIDIAN BOOKS
are published by The New American Library, Inc.,
1301 Avenue of the Americas, New York, New York 10019

FIRST SIGNET PRINTING, NOVEMBER, 1978

1 2 3 4 5 6 7 8 9

PRINTED IN THE UNITED STATES OF AMERICA

For Jerry Ludington—hats and horns

1.

There were two dreams she had regularly. Actually nightmares. In one she was in the ship's lounge—as she'd been in reality—sitting on a banquette neatly tucked away in a dark corner, sipping a large scotch, watching as people ran through screaming in panic. She sat watching, her legs up on an adjacent chair. Unconcerned. The ship was sinking. She didn't care.

In the other she was on the upper level of the number 73 bus—having gone up there, as always, to smoke—and stood silently screaming, not a sound emerging from her mouth.

She'd sleep through that first dream. Just tell herself, This will only last a moment. Her waking self talking to her sleeping self. Sending messages from here to there, saying, You can sleep through this one. It's all right.

But the second one had her up instantly. The back of her hair wet against her neck, the nightgown clinging, soaked, to her body. Up and putting on the light, reaching unsteadily for her cigarettes. Getting out of

1

bed to walk through the at-last-completed first floor of this house she'd bought. Going back and forth between the rooms. Sometimes hearing Mrs. O'Brian moving about upstairs.

Mrs. O'Brian claimed not to sleep for more than three or four hours a night. Saying, "I used to be a positive champion at sleeping. Could sleep the clock round. Now here I am in bed at ten, up again at three or four. Sometimes as early as two. Wide awake. So I have a cup of tea and a good read. Then nap a bit until it's decent time to be getting up."

Mrs. O'Brian.

When it sometimes seemed too silent up there, Gillian would go quietly up the stairs to stand on the landing, listening, waiting until she heard some indication of life inside the apartment. Then, relieved, go on down again and get on with her work. Mrs. O'Brian was seventy-one and although she didn't look or act elderly, Gillian couldn't help occasionally worrying about her. She was seventy-one, after all.

She had to smile every time she recalled the day Mrs. O'Brian had come around, pointing out the newspaper ad with surprisingly pretty, well-tended hands, asking, "Have you anything against old people? Because I'm weary to a fare-thee-well of looking at apartments, then having the landlords tell me sorry but it's already taken when they find out it's myself I'm wanting it for."

Gillian had said, "Not at all," and showed her up the stairs to the second floor, where Mrs. O'Brian had exclaimed, "Oh, now! Isn't this just too lovely! All so bright. And the floors just magnificent. How much might you be asking?"

She'd planned to ask two hundred and fifty a month—as she had for the third floor—but something told her

Mrs. O'Brian wouldn't be able to afford that much. And she'd liked her. So, on impulse, had dropped her asking price, saying, "One hundred and fifty a month." At which Mrs. O'Brian had turned with a look bordering on amazement, asking, "Are you sure of what you're saying? Is it you who's the landlady?"

"I own the house, yes."

"You're asking far too little."

"P . . . perhaps."

"Mind you"—Mrs. O'Brian had moved into the center of the living room, turning slowly as if mentally placing pieces of furniture here and there—"it's just what I've been looking for. Not that I ever expected to find it. What about a lease?"

"As long as you like," Gillian had said, leaning against the doorframe, watching this meticulously turned-out woman run her hand across the newly refinished mantel of the fireplace.

"I'll take it, of course," Mrs. O'Brian had said, turning to look once more at Gillian. "But I have to tell you I think you're just the slightest bit daft. I could move in at once?"

"Any t . . . t . . . time you like."

"Done, then!" Mrs. O'Brian had come back across the room to shake Gillian's hand and to ask, "Might I sit upon occasion in the garden?"

"Of course. And I've a washer and dryer, a laundry room of sorts in the cellar."

And that was how Mrs. O'Brian had come to be her tenant. Four months earlier. So now, when the dream got her up, had her pacing at two or three in the morning, she was always somehow reassured by the knowledge and movement of Mrs. O'Brian overhead.

Her tenants. Her house.

3

She'd started on the top floor and worked her way down through the house. Knocking down the multitude of partitions that had, over the years, turned the once-gracious nine-room house into a fifteen-room rabbits' warren. Working with the original plan, one by one locating the supporting walls. With a crowbar, a hammer, and, at times, an electric saw. Pulling the shabbily done sheetrock partitions down, away, seeing how the light slowly spread from room to room until the entire floor was sun-filled. Open expanses leading one into the other. Three large, high-ceilinged rooms flowing into one another. The bedroom at the rear, the living room with its fireplace in the middle, the kitchen at the front. And adjoining the bedroom, the bathroom.

The bathrooms had driven her half mad. Four of them, counting the spiderwebbed, foully filthy one in the cellar. She'd started out thinking she'd simply strip them back to the walls, retile, and use the original fixtures. But had seen almost at once how impossible that would be. Upon pulling up the moldering linoleum, she'd discovered ancient leaks had rotted out some of the underflooring. And newer leaks were compounding the damage. So she'd called in a plumber, received what she thought a satisfactory estimate, and set him to work tearing out the fixtures in all four bathrooms. Then, with nothing more than exposed pipes awaiting reconnection to the new fixtures she'd ordered, she'd set to work removing the rotted sections of underflooring, replacing them, laying down a new subfloor. Then started in on the walls and ceilings. Ripping them back all the way to the lathing. Replastered. And had a tiling man come in to do each bathroom, floors and walls. So that they, too, were sunny and gleamed with freshness.

She'd come to know the men who worked at the lumberyard. And after their initial mix-ups—amazing how people all speaking the same language could manage to misunderstand one another so completely—had come to know them by name. And could speak to them more easily, without falling over every word. Going back time and again for lumber, nails, huge sacks of plaster of Paris. Any number of items. Had the dressed lumber cut to size where possible, then delivered—first to the third floor, then to the second, and lastly to the main floor. Another mix-up there, too. Because she'd automatically called the third floor the second, as they did at home. And had to shift all the delivered materials to the third floor herself. Quickly learning to rethink her numbering. Along with all sorts of other new pieces of information. Lumberyard terminology. Two-by-fours, Spackle, and so forth. Still, it all served to keep her very, very busy. And so exhausted at the end of each day she was able to collapse into bed and sleep. Something she'd been unable to do for well over a year. Months when she'd paced out the nights, getting through them as best she could. Selling off the house, most of the furnishings, then living in that tiny flat off the Fulham Road waiting for her visa to come through, waiting until her papers were in order and she could leave, get out, try to put it all behind her.

Except that she couldn't. The dreams came over and over and over. Initially she'd tried returning to sleep afterward. But couldn't. Eventually giving up, giving in. Getting herself some tea, taking a bath, pulling on some work clothes, and then sitting down at the dustcloth-covered escritoire—Mother's, she'd steel herself not to think about it—to note down her list of the continuing expenditures in the small ledger book she kept throughout her year-plus redoing the house. That done, she

5

might write a letter to Uncle Max, telling him of her progress. Or to Michelle. Occasionally to Hugh. Not feeling anything, just staying in touch. Mechanical exercises of good manners.

She'd rented the third-floor apartment to a young, unmarried couple. Genevieve, who called herself Jenny. And Harold, who was nicknamed Sandy, claiming a great feeling of fondness for some comic-strip dog of that name. To Gillian it was all amusing nonsense. But they were reasonably considerate tenants. Frequently entertaining their friends but keeping the noise level bearable. Jenny worked as a window dresser at Hamilton's, downtown, and took painting and drawing classes at the art college three nights a week. She aspired to fashion design. Or perhaps to one day being the head of the window-dressing department. She was small, even slight. With that long, dark straight-hanging hair that so many of the girls seemed to have. But fine features and exceptionally long-fingered hands. And lovely, cascading laughter.

Sandy was very tall, massively built. And he, too, had a wonderfully infectious laugh that bubbled and built and spilled like music. She liked to hear the two of them laughing upstairs, liked to see Jenny—always dressed in some fairly outrageous outfit—come skipping down the stairs on her way to work in the mornings.

She'd only just finished her own flat—apartment, she kept telling herself to stop calling them flats—the month before. The smell of newness still clung. The varnish on the sanded and refinished floors. The fresh paint on the newly plastered walls and moldings. And with the rear bedroom windows open, garden scents from the minimal planting she'd done. With plans for next summer to lay down a proper patio, acquire some garden furniture, put in beds of flowers and a small vegetable patch off to the side there. A compost heap she'd started with her preliminary weeding, clipping.

She loved the garden. With its four huge old trees and the expanse of grass. A very English garden, really. It so reminded her of home. Nicely so. Not like so much else that seemed to stab at her. Needles piercing her chest and arms, her throat; a clamp applied to her lungs, her heart. But certain things were quite comforting. Her cache of Twinings. English Breakfast, Earl Grey, and orange pekoe. Twelve half-pound tins that should last years before she'd have to begin buying replacements from the imported-foods department downtown at Hamilton's. The old teapot she'd carried along in her hand luggage, wrapped in three linen tea cloths. Idiotic, some of the things she'd chosen to bring; items that comforted, reminded, yet mercifully revived no particularly painful recollections.

Mother's watercolor. The one she'd done in Sussex before she'd married and come up to London. Of the garden at the back of the old house, a ribbon strip of the river at the edge. A bit too architectural. But lovely, a lightly moody piece. Very unlike those last, later works. When she'd found "the rhythm," as she'd called it, and produced large, vibrantly colored canvases.

Megan's little crayon drawing. Done at age five. Of a funny, smiling, female creature with fanglike teeth and tiny, knobby leg and foot attachments, no hands. A big purple dress.

The escritoire. One or two other small pieces. She'd sold all the rest. To a flock of greedily fawning antiques dealers who'd descended on the house with all the avidity and glinting-eyed avarice of vultures. Sold the lot. And used the bulk of the money to buy this once-decrepit house just to the north of Remington Park. On Pleasant Avenue. The name irked her. Such a silly, pretentious name for a street. Certainly it was pleasant. It was just such a witless name.

In any case, Pleasant Avenue was where she now resided. As a landlady, at the age of twenty-nine. To an unmarried couple. And an elderly Irishwoman. A young man of twenty-seven, a girl certainly no more than twenty. And Mrs. O'Brian. With her exquisite hands and long, carefully manicured fingernails. A very much uplifted pair of breasts on a narrow, quite tall body.

And now that the house was finally finished, with little beyond the garden left for her to do—being far too late in the year to attempt any further work out there—she was going to have to do something about all the suddenly empty hours. Because if she remained indoors, puttering around, attempting to kill time, she'd sooner or later find herself sinking back into that dreadfully apathetic, lethargic state it had taken her close to a year to climb out of. It frightened her just to think of it. Better to keep on the move, active. And since her previous credits would mean all too little here and she hadn't any contacts, she'd have to hire herself out as a junior and work her way up once again.

The thought of job interviews frightened her. She became hopelessly thick-tongued, inarticulate, unable to give the chatty, bright sort of interviews expected. But sat instead doggedly pointing out the projects she'd seen through to completion, explaining, "That was a small job. A shoe shop in Huddersfield. And that a school in Twickenham. Lady Addington did primarily schools, you see."

Lady Addington.

With her inherited title—she'd done an incredible

8

amount of backstage legal work to acquire it—and the affectation of her malacca cane, and her ten-years-younger lover. Lady Nora, who dropped parcels of work on her four assistants, the thirteen draftsmen, the two frazzled and overworked secretaries. Lady Nora, who doled out the jobs, then made aristocratic appearances upon completion of the jobs, graciously accepting the accolades and credit for work almost always done by others. She hadn't done an original design in twelve years at the time she'd taken Gillian on. And in the course of the three years Gillian spent with her in the offices on Oxford Street, Lady Nora had done nothing more than scatter ashes from the end of her long cigarette holder and "Yes, yes, yes" all over working drawings, models, and whiteprints. Gillian, Michelle, James, and Edward had done it all. Schools and more schools. An occasional shoe shop or boutique. But mainly schools.

At the end, she'd been at work on one of the schools. And had had to stop. She'd telephoned Lady Nora at her Mayfair flat to say, "I'm sorry. I thought I could but I can't keep on with it. Michelle and Edward will see it through to completion." And Lady Nora, in one of those surprising emotional responses she displayed every so often, had said—not without considerable passion—"Get away, Gillie! Get clear away. And don't look back. Ludicrous to tell you to forget it. But get yourself away. I'll help in any way I'm able."

And she had. She'd used her considerable influence in order that Gillian might obtain her working visa, emigration papers. Then she'd been there at the boat train with an armload of freesias and several architectural journals, saying, "I shall expect to see your work in here," tapping the cover of the American Institute of Architects' yearbook. Smiling, showing her large teeth. "Do take good care. And God bless, Gillie." Then, astonishingly, atypically, had burst into tears, thrown an arm around Gillian's neck, and kissed her before hurrying off home to seek comfort and consolation from her thirty-five-year-old lover. Amazing Lady Nora. Arrogant, exceedingly self-centered, yet possessed of surprising passion and kindness.

But here, would they know Lady Nora? It seemed highly doubtful. Yet the credits were good. And she could no longer occupy herself putting finishing touches to the house. It was finished. Done. Complete. With tenants. She'd have to arrange her portfolio, her résumé, and begin making job applications.

She listened, hearing Mrs. O'Brian above. Six-forty-six. A decent enough hour to be up and about. On impulse—suddenly frightened of being alone, telling herself, Just for a bit—she went upstairs to knock at Mrs. O'Brian's door and invite her down to breakfast.

"I've been wanting to try my hand at crepes. I thought perhaps you might risk sampling them."

Mrs. O'Brian, in a good-looking robe and slippers, very wide awake, smiling. "Lovely," she said. "Just get my smokes and I'm right with you." White hair and startling green eyes. Someone who, once upon a time, had been young and very, very pretty. Widowed now. With five children in as many countries. None of them within touching distance. "They don't need me fussing over them," she'd told Gillian that first week when she'd been moving in. "And I always did want to see America. I've been here nine years now. Never going back and that's a fact. Too bloody cold over there. In every way. Cold. People here might not have any great interest in how

10

you actually are, but at least they smile and ask how are you."

Perhaps, Gillian thought, readying the crepe pan, I like you because you have the wits not to ask questions. As to who I am or what it is I'm doing playing at being a landlady or why every so often I feel I will go quite, quite mad if I stay alone here one minute more.

I like you because behind the soft, aged quality of your face is someone intelligent, immediate, and oddly diplomatic. I like you.

"Do you fancy apricots?" she asked Mrs. O'Brian.

"Oh, indeed."

Gillian laughed. Mrs. O'Brian busied herself setting the table. Gillian watched her for a moment, then returned her attention to the stove.

She went at it slowly, arranging items in the order of their importance in her portfolio, sitting for quite some time looking over her résumé. The one she'd presented Lady Nora at the time of her first interview. Lady Nora hadn't even looked at it. All that needed doing now was the addition at the bottom of Lady Nora, the dates of her employment, and it would be current. But how would she explain if they asked about the gap of close to three years? What would she say if they were to ask what she'd done since leaving Lady Nora's employ?

It alarmed her to an unreasonable degree. And so she sat for a considerable length of time over a third, then a fourth cup of tea, staring into space trying to think of what she would say. Certainly they'd ask. Tell the truth? She couldn't. If she so much as thought about it in the course of an interview, she'd go speechless, mute, unable to think rationally, let along speak. No. She'd have to think of something else.

Charlotte Vale Allen

You'll simply say you were selling the London house,
working at getting your papers. Then you were settling
in here. It's fair. It's the truth. To a degree.

She lit another cigarette—still finding the taste of the
tobacco strange, wishing she had a pack of
Player's—noticing a tremor in her hands. Wishing none
of it was necessary, that she needn't go through interviews, meetings with strangers who'd ask any number of
questions she might falter in answering. Needing to
work. Needing the additional income the work would
bring. The income from the tenants taking care of the
better part of the mortgage. But there was very little left
in her account at Barclay's now. And Michelle had to be
getting put off making the transfers. She'd have to clear
out the balance, deposit it in her account here, sever
that last, tenuous connection. She'd ask Michelle next
time she wrote.

Get on with it! she told herself. It'll do you no good
sitting here fretting over questions that might be asked.
You'll simply have to answer as best you can and stop
anticipating they'll ask you the worst conceivable questions.

Getting up, carrying her cup of tea and cigarette out
to the garden, walking through the still-wet grass wishing she could simply stay here in the garden or safely inside her apartment without ever having to go outside,
without ever having to answer to strangers. But that
really would be mad. Dangerous. She might end up one
of those batty old women with dozens of cats and di-
sheveled hair, mad eyes; women writing strange, dis-
torted letters to their MP's or the local newspapers.
Demanding antivivisection laws and cat shelters. All
sorts of irrational acts. Their focus turned entirely to the
cats. Spending their few-pence income on cat food and

12

gravel for the litter boxes. Old Miss Westcott had been one of those. Living in one of the council flats—the older ones with the treacherous outdoor stairways—with all those cats. Mother had visited her regularly, giving her a pound here and there, brought her fresh vegetables from the greengrocer, a packet of Starbursts.

Mother. Hanging away her mink, getting down the cloth coat. Saying, "She minds the coat, thinks it's cat fur." Laughing. "I suspect it may be. Be a little charitable, darling. Don't judge. She hasn't anyone."

Later, taking Megan there, too. They'd had a dreadful argument about it. Not wanting Megan to go there. Thinking she might somehow be contaminated.

"By what, for God's sake!" Mother had demanded, very angry. Unusually angry. "There's no sin to teaching a child a bit of kindness. And what on earth do you suspect she's going to come away with—a fondness for cats or sad elderly women? It's the most that'll happen to her, you know. One day it might be me, Gillian. Am I to interpret all this as meaning you'll not come to visit me when I'm old and a bit mad, giving all my affectionate attention to a dozen scruffy cats? I don't understand this in you. What is there about Miss Westcott, of all people, to frighten you? Perhaps you'd care to explain it to me. The rest I understand. You know that I do. I understand how terribly difficult it is for you, Gillian. But you haven't any perspective. And you simply must acquire some!"

Is it penance? she wondered now. Is Mrs. O'Brian my way of doing small penance for Mother, Megan? I don't know. I was so young. I didn't know then. Now I'm no longer all that young. And I suppose I do know. I wonder if she's dead by now, Miss Westcott. If she's gone, what happened to the cats?

Megan saying, "She's got ever such a pretty orange tabby. I'd so love an orange tabby."

She dropped the cup. It fell soundlessly onto the grass. The tea gone. Tea leaves clinging to the bottom in a starlike pattern. She bent to retrieve it and returned indoors. I should've got you the bloody cat. I'm sorry. God, so sorry! No, no, no. Putting the teacup in the sink, she held her cigarette under the cold water, then dropped it into the trash. I must redo this damned résumé and get on with it.

Responding to advertisements in the back of a recent architectural journal. Six at one go. She was on her way out to mail the letters when she met Jenny coming in.

Jenny always looked so fresh. First thing in the morning or late in the evening, she looked as if she'd just emerged from the depths of a most refreshing sleep. Bright-eyed, enthusiastic. She even looked cheerful carrying her trash out to the bins.

"Hi!" she said, dropping her front-door key into her pocket, holding a large bag of groceries with one arm. "How's it going?"

"Oh, fine. Very well. Thank you."

"Listen," she said. "I was talking to Sandy this morning and we thought maybe you'd like to come for dinner. Would you like that?"

Gillian flushed. Felt the heat rising into her face and thought, How bloody stupid I am! No grace whatsoever. A giant, inept clod.

"You're very sweet," she said, taking her time with the words. She hated seeing what happened to people's eyes when she started that bloody stammering and had to stand there in front of them with her mouth open, trying frantically to push the words out.

14

"I *know* I'm sweet." Jenny laughed. "But d'you want to come for dinner?"

"That would be very nice."

"Okay. Seven-thirty?"

"Tonight?"

"Right."

"I didn't realize you meant this evening. . . ."

"Oh." Jenny's face dropped with incipient disappointment. "No good tonight?"

You're getting involved with these people, she warned herself. First Mrs. O'Brian, now these two. This wasn't the way it was supposed to be. You were to maintain a polite, friendly distance. It's not happening. But I hate staying alone night after night. Feeling so alone it's in my mouth, my ears, my eyes. It can't do any harm having dinner with them. It'll be pleasant. They're so young.

"Yes, all right. Thank you very much."

"Okay." Jenny brightened again and moved toward the stairs. "We'll see you later."

"Yes."

Jenny stood on the bottom stair watching Gillian go out the door. She just couldn't get over it. The same every single time. Thinking someone who looked like that and could smile the way she sometimes did, thinking someone like Gillian would be so easy, so friendly. But if you said something to her—something not even important—she'd get all red in the face and start to stutter. So that every time she talked to Gillian she felt her own self getting all tight inside, hoping Gillian would be able to say what she wanted without looking so miserable, stumbling all over her words.

It really bugged Sandy, she thought, continuing on up the stairs. She couldn't figure that out. That first time they'd come to look at the apartment and Gillian had gone back downstairs so they could look around, take their time, Sandy—the minute Gillian was gone—had said, "Do you *believe* that?"

"What?" Jenny had asked, looking out each of the windows in turn.

"*Her*. When she opened the door down there I nearly fell over just looking at her. I mean she looks like a *Vogue* model or something. And then, when we got to talking and I asked her was she Mrs. Blake of Miss Blake and she got so red and started that stuttering business. 'J . . . j . . . just c . . . call me . . . Gillian. Soft G. L. . . . l . . . like Jill."

"Don't make fun of her!" Jenny had snapped. "That's *not* funny! She can't *help* it!"

"I'm not!" He'd defended himself. "It's just . . . I don't know. Spooky, kind of. I mean, she wasn't stuttering before."

"She's just shy, Sandy. Sometimes I think you're a real prick."

"Why're *you* getting so mad?"

"Because. You think you're being funny but you're mean. You do that, you know. Thinking you're so funny. But it's just mean."

"Hey! Take it easy! I wasn't doing a number on her. I mean, Jesus! I won't mind one little bit giving her the rent check. Just so I can look at her. Too bad she's got kind of thick ankles. Otherwise, boy!" He'd shaken his head and let the matter drop. And they'd taken the apartment. Watching him sign the lease, she wasn't so sure it was such a good idea after all. They'd known each other only a couple of months. But it turned out to be not so bad.

And every time they encountered Gillian she smiled and asked how they were getting on, was there anything they needed. But as soon as Jenny tried to be a little friendly or thought about maybe saying, Come on up for coffee tonight, it was like Gillian could feel what was coming and hurried away before Jenny had a chance to say anything.

She stopped on the second-floor landing to shift the groceries to her left arm, looking at Mrs. O'Brian's door. Jenny liked her. Mrs. O'Brian reminded her of her gran. Her mother's mother. Died when Jenny was almost seventeen. And thought about Gran every single time she saw Mrs. O'Brian. Maybe Sandy wouldn't be too bugged if she asked Mrs. O'Brian to come tonight, too.

She could never figure out what Mrs. O'Brian did all the time. She'd get all dressed up and go out a couple of times a week. And the rest of the time you'd never even know she was in there. Unless you pressed your ear right up against the door—Jenny'd done that one time, feeling supersneaky—you couldn't even hear the TV going. And her telephone almost never rang. What do old folks do with themselves all day long? she wondered.

Better hurry, she thought, letting herself into the apartment. Set the bag down, then raced back down the stairs to knock at Mrs. O'Brian's door. And wait, feeling kind of high, hearing footsteps inside the apartment; the door opening.

She looked, Jenny thought, like a movie. Or something. One of those English movies where the lady of the manor always looked so important and dignified, all duded up in cashmere sweaters and pearls. And here was Mrs. O'Brian with what looked like a real cashmere sweater and real honest-to-God pearls.

"Hi." Jenny smiled, feeling like a little kid. Old folks always made her feel that way. "I thought if you haven't already started cooking or anything you'd maybe like to

17

come up and have dinner with me and Sandy. Gillian's coming."

"Well, now." Mrs. O'Brian smiled, showing what looked like too-perfect teeth. Jenny wondered if they could be real. "Aren't you dear." She laughed. And for just a second Jenny thought maybe she was a little on the nutty side. But then Mrs. O'Brian explained, "My second meal out today. I had lovely crepes with Gillian for breakfast this morning. Lovely, they were. I'll come, of course. If."

"If?"

"If you'll allow me to bring along the dessert. I've been baking this afternoon."

"Oh, sure! Okay. About seven-thirty, okay?"

"Just fine. That'll give me time enough to put on the finishing touches."

"Good. See you later."

Mrs. O'Brian returned inside and Jenny ran back upstairs feeling very good now. It was starting to feel like a family dinner. Or a celebration or something.

Well, well, well, Mrs. O'Brian thought, setting out the ingredients for her favorite chocolate butter icing. Isn't this working out wonderfully well? That one downstairs. And the two upstairs. She'd had a feeling when she'd first come round that afternoon to have a look at the place. Something about the one downstairs. Gillian. Clever girl to have done the work all on her own. And the lovely face on her. But such a sad, silent creature. Not, she'd initially thought, the sort you'd sit with in front of the fire for a cozy chat. Yet that's just what they'd done that morning. So surprising, people. It shows, she thought, you just can't go about passing judgment. Prove yourself wrong every time out.

18

Now, take Gillian. Wouldn't you think a lovely-looking girl like that would have them coming round all hours of the day and night? But no. Never a soul knocking at the door, the telephone never ringing from one month to the next. Occasionally an air letter from overseas on the downstairs table, a few bills, and nothing more.

Of course there was that sad business of the stammering. Such a pity. Still, she didn't do it all the time. Could talk quite effortlessly at times. She'd been so very pleasant this morning. And it was a delight simply looking at her.

She smiled to herself thinking about that matter of the rent. Of course the apartment was worth far more than Gillian had asked. It was all so obvious she'd dropped her asking price. What a strange, generous girl. And those two children abovestairs now, with dinner. Well, fair enough, then. Next week she'd do up dinner for the three. Get a lovely big roasting chicken, do her chestnut stuffing. That's it. With roast spuds and gravy, the lot.

She took a sip of her sherry, smiling again. Thinking, Isn't this grand? A proper little family in the making. She did like the idea of that. Particularly after that frightful place in Wellington Road. With the heat and hot water off half the winter so she'd frozen near to death and had had to spend hours at the cinema or shopping the stores just to get a little bit of warmth.

This place. So good to see all the old bits and pieces again. Room enough for the furniture she'd been storing for so long. Mam's old rocker and the Queen Anne chairs, the good Persian carpet from Father's study. I'll not be moving from here, she thought, running her fingers down the polished arm of what had once been Da's seat at the head of the table. Seeing her child self down at the foot, playing at being Mam. Seeing and feeling the way she'd started when he'd come into the dining room, bellowing. He'd frightened her half to death.

No, she'd not be moving. It was good to be settled at last, have a bit of warmth.

Gillian paced back and forth in the living room, her arms wrapped around herself, thinking she should've refused the invitation. Thank you, but no, thank you very much. So hopeless in social situations. Being expected to make cozy conversation when she simply couldn't, hadn't ever been able to chatter effortlessly the way other girls could, the way Mother and Megan could. With strangers. Anyone.

And Brooke with his face very close to hers, saying, "Come sit with me, Gillie. We'll talk." Drawing her down by his side, making her feel as no one else ever had. So that she'd suddenly started talking and had gone on and on, saying such a lot of silly-sounding things he hadn't seemed to think in the least silly. Perhaps because he'd wanted something else and had thought the simplest way to get to that was by encouraging her to prattle on about her schoolgirl ideas. But he'd seemed so kind, so very interested. Where did you go, Brooke?

Year in, year out, wondering where he'd gone, why he'd gone, or if he'd gone anywhere at all. Had it been real or simply some heartless game? No point to this. She'd never know. Unless ... No.

Dinner. She looked out through the bedroom window, having wandered out of the living room in her preoccupied state. The last of the mums were in bloom. Perhaps ... She found the shears and went out to clip a dozen of the best blooms, wrapping them in wet newspaper. They might like the flowers.

2.

"An architect? I didn't know you were an architect." Jenny looked awed.

"Oh, yes. My mother was as well." Gillian laughed. "I come from a long line of architects, actually. Mother's brother Max. And my grandfather. Passed down the family passion for the beautification of institutions rather than the family jewels, heirlooms. That sort of thing."

"Now, isn't that fascinating," said Mrs. O'Brian. "And what sort of buildings did you do?" She wondered why she'd used the past tense. Yet it seemed somehow appropriate. Everything about Gillian seemed to be of the past. Which was all wrong for someone her age. Some sort of mystery here.

"Schools." Gillian smiled. "Bloody schools. An odd shoe shop or boutique. But mainly schools. Lady Nora—I was with her for three years before coming here—made herself a comfortable reputation doing schools. Of course *she* didn't do them. We did. Michelle, Edward, James. And me."

"Didn't you like it?" Jenny asked, refilling the wineglasses while Sandy dropped another piece of wood on the fire, then sat down to continue staring at Gillian as he'd done all evening.

"Oh, I did really. It's just that after a time I began to fancy doing something different. Something with a bit of a challenge to it. There's really only so much you can do with a school. Well, no. That isn't strictly true. What I mean is there was only so much they'd *allow* us to do. None of them was really right for the children. Still . . ." She shrugged her shoulders as if to say, It was out of my hands, you see.

"What about your mother?" Sandy asked, settling himself more comfortably, picking up his wineglass. "What kind of buildings did she do?"

"Oh, Mother did several office blocks. One really lovely place. A nursing home, actually. But very inspired. That was very early on, though. Soon after she and Father were married, she had to give it up. He was in the Diplomatic Service, you see. And was posted to the West Indies. Naturally, there wasn't any sort of work for her to do there. So she took up painting in earnest. Watercolors. Later on, she switched over to oils."

"Were you born in the West Indies?" Mrs. O'Brian asked interestedly, wondering why Sandy was staring at Gillian that way. It was really very rude of him.

Why am I doing such a lot of talking? Gillian asked herself. The wine. I'm drinking too much. Drink more slowly.

"No, in London. But I grew up in Antigua. Father was originally to be there for four years. Trying to help them sort out the sugarcane problem. He was an economist, you see."

"Wow!" Jenny said. "I'd *love* to go to the West Indies. How old were you when you left?"

"Almost twelve."

"Do you remember it?"

"No, not really." That was a lie. Why was she lying? "No, actually I do. I went back to visit when I was sixteen. I'd thought I might prefer living there with him. They were divorced. And I'd returned to England with Mother. But it didn't work out with him. He'd remarried, stayed on the island. It really wasn't the way I'd thought it would be." Brooke had been there. She'd gone home to England with his promises echoing in her ears. "He's still there," she said. Thinking, Why am I going on and on? Why don't I stop? "I have two half sisters. He married an Antiguan woman. They live in quite a beautiful place. Really very beautiful. Near English Harbour. He keeps a boat at Nelson's Dockyard." She laughed again. "I suppose that sounds funny. But he does keep his boat there."

"I've been to Bermuda," Sandy said, finally looking first at Jenny and then at Mrs. O'Brian.

"You never told me that," Jenny said. "When?"

"My mom and dad took me when I was about six or seven. I forget. But it was great."

"You children go on talking," Mrs. O'Brian said. "It's bedtime for me, I'm afraid. Old bones." She got up, reaching for her handbag. "You'll all come to me for dinner Wednesday next. All right?"

"Sure," Jenny said eagerly. "I'll bring something. What should I bring?"

"Why not do another salad?" Mrs. O'Brian suggested. "It was first-rate."

"Shall I bring something?" Gillian asked, looking a

23

little stunned, so that Mrs. O'Brian thought, You've had a drop too much of the drink.

"You just bring yourself," she answered Gillian.

Gillian looked at Jenny and Sandy, suddenly alarmed at the prospect of remaining here alone with them. She'd drink more wine, say too much. So she, too, got up, saying, "I think I'll just go along now. Thank you so much for a lovely evening."

"Did you notice that?" Sandy said.

"Notice what?"

"Didn't you notice how she didn't stutter one bit after the second glass of wine? Not once. She even laughed, for chrissake!"

"You know you make her sound like a retard or something! So she didn't stutter and she laughed. What's the big deal? And how come you sat there the whole time gaping at her that way? Man, it was so embarrassing!"

"I think you misunderstand me on purpose," he said angrily. "I'm interested, that's all. It's *interesting*. A couple of glasses of wine and she really unbent. *That's all*. What the hell's the matter with you?"

"What d'you mean what's the matter with me? What's the matter with *you*? You were so *rude*! Sitting there staring at her like she was some kind of freak or something."

"What're you, her mother or something? What's the big deal if I looked at her?"

"You weren't looking, you were *staring*. I'm not her mother. But I like her. And all you ever seem to do is talk down about her. Making her sound . . . I don't know. Like she's some half-wit or something. And I don't like it. I mean, I'd like to see *you* do over a whole

24

house all by yourself. I'd like to see *you* design a school or something. You're really something!"

"*I'm* really something? *You're* really something! Let's just drop the whole thing, okay? I'm not in the mood to argue. I'm not an architect or a carpenter, so making that kind of half-assed comparison's really idiotic. I'm not in competition with her."

Oh, yes, you are! she thought. But didn't say it because she wanted to think about that a whole lot more.

"Oh, beautiful!" he said. "Now you're going to give me the silent treatment."

"I was just thinking."

"Yeah, I can tell."

She looked up at him, her eyes flashing. Danger signals. He really wasn't in the mood for hassling.

"Okay," he said, backing down. "Okay, okay! Leave the goddamned dishes! Come on to bed."

"It'll only take me a minute to get the machine going. I don't want to have to get up to them in the morning."

"Okay," he said impatiently. "I'm going to bed."

"I'll be in in a couple of minutes."

He went out and she finished loading the dishwasher. Trying to understand what was coming down. All of a sudden, there was too much bad air circulating between them.

And when she climbed into bed and he immediately threw himself on top of her, she felt really scared. Coming down too fast off such a nice high. She was really starting to hate the way Sandy would come on all animal. Lately he'd been doing it a lot. Throwing her around like something he'd bought on a sale counter and didn't have all that much use for. Except as a convenience. Which was too bad. Because she was back

25

to thinking maybe the whole idea of taking the apartment together had been a really rotten one.

He could get to her, though. It was happening now. And it brought her down even harder. Because she wasn't in the mood. Hadn't been in the mood. He was presenting her with the mood. Getting her down, telling her what he wanted—hating the way his voice sounded when he hissed out his wants, not-wants—pulling her down on his mouth. Maybe it was because she was still so bugged with him that the whole thing turned so explosively hot all of a sudden. Whatever the reason, she stopped thinking and got into it.

As they arrived at the second floor Mrs. O'Brian said, "Don't go rushing off! Come have a cup of coffee with me."

She looked at the woman's face, her green eyes, expecting to see something there. She had no idea what. There wasn't anything out of the ordinary there. Simply a smiling invitation. Extending from her mouth to her eyes. Green like the sun on emeralds.

"Thank you," she said. And Mrs. O'Brian opened the door.

Gillian walked into the living room, admiring the beautifully preserved, gleaming antiques.

"You do have some truly beautiful pieces, Mrs. O'Brian. The Queen Anne chairs. It's . . . lovely."

"Pat," Mrs. O'Brian said. "The name's Pat. Makes me feel older than God being called Mrs. O'Brian." Makes me feel strange to myself, she added silently.

"Pat," Gillian repeated inaudibly, looking at the rug. Silk threads. A very fine, very valuable rug. Why had she thought Mrs. O'Brian hadn't any money? Obviously she had money. She sat down wondering why she felt invisible. She was here, invited in, yet felt she oughtn't to be here. And couldn't understand why she felt so distant, removed. Yet when Pat returned, setting down a tray bearing a coffeepot, cups, the woman seemed suddenly very familiar to her. As if she was remembering all sorts of things that hadn't ever happened, shared memories they'd never shared. It was odd. But it was Pat whose footsteps were such a source of comfort in the dark early-morning hours. And perhaps that accounted for the sense of familiarity.

Settled in the chair opposite with her cup of coffee, Pat said, "Your mother, is she living still in London?"

Gillian shook her head, her eyes on the coffeepot, then on the cup in her hand. "She w . . . was . . . she died."

"Oh, I am sorry," Pat said, studying Gillian's expression, which had gone childlike and grief-filled.

"Thank you." She swallowed the clot of emotion in her throat and sipped at the coffee.

"I have a daughter your age," Pat said.

"Oh?" Gillian looked over at her.

"A husband, three children, and a practice in Wales. She's a physician."

"Isn't that fine. You must be very proud of her."

"Oh, indeed. I am."

"Where are the others?" Gillian asked, grateful for the change of subject.

"Another daughter, my eldest, is married to a solicitor. They live in Manchester. My one boy's an engineer, working in the Middle East. The next lad's a pharmacist. Moved to Vancouver, married a lovely girl there. They have two kiddies. And the last lad's a veterinarian. In Scotland. Aberdeen."

"They sound wonderful. Do you visit them often?"

"From time to time." Pat toyed with the spoon in the sugar bowl.

A silence.

Gillian drank some more of the coffee, thinking about Wales. They'd driven to Aberystwyth. Not for any reason. Except that Mother loved to drive, so enjoyed being in control of the Rover. And Megan had simply loved going places. Anywhere. Excitedly commenting on everything from the narrowness of the roads to the sight of sheep grazing in a fogged-over field. She could close her eyes now and see Megan kneeling on the backseat, her hands pressed flat against the window. And Mother. The cat-fur mink draped around her shoulders, leather driving gloves—another gift from Hugh—her profile and the fall of her hair so perfect, so perfectly beautiful.

Pat sat watching her, seeing her eyes go distant. Was it the third or fourth time Pat had seen this happen? What do you see? she wondered. Are there pictures you see again and again? Like mine. A sharply defined image of Peter Flannigan. The doctor. She'd been so young. In retrospect, she could see with alarming clarity how very young she'd been. And the shape and feel of his mouth, the twisting pleasure of that kiss. Whispering into her ear, saying words that made her feel she might melt with the heat and embarrassment. The temptation itching in the palms of her hands, in her thighs. But no. And finally he'd gone on his way. Looking bewildered, disappointed.

Gillian looked up, smiled, and sat down her empty cup, saying, "I'll run along now. Thank you for the coffee."

"My pleasure, dear," Pat said, looking distant all at once. Almost melancholy. "I'll see you out."

Gifts of Love

She decided to have another glass of wine. Just to perpetuate the pleasant feeling that had begun upstairs with dinner. Poured herself a glass, then went into the bedroom to undress and stand naked in front of the mirror, holding the wineglass, looking at herself critically. Hating her legs. Thinking of Jenny's beautiful, slender legs. Pat's trim ankles. Looking at her own legs and ankles. Wrong altogether. Breasts so silly-looking. All of her. Bloody silly-looking. Then she laughed, taking another swallow of the wine before turning away. Going to the bathroom to run a bath, absentmindedly dropping in a bath cube—the last of the supply she'd brought with her—watching it dissolve under the flow of water, thinking about Brooke, about how she'd felt.

Sitting on the sand at the far end of Half Moon Bay. Not another soul on the entire beach. The water so beautiful. Sun glints, diamonds. The sun hot, hot. And Brooke sitting beside her, his arms folded around his knees, looking at the water, then at her, then back at the water. Talking. She'd listened, not really hearing, studying the hair on his chest, on his legs; the Bermuda shorts, his arms. His face. He'd never seemed old to her. Her brain had told her he was. He'd admitted to being forty-four. Yet her feelings couldn't accept that vast difference in their ages. Not even seeing the gray mixed into his hair or the crinkles around his eyes. His voice had sounded young, rich and fluid and young. And his interest, his enthusiasm.

She sat down in the hot water realizing she'd forgotten to pin up her hair. She'd have to dry it or sleep with a wet head. Too pleasantly drowsy to think of drying it. She'd sleep with it wet.

All those children Mrs. O'Brian—Pat—had. Five of them. It sounded not quite right somehow, hearing her speak of them. Something missing there. Visiting them from time to time. And no photographs. Not anywhere. Closing her eyes, letting herself drift, wondering about that. Thinking about the album, the box of photographs. Hidden away at the rear of the shelf in the bedroom closet. They were there. People in a book, a box. Drifting away. And awakened with a start sometime later, realizing the water had gone cold. And realizing, too, as she let out the water and wrapped herself in a towel, she'd had a pleasant evening. Really very pleasant. Except for the way Sandy had stared at her. Had he not stopped when he had, something might have been said. But he'd stopped. She was overreacting. Thinking she ought to be accustomed by now to people, men, staring. But she'd never become accustomed to it.

She switched off the bedside light wondering if she'd get any response to her letters. A shooting spark of apprehension at the thought that she might.

Monday, in the late afternoon, she was about to change, clean up a bit before starting her dinner, when there was a knock at the door. Tucking her shirt in at the back of her jeans, she went to open the door.

"Your check," Sandy said, waving the paper in the air. Smiling. So huge he seemed to fill the entire doorway.

"Oh, yes," she said, accepting it from him. "If you'll wait just a moment, I'll write you out a receipt." Leaving the door wide open, she crossed over to the escritoire to get the receipt book. She started to write the date and heard the door close quietly, the lock click. And was afraid. For no special reason. Just afraid. She kept writing, trying to hurry. Get it done, get him out. But her hand didn't want to seem to work properly. His presence in the apartment was ominous. He was being too quiet, she thought. Signed her name, tore the receipt from the book, and turned to find him standing so close her arm bumped him as she turned.

Moving sideways away from him, she tried to smile, holding out the receipt.

"Thanks," he said, taking it, jamming it into his pocket. Staring at her the way he had the previous Wednesday evening.

Why is he back from work so early? she wondered, glancing at her watch. Just gone five. Why doesn't he go?

She started to go to the door, thinking she'd open it, he'd leave. His hand came up and closed around the lower half of her face. Hard. She was terrified and stood immobilized, trying to think what to do, imagining what was going to happen.

"It's wild," he said, "how you turn me on. You know it, don't you?"

With difficulty, his hand holding her captive, she shook her head, eyes staring. *Leave me alone, leave me alone!*

"Don't play dumb." He smiled, dragging her against him so abruptly the air was knocked out of her lungs.

"Pl . . . pl . . ." She couldn't speak. Wanting to beg him to go away, leave her alone. *Please!*

"Dynamite body," he said, his hand still so tight around her jaw she could scarcely open her mouth. "One bitching body."

"S. . . S . . . S . . ." Help!

"Don't get so worked up," he said softly, slowly bringing her head forward. The strength in his one hand overpowering. She strained away but he kept her coming forward, then clamped his mouth down on hers. Wet. His tongue pushing into her mouth. His hand fi-

31

nally leaving her throat, closing over her breast. She shoved at him. Like trying to push down a stone wall. He didn't even sway under the impact.

He let her go and she staggered back from him, gasping. Her eyes going to the door. She could get to the door, run outside. He wouldn't dare follow. Pat was upstairs. Running her vacuum cleaner. She could hear the hum of it.

"Take off your clothes!" His mouth wet, his eyes determined.

She shook her head back and forth, back and forth, her mouth opening and closing. Sounds emerging, no words. *I can't scream if I scream Pat'll hear, Jenny will find out it would be so terrible for her what can I do?*

"Come on!" His voice lightly menacing now. Advancing toward her. Blocking off the path to the door. Shaking her head so violently everything was out of focus. Hair in her eyes. How could this happen? Her throat hurting with the effort she was putting into trying to speak. If she could just get out the words. All the words having to do with Jenny, this house, living here. He'd have to leave. She couldn't have him here. But if he'd just stop now, they could perhaps forget it. Before any damage was done. He'd go away.

"Okay," he said. "Just have to *make* you take 'em off!" And he leaped through the air between them, his arms flying, hands grabbing at her shirt, ripping, the buttons resisting, buttonholes tearing. Pulling at the shirt, getting it open while she tried to twist away, pushing at him. Using every ounce of her strength trying to hold him off. A squeaking noise coming from her throat. Hitting his chest with her fist, then his ear. He stopped. His arm swung out and he slapped her across the face. So hard her head snapped around. Blinding. Then a collision with the floor. Banging the back of her head, her elbow as he knelt over her, yanking the brassiere up, exposing her breasts. She caught handfuls of his hair and pulled as hard as she could. He slapped her again. Trying now to get her jeans down. She closed her eyes for a moment, heard the sound of zippers. Hers. His. Opened her eyes, saw him exposed. A moment of advantage. Brought both knees up suddenly, fast, hard. And sent him over backward, crashing into the andirons, sending them loudly to the floor.

"Out out *out!*" she cried in a voice crushed, muted by fear. "*Out!*"

Glaring at her—she'd grabbed up the poker and was standing clutching it, trembling—he got to his knees, his hands between his legs.

"Cockteasing cunt!" he hissed, tears of pain sitting in the rims of his eyes as he struggled to his feet, turned away. The sound of a zipper. The poker was bobbing up and down. She tightened her grip on it. Standing hunched over, panting, ready to hit him, beat him to death with the poker. But he straightened, marched over to the door, flung it open, and went bounding up the stairs. Gone.

She couldn't move for several moments. Then dropped the poker, raced across the room to close and double-lock the door. Stood against the door for several moments more trying to catch her breath, her heartbeat still wild. Stood there until a sob erupted out of her mouth, then another. And, hurting all over, moved stiffly into the bedroom. Pulling down the shades, drawing the curtains. Taking off the ruined shirt, readjusting her brassiere. Finding a sweater in the drawer, pulling it on. Feeling cold. Frozen. Her stomach churning. She lay down on the bed, pulling the blankets around her. The crying hurting her chest. Her face burning where he'd hit her. Touching her face, feeling how hot it was. Then tucking both hands between her thighs, trying to get warm.

They'd have to go! But how? Poor Jenny. She wouldn't understand, couldn't be told. But he was a monster. Stupid of her to think she could carry this off on her own. Anyone might come in off the street and molest her. Her own tenant. And how had she teased him? What had he meant? She'd done nothing, nothing. It was all in his mind. Saying such dreadful things to her. What will I do? I never want to have to see him again, not look at him. Never.

Beginning to feel a little warmer, the bulk of the blankets, their weight calming her. She got up to go into the bathroom, look at her face. Still red. But, thank God, there'd be no bruises. He'd hit her hard but not hard enough to bruise. He'd have raped her. The thought setting her to trembling again. To be raped. Right in her own home. She shuddered and went back to the bed, once more drawing the blankets over her. She'd have to think, decide what to do. There was no way on earth she could tell Jenny. Jenny would be shattered. To think she was living with a man who would try to rape another woman.

Seeing again the way his eyes had gone at the sight of her exposed breasts. How could he? Under the sweater, arms crossed, she covered her breasts with her hands. Protecting them. Deciding if he didn't leave of his own accord, she'd have no alternative but to ask them to go. If only she could get him to leave, have Jenny stay. Liking Jenny. Convinced of Jenny's outrage should she learn of what Sandy had tried to do. Dear God! Right there, in the living room.

"I'm going out!"

"What d'you mean you're going out? I've got everything ready for dinner. It's all cooking. Why didn't you tell me before I started you were going out? What'm I supposed to do, eat all this stuff myself?"

"You can stick it up your ass, for all I care. I'm going."

"What the hell's the *matter* with you? You've been acting weird ever since I got home."

"You might as well start getting used to the idea," he said. "I've about had it with this scene."

He slammed out and she stood there, open-mouthed, trying to figure it out.

"Son of a bitch," she exclaimed aloud, sitting down, staring at the door. "What's going on around here?"

He was getting weirder by the minute, it seemed. And she wished she'd never managed to get herself into all this in the first place. Because he was definitely up to something. Probably going to throw her out, damn it. Now she'd have to go hiking all over town trying to find someplace to live. Goddamned stupid men! All so fucked up.

She didn't feel like sitting around and she sure couldn't eat all that food by herself. Maybe Gillian . . . No. It'd probably send her into fits if she just casually knocked at the door, asking, Want to eat with me? But Pat. Maybe Pat would. She got up—feeling angrily defiant—put the door on the latch, and went down to knock at Pat's door.

"Have you eaten yet?" she asked Pat, who'd smiled upon opening the door.

"I was just about to," she said.

"You haven't already started or anything yet, have you?" Jenny asked hopefully.

"Not yet, no. Is something wrong?"

"It's no big deal. But right in the middle of dinner that idiot went marching out. Now I've got this whole pot of spaghetti. I can't eat it all myself. Would you like to have some with me?"

"We're getting to be quite a community kitchen." Pat laughed. "Why don't you just go along and bring your pot of spaghetti down here? I'll open a bottle of wine."

Her face lightening, Jenny said, "Great! I'll be right back. Thanks a lot," she added, hurrying toward the stairs. "I really wasn't in the mood to eat alone."

I am never, Pat thought, in the mood for eating alone. But one can become accustomed to all sorts of things. All sorts. For example, not asking questions. Especially questions having to do with some sort of altercation that had taken place earlier downstairs. Between Sandy and Gillian. That lad up to no good. She'd seen it in his eyes last Wednesday. The Lord only knew what he'd been doing down there. She'd heard him go down. Then she'd heard him come up again some fifteen minutes later. Muttering to himself as he stamped his way up the stairs. And Jenny, caught somehow in the middle. She hoped Gillian was all right down there. Looking out the kitchen window, she could see the spill of light on the front lawn from Gillian's kitchen window. Which was a good sign. Because it hadn't been an hour earlier when she'd looked out. At the very least, it meant Gillian was up and about down there.

Not a nice lad at all, that one. A definite meanness to the eyes and mouth. Curious how a gentle, fun-loving girl like Jenny could tolerate—perhaps even enjoy—the company of a one like that. Still, it's none of my business, she told herself, unearthing the corkscrew. Not at all.

She spent all day Tuesday in bed. Getting up only to fix herself a bowl of soup, some tea. Returning to bed at once. Sitting gazing at the little television set she toted from room to room when in need of company. Watching quiz shows, films throughout the day. Slowly returning to herself, feeling a little calmer, a little less afraid he'd return to finish the job. He'd not dare, she told herself. Not in broad daylight with Pat up above, people out walking on the street. And if he came again to the door, she'd keep the chain on, not allow him in.

By late afternoon she felt sufficiently restored to herself to get up and make herself a proper dinner. A steak she'd intended to eat the night before. Some salad. With endive and watercress. Mother's recipe for salad dressing. Oil and lemon, a bit of crushed garlic, ground pepper. She ate with appetite and felt better still. She'd simply have to handle this. Go up when both of them were there, ask them to leave. Say she'd prefer not to discuss the reasons why; it would just be better for all concerned if they'd go.

But she'd miss Jenny. It surprised her to realize this. In the seven months of their tenancy she'd come to rely on the daily sight and sound of Jenny, her bright hello's and good-natured cheeriness. Why did things have to turn so ugly, so impossible? She'd miss Jenny.

The next morning there was a telephone call. Asking her could she come in that same morning and see Mrs. Brewster. She could? Good. Come and please bring whatever working drawings and letters of reference she had available.

She was very nervous. Worrying over what she'd wear, what she'd say, what they'd ask. Arrived at the given address in an agitated state, chain-smoking in the waiting area, perspiring heavily. But as it turned out, Mrs. Brewster was only slightly older than Gillian, an architect, too, with a surprisingly frequent smile and a pleasantly aggressive manner. Just the right amount of push without being overbearing or condescending.

"I'm not interested in all that," she said, dismissing the shoe shops, the boutiques. She said it not unkindly, so Gillian didn't mind. "We need someone for a school. We lost one of the senior partners right in the middle of this stinking project and we're desperate for someone who knows how to get it finished."

A school. Gillian felt her insides dropping. Another school.

"These people are so desperate to have the building finished, you just wouldn't believe it. Call me Jane, by the way. Anyway, they're so hung up and antsy, they're calling practically every hour on the hour trying to get us to hurry things along. And we've been totally screwed up on site for the last month because Bruce suddenly decided to split. You know contractors. Unless there's somebody out there keeping them going, they'll just diddle around, dragging their feet. That idiot Bruce. Gone off to smoke pot and look at the Rockies or some such silly shit. Probably listened to too many John Denver records and felt the call of the wild. Anyway, when your résumé came in, we all flipped. You're exactly what we've been looking for."

Her smiles seemed so real, not the result of some social program that had been computed into her. Gillian couldn't help liking her. And thought, I could handle another school if I'm to work with people I like, in an easy atmosphere.

"Carl, my husband, is out at the site right now or you'd meet him. He's doing a church. Very interesting. A lot of scope. Anyway, I like your stuff and your credits look great. Really!" Another of those smiles. "A lot more than this particular job needs. But we're still pretty new and there's room to move in if you're interested in moving."

"How far along is the school?"

"Just over halfway. We had some flak from a couple of the subcontractors, so we've had to have a couple of new companies submitting estimates. They're in now and we've got everything set to go. That idiot Bruce, going out there doped out of his mind. The thing is, somebody's got to oversee, keep these men moving, or the damned thing'll just keep grinding down to slow and never get finished."

She knew she was going to accept the position and sat listening to Jane go on about the job, liking the look of her, her immediacy. Not tall, not short, not thin, not fat, with short, shaggy-cut black hair. Very white skin and large almost-black eyes, a wide mouth. Strong, able-looking hands.

"So listen," Jane said, "d'you think you're interested?"

"Oh, yes." Gillian returned her smile. "I think so."

"Great! God, that's great. We can't pay a fortune but we'll take care of you. We've got group insurance, a profit-sharing plan. And a really good bunch of people here. I don't suppose you'd be interested in starting right now?"

"Well . . ." Gillian looked around. "Since I'm here, I might just as well."

"Great, great. Carl's going to be so pleased. Come on, let me show you where to put your jacket. Then I'll get you organized, introduce you to everybody." Jane stood up, smiling, smiling, and held out her hand. "Happy to have you," she said. "I just know this is going to work out beautifully."

Flushing, thinking, I *wish* I could stop doing this! she returned Jane's handshake, then followed her out of the conference room.

Like an old friend, introducing her around to everyone as if she'd known Gillian for years and was very pleased to have all her other friends know her, too. There were four junior architects, four senior partners including Jane and the absent Carl, five draftsmen, a bookkeeper, a receptionist-typist, and—inevitably—an overworked secretary.

"We're going to have to hire another secretary," Jane explained, showing Gillian into one of the cubicles off the main area. "This'll be yours. For the moment you're going to be kind of in the middle. You're way too qualified to be a junior and too much of an unknown quantity to have your name on the letterhead. But we'll work things out as we go. Let me just go get the drawings and some coffee for us and we can get started. All the supplies are in that room over there. You should find everything you need. Anything you can't find, just sing out."

On her lunch break, she completed an insurance application and several other forms Renée, the bookkeeper, brought in and set down on Gillian's board.

"Just when you get a minute, you'll fill those out, eh?" She smiled, then bustled away. A round, bleached-blond woman in her early fifties. With an accent somewhere between French and German. Swiss, perhaps, Gillian thought, carefully completing the forms one after the other.

The atmosphere was very informal, busy. Most everyone wearing jeans, T-shirts. There were three other women. One of the juniors and two in the drafting pen.

And one of the seniors was perhaps one of the most beautiful men she'd ever seen. With a close-cropped Afro, creamy-coffee skin. Lovely large eyes and an utterly disarming smile that turned him from a prepossessing man into someone whimsical and probably good-humored. In gold-framed aviator glasses. Chocolate-brown corduroy trousers, a V-neck Shetland, and open-necked shirt. The other senior looked very young. In denim overalls, shirt sleeves rolled above his elbows, long curly blond hair and long-lashed blue eyes. A look of ingenuousness. She wondered what Carl would be like.

The school.

A simple design. Nothing very inspired about it. Functional. A small suburban institution. Grades kindergarten through six. A cafeteria, an auditorium, a small gymnasium, a central corridor. Expanses of glass and a vaulted front entranceway to be floored in brick. Brick? She picked up the specification and flipped through. Brick. From the already-demolished manual-training building adjacent to the old school. A sentimental nicety requested by the parents' association and approved by the school board. Brick. What other oddities? An oak tree around which the school was being constructed. In order to accomplish this, the original architect had bent the school, the corridor, wrapped the building halfway around this tree, set two long concrete benches facing each other on opposite sides of the tree, approachable only through emergency doors. A useless walkway outside. There wasn't anything she could do about the design. The building was under way. But what a sad waste of a potentially beautiful setting. A wonderful play area. But when she asked Jane about it, Jane said,

"Isn't that a bitch? But it's what they wanted. They don't want the area *used*. They want it *admired*."

"It's a pity, really. Such a lovely area for the children to play in." She thought of Megan. On her hands and knees, scooping dirt into little hills. Sprinkling them with a watering can. Intent on her work. Dirt in her hair, up her arms, all down her legs.

"I know," Jane agreed. "What can I tell you? My kids would love a place like that. But what do the parents remember? Nothing. They're all hung up on exercising their little bit of power."

"You have children?"

"Three." Jane smiled. "Nine, seven, and five."

"That's very nice." Gillian's voice emerged thin.

"You'll want to make a visit to the job site. D'you have a car?"

"N . . . n . . . no. I ha . . . haven't."

"Problem. Well, I suppose you can use mine."

"I d . . . don't drive."

"Oh! That's really a problem."

"Couldn't I go by bus or perhaps a taxi?"

"It'd take you several days. I guess I'll have to take you out there myself. I don't suppose you'd consider getting your driver's license?"

Gillian shook her head. "I'm afraid not," she said, her voice now thinned down almost to nothing. "I couldn't."

"Well," Jane said, studying her face with interest, "we'll work something out. Don't worry about it."

"She's terrific," Jane was telling Carl that evening. "Unbelievable background. I know you'll like her."

"English?"

"Right. Gillian. With a soft G. I'm taking her out to the site tomorrow."

"How come you're taking her?"

"No car, doesn't drive. That was really something," she said, remembering. "I asked her if she might consider taking driving lessons and she went absolutely white. I've never seen anything like that before. Scary. She went white white and said she couldn't. I had this feeling if I pushed the point she'd really freak out."

"Lots of people have a thing about cars," he said, cutting the last of Lissa's meat. "If she's as good as you say, we'll just work around the no-car business."

"She's beautiful, Carl."

He looked up at her, caught by her tone of voice; his eyebrows arched, questioning.

"I mean it. One of those English complexions you hear about. And this long, thick-looking silver-gold blond hair you can't get out of a bottle. Really beautiful. And so shy you want to do her talking for her just to help her out. I know you'll like her. Andrew! Eat your own food and leave Lissa's alone! She's very . . . I don't know. Tentative. But once she started in to work all of a sudden she was entirely different. Confident and very capable. She knows what she's doing. And one thing for sure, Gabe Hadley's going to have a hell of a hard time exercising his temper on her."

"Oh?"

"I hope to God he's going to have a hard time. If he scares her off, I'll *murder* him."

She put down the drawings and specification she'd brought home and stood looking at the living room. Feeling exhilarated. Glad to be working again. She hadn't thought she would be. But she was. Glad. Feeling pleasantly tired, thinking she'd light a fire after dinner, sit down to read through the specification, make notes, go over the drawings thoroughly, familiarize herself with the project.

I'll have to write Michelle, tell her I've been taken on. She'll laugh when she learns it's another school.

She hung away her jacket, lit a cigarette, and carried the spec and drawings through to the drawing board in the bedroom. I do love this house, she thought, stepping out of her shoes. My house. The walls, the windows, the garden. Feeling so much better now. Determined nothing and no one would destroy her pleasure in the house. The routine would come, the days would get filled. No more killing time puttering about with last, really unnecessary tasks.

Thinking again of the face of the beautiful black man. What was his name? Pierce. All of them. So fresh-looking, young, informal. And Renée. Motherly, overseeing the lot of them. I will like it there, I know.

A knock at the door. Her heart seized up. She whirled around, terrified. Had he come back? Oh, my God! Trembling, she didn't know what to do. Another knock. She went shoeless through to the living room, shakily putting the chain on the door before opening it a crack.

Jenny. Saying, "You didn't forget, did you? About dinner?"

"Oh!" Sighing with relief. "Just one moment." Closing the door to remove the chain, then opening it to allow Jenny in. "I did forget," she told her. "Completely. Is it time? What time is it?"

"It's okay," Jenny said easily. "There's plenty of time."

You want me to ask you in, Gillian thought, seeing Jenny looking past her. Saying, "Sandy's not going to be here."

"Oh? Would you like to come in, wait, and I'll go up with you?" He wouldn't be there. Further relieved.

44

"Sure, okay. I have to admit I was kind of wondering what kind of stuff you'd have. It's nice. I really like it."

"Have a look around. I won't be long."

She hurried into the bedroom, looking back before closing the door to see Jenny—with such little-girl curiosity—examining a lacquered papier-mâché egg. And changed quickly out of her interview dress, setting out one of her favorite caftans. Liking them because they hid her legs. Went into the bathroom to have a hurried wash. Thinking it was growing colder. She'd soon have to put on the heat.

Jenny sat experimentally in the bentwood rocker beside the telephone, then got up and walked around it before making her way to the sofa. Very square lines. Wicker or rattan? Whatever it was, she liked it. And sat down, surprised at the accommodating softness beneath the rough-woven cream-colored fabric. Big and wide, like a bed. And the rug. She'd never seen one like it. All light browns and beiges, fat and skinny wool woven together. A zillion baskets. Some on the walls—round, flat, ones and big shallow square ones. By the front windows in the kitchen a whole row of plants in more baskets. Kindling in a great big basket beside the fireplace. A whole wall of shelves on brackets with books separated by baskets or more of those lacquered pieces. Square boxes, round ones, oval. A watercolor over the fireplace. And there—isn't that odd? she thought—just to the left of the door. Looking like something a really little kid would do. She got up and walked over to have a look, deciding Gillian had probably done it in school or something. But no, in big, uneven letters, "Megan."

The bedroom door opened and Gillian came out.

"That's a really pretty dress," Jenny said. "Who's Megan?"

Gillian saw she'd been looking at the crayon drawing. Sooner or later, she thought, I'm going to have to learn to talk about it.

"My daughter," she said, feeling a sudden rush of blood to her head, giddiness.

"Your daughter? You have a daughter?"

"I did."

"You did." Jenny looked at Gillian's face, then back at the drawing, and decided the smart thing to do would be to change the subject. Fast. "I just love all your stuff," she said instead. "I tried out the rocker, the sofa, and both chairs." She laughed. "Boy, I've never seen so many baskets in my life. I'd never think of using baskets the way you have. And all those neat little boxes and eggs."

"Thank you." The blood rush ebbing, cooling; thinking, How very sensitive you are, how kind. Not to ask the obvious. "Shall I bring along a bottle of wine, do you think?"

"Why not? I sure feel like getting tanked." Jenny looked suddenly angry, unhappy. "He's paying me back, I'll bet."

"For what?"

"Oh, nothing. Sandy's such a childish idiot sometimes. You can't argue with him or he just thinks up some way to get back at you for disagreeing. He acts more like five than his age. He makes me so damned mad."

"How old are you, Jenny?"

"Nineteen. How old are you?" she responded with what Gillian was coming to see as typical candor.

"Almost thirty. Shall we have a quick glass of wine before we go up? I should celebrate. I started work today."

"No kidding!" Jenny was bright again. "We definitely should have a drink, in that case. Isn't that neat?"

"It is, actually. I think it's going to work out rather well." She poured two half glasses of wine and handed one to Jenny. They clicked glasses.

Jenny said, "Happy days!"

"Cheers!" Gillian said. Then had that New Year's Eve feeling that she might cry. It happened every year without fail. Her throat would close and she'd start crying for so many reasons. A multitude of reasons. The end of another long, long year. The start of one more. Feeling the cumulative weight of all those weeks and months alone burying her. She forced herself to smile, then drained her glass in one swallow.

"We'd best go up now," she said, setting down her glass, picking up the bottle of wine and her handbag, her keys.

"Oh, boy! I left the *salad* in the *fridge*. I'll meet you there." She tossed down the wine, handed Gillian the glass, and dashed out.

Gillian stood very still for a moment, then smiled.

3.

"When she was a tot," Mrs. O'Brian said, "my Mary loved nothing better than to take off her clothes, slip out of the house, and go running up the road. Knowing full well she'd caught my eye and would be right after her." She laughed. "Off she'd go, turning round to make sure I was following. Laughing her head off. With those chubby legs. Lord, she was a one!"

They were having coffee. Jenny curled up on the floor with her back against the sofa. Gillian on the sofa with her shoes off, her legs tucked under. Mrs. O'Brian in the armchair. Talking. And as she talked, noted—for the second time—the transformation in Gillian wrought by several glasses of wine. With each glass she became more open, expansive, talked without hesitance, laughed.

And Jenny, in sharp contrast, was becoming melancholy, silent. Bothered, Mrs. O'Brian decided, because her young man hadn't come along. Strange, she thought, the effects of drink. Making the one chatty and gay. Making the other sad and moody.

"I've eaten too much," Gillian complained with a smile. "But it was so good. Just what we'd have for Sunday lunch. Roast chicken with all the trimmings. I think since you and Jenny have both done dinner now, next time really should be mine. Shall we make it next Wednesday?"

"Fine with me," Mrs. O'Brian said, turning to look at Jenny, who'd been staring fixedly at the floor and now lifted her head, asking, "What? Sorry. Did I miss something?"

"Next Wednesday evening," Gillian said. "I'll do dinner and all of you will come."

"Sure," Jenny said absently. "Okay."

"What is it?" Gillian asked her, touching Jenny's shoulder.

"That bastard's winding himself up to do a split!" she erupted. "I just *know* it! He'll take off and leave me with everything."

Both Gillian and Mrs. O'Brian looked at her, neither of them able to find anything appropriate to say.

Jenny blinked, looking from Gillian to Mrs. O'Brian, then down to her hands.

"I'm sorry," she said unhappily. "I'm just so mad because it's so unfair. How'm I going to pay the rent on my own? I don't even make enough money to pay two weeks' worth. And I *like* living here," she wailed.

"Are you sure that's what he intends doing?" Gillian asked. How perfect if he'd go without having to be asked! Not perfect, of course, for Jenny. But he really was a bastard and Jenny could do far better for herself than someone like Sandy.

"I can tell!" Jenny insisted. "Believe me, I can tell. He's slamming around dropping large hints here and there."

"Well, if that's the case, perhaps you could find another girl who'd share the apartment with you."

"I guess I could. It's just that I *hate* living with other
girls. I tried it last year. They're always moving things,
never putting them back the way they were. Or bor-
rowing your clothes and makeup and stuff and returning
everything all crapped up. I don't know. I mean, Sandy's
bad enough, but another girl. I don't know. I'd rather
stay by myself. Except that I can't. And I love this
house. I don't *want* to move. It's the first place I've lived
where I've been happy since I left home. Before that,
even. Since Gran died."

"Don't you think it would be wisest to wait and see
what happens?" Gillian said carefully. "We'll work something out."

Mrs. O'Brian wet her lips, started to say something,
then took a sip of her wine, set down her glass, and said,
"If you find yourself hard up for a place, I'd be happy to
have you come stay with me. There's more than enough
room for one more."

"Honestly?" Jenny asked, her spirits rapidly lifting. "I
could come here?"

"It would be my pleasure."

"Boy! That's great! That's really great."

Appearing satisfied, Mrs. O'Brian said, "Now you
haven't a problem. If your young man does decide to
leave, you'll just come on down here to me and we'll
move you right in."

"That's very kind of you, Pat," Gillian said, wondering
why, with five children she was finally free of, she'd volunteer to take in another. Not that Jenny was a child.
But still.

"Oh, not at all," Pat said. "I'd enjoy the company. And

it's not as if she'd be underfoot constantly. Jenny goes
off to her work every day."

"Well, until I found someplace on my own or something, it'd be really nice," Jenny said, her smile returning. "Like home," she added. Hoping like hell what she
thought was happening wasn't happening. Because it
would be such a big, stinking mess.

She was in her nightgown, sitting on the rug in front
of the fire reading through the specification, when she
heard the front door open and close. Sandy coming in.
She tensed, hearing his footsteps in the hall. And
glanced at the clock—Mother's four-hundred-day domed
clock she'd carried over with her wrapped in a blanket.
Twelve-fifteen. She relaxed slowly as his footsteps
continued on up the stairs, sitting listening a moment
longer. Then yawned, deciding she'd finish her wine,
have one last cigarette, and go to bed. Must remember
to set the alarm, she reminded herself. It wouldn't do to
arrive late on her first official day of work.

Silence above. Pat must be sleeping. How very generous of her, offering to take Jenny in. And Jenny, having
the sense to know when not to ask questions. Had Pat
not made her offer, what did I have it in mind to do?
Lower the rent to a price Jenny could afford. Such a bad
businesswoman. But what is it, being good at business?
Profiteering. No, I want to keep them here. Pat and
Jenny. Beginning to know them. And knowing them,
needn't suffer over the unpredictable things they might
do. Not like newcomers, strangers. Doing things you
don't want them to do. Forcing you into positions where
you've no options—either be hurt, or hurt first. Men.
Like Sandy. Putting you totally on the defensive. Because you don't want them and they take your words

away. And the others, trying to say no without offending them. Or some you want, then have, then hate the sight of, comes the morning. Longing to see them out, away.

In the sudden absence of fear she felt warm, languid. Dangerous signs. The heaviness in her breasts, the loose weight sitting on her pelvic bones. Looking around the room as if there might suddenly appear a group of people who'd all sit smiling derisively, nodding knowingly. Mocking her desires. Knowing she'd attend to it. And hating the dreadfully transparent feeling given her by her own needs. Self-humiliation in the presence of no one but herself.

Her concentration was gone. She slipped a piece of paper into the spec and closed it, stretching out her legs, gazing into the fire as she savored the last of the wine, the cigarette. Megan clutching at her legs. "Come paint pictures with me, Mummy. Do, let's." Or "Come read to me, Mummy. This book, this book!"

Returning from the island. Knowing. Trying to think what to do, how to tell; so frightened. Finally blurting out the whole story. Hysterically. Tripping over the words, sobbing with the fear, the shame. And Mother quietly asking, "What would you like to do about this, Gillian? What are your feelings?"

"I don't know. I don't know!"

"Let's try to think this through logically, darling. You've only just turned sixteen. You've a good number of years of school ahead of you. Is this child something you're going to want?"

"Oh, I couldn't *kill* it! I *couldn't!*"

"I'd say that answers it, then, wouldn't you?"

"You mean I'll keep it? You'll allow me to keep it?"

"You make me sound a monster, Gillie! I wouldn't dream of forcing anyone, let alone a child of mine, to do

52

something so utterly against her wishes. If it's your intention to keep the child, we'll have to work it out. But you're sure this is what you want?"

"Oh, Mummy, it is! I'll write him and when he knows, I'm sure he'll come fetch us back, take care of us. I know he will! He promised me he'd come."

"Yes. But for now I think we'd best just make our plans and worry about what will happen when it happens."

Mother and the midwife. Mother saying, "That's a good girl, *push!* Come on, darling, *push!*" So hard, pushing. Mother's eyes down there, watching, her hands so solid, strong. The midwife murmuring, saying the same things. The two of them. And me. On my mother's bed. In the middle of the morning with the sunlight blinding. Naked, spread on my mother's bed, the midwife saying, "This is bloody ridiculous. Come on down here. *Come!*" Spreading newspapers on the floor, a sheet on top. "Squat down here now and push like the bloody devil, child. Better, isn't it? Isn't that better?" God! On my haunches on the floor. Mother watching, watching. And the midwife sitting there between my legs, her face so serious, saying, "That's the way, now. Come along. Good! Here we go, here we go!" Oh, *God!* The pain, the monstrous shuddering push, pushing everything out. The baby slithering into the midwife's hands. Megan. Mother wept. The only time I ever saw her cry. Lay beside me on the bed while the midwife cleaned Megan. Lay with her arms around me, holding, the tears falling down my neck, on my shoulder. Holding her, so exhausted, awed by this woman, my mother. And her tears.

She tossed her cigarette into the fire, set the screen in place, carried her glass to the kitchen, then switched off

the lights and went into the bedroom. To take off her
nightgown—feeling stealthy—before sliding under the
bedclothes, turning the last light off. Eyes closed, hands
holding her breasts. Thinking this made things both better and worse. Better because it proved she was still all
right, only superficially damaged by Sandy. Worse because. Pairs and pairs of hands that had held her
breasts, touched and tasted them as if searching for their
mothers through her breasts, emitting satisfied sighs
upon gaining access to her breasts. Slipping down over
her ribs, belly, across her hips, down. Momentous instant parting her thighs, one hand dipping down, the
other circling her breast, moving, moving. So easy, easy.
Brooke, the tickle of his chest hair on her breasts. Heat.
Tremendous heat.

And after, feeling so lonely, so deathly alone. A sob
like the aftermath of tears, shaking her violently, just
once before that solo flight into sleep.

"Where did you go?"

"None of your fucking business where I went!"

"It certainly *is* my business. What's coming down
here? Don't you have the goddamned decency at least to
let me know?"

"Okay, okay, okay! I'm moving out. Okay? That answer your question?"

"I *knew* it. You son of a bitch! Where do you get off
treating people this way? You can't just leave and stick
me with this place."

"Oh, no? Wanna watch me? I can do any goddamned
thing I feel like doing. You get on my nerves. You really
get on my nerves."

"You're so small," she said, her eyes narrowed. "So
fucking *small!* You can't be king of the castle, you'll go

someplace else where you can be. I don't care. Go on. Take your stuff and go."

"Tomorrow."

"The hell! You're going, go now. I'm not sleeping in that goddamned bed with you. Go sleep somewhere else!"

His face turned so mean it scared her. Menacing.

"I'll sleep where I fucking well *want!*" he said, advancing on her. "You don't like it, sleep on the fucking floor. But I'm sleeping in the fucking bed I fucking paid for. Got that?"

He'd hit her. She could see that. Enraged, she stomped through to the bedroom, grabbed her pillow and one of the blankets, carried them back to the living room, and threw them on the sofa. He glared at her for several moments, then turned off the lights and slammed into the bedroom. Leaving her alone in the dark. She collapsed on the sofa, mouth quivering, determined not to cry. But so scared. What a mess! What was she going to *do?*

She could see at once how impossible a bus or taxi would have been. The job site was miles outside the city. Jane drove well, with obvious pleasure—that image of Mother driving to Aberystwyth flickering on and off in Gillian's mind—talking about the boiler installation. Then saying, "The principal's planning to meet us at the site this morning. To meet you. He really doesn't like it but the school board's on top of him to keep the whole thing moving. He comes on like gangbusters every now and then. But I think you'll like Gabe. Underneath all the hue and cry, he's a really decent guy. I think it's just the pressure, you know? All that upper-level political bullshit. Insisting he get out there and make sure the job's getting done."

"I do know," Gillian said, reminding herself to have a look at that tree, the walkway.

"By the time we get back to the office," Jane went on, "Carl should be there. He's really looking forward to meeting you."

"And I, him," she lied. Pained by the idea of another new person to meet in a day that would be filled with little else.

"Let's have lunch before we go back," Jane suggested.

"Yes, all right. That would be lovely."

"I don't make you nervous, do I?" Jane asked.

"Oh, no," she answered quickly, smiling across at Jane. "*Everyone* makes me nervous, actually. I'd so adore being the cool, blasé sort. But I'm never going to be, I'm afraid. I am sorry."

"Don't be sorry." Jane smiled back. "Nervous is nervous. It's not something a person can help. Some people get me so uptight I can hardly function, let alone talk straight. All kinds of gibberish starts coming out."

"Oh?"

"To tell you the truth, it's usually women who look like you. The cool, gorgeous kind."

"But I'm . . ."

"You're not the type," Jane continued. "You just *look* it. I've always wondered how it must feel to be beautiful, what kind of reactions you get from people, men."

"I don't get any," she said truthfully. "As soon as they start in to talk with me they lose interest. I suppose they think I'm going to be terribly sophisticated and conversational. Because I look the way I do. But I don't see it. Do you follow? Because I know how I am. And I know they'll go off again straightaway they've tried to chat me up."

"Chat you up?" Jane laughed. "I like that. I guess you've got a point," she said, considering it. "It must be rough. I don't mean that sarcastically. I mean, it must be. Finding it so hard to talk to people. I guess you've always been that way, huh?"

"Oh, yes, *always*. I so envied my mother. I think she was the sort who'd have made you nervous. Lovely to look at and so wonderfully confident. But she wasn't what you might have thought, either. She was lovely, warm. Lovely."

"She's dead now?"

Gillian nodded. "Yes."

"Was she young?"

"Yes. Almost forty-six."

"God, that's too bad. What was it, cancer or something?"

"No, not that." Please, let it drop. I can't, *can't!*

"Oh," Jane said soberly. "There it is." She pointed.

Thank God! Gillian thought. And shakily lit a cigarette.

The site was covered with mud. Odds and ends of plywood and lumber had been laid here and there to form a perilous walkway from a free-form parking area—also in the mud—to the construction.

"I should've told you to bring boots," Jane said, picking her way along the walk. "Next time you'll know. Every time it rains out here this loose ground just sucks it all up like a giant sponge."

Jane introduced her to the contractor, half a dozen subcontractors. And, finally, to a tall, dark-haired, an-

57

gry-eyed man in a good-looking tweed overcoat and slouch hat.

"Meet Gabe," Jane said. "This is Gillian, our new arrival. She's taking over the project."

"How are you?" he said, giving Gillian's hand a hard, brief shake. "I want you to come have a look at this idiotic outside walkway."

"Go ahead," Jane said. "I want to check with Frank about a couple of things."

Frank. The heating and ventilating engineer. I must remember the names of all these people. Who they are, what they do.

Gabe was walking fast through the already-completed section of the building and she followed along after him on her mud-spattered shoes wishing he'd slow down.

"Look at this!" he barked, stopping before an open section, pointing out the tree. "Some half-assed son of a bitch parked his goddamned cement truck right there. Now look at it!"

The earth was horribly ground up, small piles of gravel here and there.

"I'm certain it can all be repaired," she said, starting to perspire. He seemed so unreasonably angry.

"Sure it can be repaired!" he near-shouted. "But the point is that fucking tree's a goddamned totem to those idiots on the school board and the parents' association. I don't want to find my ass in a sling because the damned *tree* got damaged! Somebody's got to be out here regularly overseeing. I've got a lot of other things to do. I can't hang around here all day every day making sure these clowns don't destroy the sacred tree. I've got *work* to do, a school to run."

He whipped around, saw the expression on her face,

58

heard the echo of his words inside his skull, and thought, Jesus! What the hell's wrong with me?

"I'm sorry," he said. "That's a great way to begin: shouting at you. Understand. I'm just so fed up with the whole thing, getting stuck playing supervisor. I don't know a damned thing about *any* of this. And that pot-smoking fool was absolutely *useless*. Please"—he smiled, showing his teeth—"please, be useful. I've got a job to do and it's not getting done." Jesus, you're beautiful. And I've made one wonderful first impression. You look as if you expect me to whip out a gun or a knife.

"I will t . . . t . . . try," she said, looking away.

He studied her profile, wondering if she really knew what she was doing. So beautiful. It was just incredible how beautiful she was. He reached inside his coat pocket for his cigarettes. Looking at her was like being kicked simultaneously in both kneecaps so that he wanted to sit down.

"Cigarette?" he offered.

She turned, looked at his face, then down at the pack of cigarettes. A brand she didn't know.

"Yes, thank you." She removed her glove, took a cigarette from the pack, held it to his extended lighter. "Thank you," she said again, watching him draw on his cigarette, his left hand pushing the lighter and package of cigarettes deep into his overcoat pocket. He no longer looked quite so angry. In fact, she thought he looked apologetic. Perhaps regretting that unfortunate outburst. She did understand, though, about the pressure.

"English?" he asked, looking out at the tree.

"Yes."

"What part?"

"London."

"What part of London?"

59

"West Kensington."

"Crazy about London," he said, smiling again. "I've been over half a dozen times. I wouldn't mind living there. Except for the state of the economy." He waited but she said nothing. "Been over here long?"

"Eighteen months," she answered, suffocating inside her overcoat. "I suppose I'd best have a look round," she said, glancing about nervously. "I promise you I will do my best to see no one interferes with the tree." And you do your best not to go about shouting at people. One needn't shout to make one's points.

"Criminal waste of space," he said, looking once more at the tree. "I don't know why in hell they think kids like to play on concrete. They'd love being out there on the grass under the tree."

"I agree," she said, looking at him. Safe now that his eyes were off her. "It is a pity. Still, it's too late to alter the design."

"Yeah," he said, sounding dispirited. "The kids'll just have to make do with the concrete play yard."

"You seem especially sympathetic to the children," she said. "Have you children of your own?"

"No." He met her eyes. "Have you?"

"No," she answered, caught for a moment by his eyes. Something there she seemed to recognize. Then, breaking it, she hurried away.

He watched her go. Then shrugged and, disgustedly, tossed his cigarette out into the mud.

"He's fierce, isn't he?" Jane said in between bites of a chopped-liver sandwich. "I think he got Bruce so pissed off it's why Bruce split."

"Why is he like that, do you suppose?"

"Who knows? A good way to drive yourself crazy, trying to figure out why people are the way they are. Do you like that?" She indicated Gillian's sandwich.

"It's very good. We call it salt beef in England. Sometimes, when we'd go to the West End, we . . . I'd have this. In a kosher restaurant on Wardour Street. Not as good as this, though. And they didn't have this sort of pickle. I adore these."

"Carl studied in England for a while," Jane said. "He was crazy about it over there."

"So, apparently, was Mr. Hadley."

"Oh?"

"He said he's been over half a dozen times and wouldn't mind living there."

"No kidding? He told you that?"

"Yes. Is that surprising?"

"It is, kind of. I mean, I couldn't tell you one personal thing about Gabe. I don't think anybody could. He never talks about himself. Ever. You'd think he'd be such a dynamite guy, the way he looks and dresses. But he keeps out of it all."

I can understand that, Gillian thought. I wish I had the discipline not to go about scattering clues everywhere so people would stop asking. Good for him!

"Think you can handle the job?" Jane asked, wondering aloud.

"Oh, yes. It's a very straightforward project. A pity, though, wasting that lovely area around the tree."

"It's what they wanted. Our original design was far nicer. We had jungle gyms and seesaws, slides out there. They axed it. 'We want the essence preserved,' they told us. *Essence.* Such bullshit. Anyway, we give them what they want."

"I know. Lady Nora was the same." Don't fuss over the niceties, Gillian. If they want it purely functional, give it to them that way. One simply cannot force one's better judgment.

Jenny was camped outside her door when Gillian arrived home.

"Jenny, what is it?"

"Didn't I *tell* you?" she said heatedly, waving her arms about. "The son of a bitch is splitting!"

So fast, Gillian thought.

"Come in," she said, unlocking the door. "I'll make some tea, we'll talk about it."

"Oh, wait!" Jenny said. "I haven't told you the really *good* part." She stood in the middle of the living room, watching Gillian remove her coat and shoes. "Are you ready?"

"I don't know that I am. Do take off your coat, Jenny. I'll put on the kettle."

"I'm pregnant," Jenny said, unable to contain it one more second. "*Pregnant!*"

"Oh, Jenny!" Gillian stopped moving and stared at her. "Does he know this?"

"The hell! I'm not going to tell him. He'd just think I was making it up or something to stop him from moving out. To hell with him. I don't need him. I knew it was a lousy idea from the word go, moving in with him. I don't know why I ever did it."

"But what will you do?"

"I don't know. Oh, *shit!* I don't know." Jenny's eyes moved, looking at the walls, the baskets, the lacquered boxes, returning to settle on Gillian's face, her mouth trembling. "Oh, shit! I don't *know!*"

"Will you get rid of it?" Gillian asked softly.

"I couldn't!" she cried. "I just couldn't!"

Echoes, echoes.

Gifts of Love

"My God!" Gillian whispered. Seeing herself, hearing herself. Opening her arms to Jenny, holding her. "Not to worry," she said, stroking Jenny's hair. "We'll work something out." Hearing and feeling Mother inside herself. Thinking, Can this be real? Am I doing these things? I haven't any more idea what to do than she has. "Have you spoken to Pat?"

"No." Jenny shook her head, feeling a little better being able to hold on to somebody. "I don't know. I kind of wanted to talk to you first, hear what you'd say. Pat's kind of old. I mean, you know what I mean. She'd maybe freak out or something. You can never tell with old folks how they'll react to things."

"I know what you mean." Think, I must think! What to do?

"I knew you would."

"Is there somewhere you could go? Family, relatives?"

"They'd *kill* me. I had to fight my way out in the first place. No. No way. I don't care *what* happens. I'm never going back."

"How far along are you?" Gillian asked, common sense returning.

"Three months."

"Have you eaten?"

"We were too busy up there fighting all day. I'm sure Pat must've heard every word. It's so awful. That idiot bastard! What'm I going to *do?*"

"I suppose the first thing will be to have dinner. Then we'll talk."

"Pat, too?"

"Of course, if you like."

"I want her in on this, too."

"Yes, all right, Jenny. We'll ring her after we've had something to eat. Have a conference."

Gillian closed her eyes for a moment, Jenny still clinging to her. I don't want this to be happening. I don't want the responsibility. She opened her eyes and looked down at Jenny.

"I'll start dinner," she said, gently disengaging herself. "Make yourself comfortable. It won't take long."

I'm starting the first in a series of complications. Whatever happened to that picture of myself as the aloof proprietress of an apartment dwelling? She went into the kitchen, feeling beleaguered. But something else, too. Needed. Of value in some small fashion. It eased the chill a bit, warming her. We'll get through this somehow.

4.

"I don't really *want* a baby. But I just couldn't *kill* one. I mean, I hardly ever go to mass anymore or any of that. Haven't been to confession since I was about fourteen. But just thinking about an abortion, I get this feeling God's going to come down out of the sky and put His finger on my forehead, electrocute me or something."

"Oh, nonsense," Pat said sensibly. "Sheer fanciful nonsense. It's your body, after all. If you're not prepared or ready for a child, you needn't have one."

"No!" Jenny said, determined. "I just can't do it."

"You'll have it," Gillian prompted, "and then what will you do?"

"I don't know. It's so far away."

"It isn't, you know, Jenny. Another six months and the infant will be very much here. You've got to know what you'll do."

Jenny looked at Pat. Another cashmere sweater. The same pearls. At her breasts. Such large breasts for someone with her bone structure. Her spine very straight, shoulders, too. Then she looked at Gillian. The two of them so much bigger than her. Gillian as tall as any guy. Taller, even. But soft-looking. And pretty big in the breast area, too. The two of them making her feel like a kid of about twelve. Too small. Everywhere. In every way.

"I don't know," she said at last. "I'll have to think about it."

"For now," Pat said, "you'll continue your job, put by your money. And you're more than welcome to move in here with me."

"Perhaps," Gillian said cautiously, "it would be best if you did, Jenny. I hate sounding mercenary, but I truthfully can't afford to carry you rent free in the apartment. I need the income to cover the mortgage. And if you're here with Pat, you'll be able to put aside most of your salary. For after the baby comes."

"Okay," Jenny said. Thinking, You care. You both care. It made her feel like crying. The two of them being so supportive, so positive about this stinking disaster. "I guess that makes sense. If you're sure it's okay with you." She looked at Pat.

"Oh, it's perfectly fine with me," Pat said, sounding so eager Gillian looked at her with interest. "Tonight, if you like. Any time at all."

"I think tomorrow might be better," Gillian suggested. "It will give Jenny a chance to sort through her things."

"He's coming back tomorrow to take his stinking furniture," Jenny said. "I can't believe any of this. I think I'd better hang around tomorrow, make sure he doesn't help himself to my stuff, too."

I can no more believe it than you can, Gillian thought. Anticipating prospective tenants coming around knocking at the door. Bloody hell! Why is nothing ever as easy and uncomplicated as you think, hope it's going to be? Now I've this pregnant girl moving in with Pat and another ad to place in the newspapers. When I thought everything was settled.

"I think we could all use a drop to drink," Pat said, getting up. "What will you have?"

"Oh, anything," Gillian replied, distracted. Wording the ad in her mind. She should have saved the original one instead of throwing it away once the place was let.

"Some wine would be nice," Jenny said in such a small voice that Gillian felt sorry for her, touched by her. So young and defiant. I never was. All I knew was that I'd keep the baby. No matter what happened. It had nothing at all to do with religion or abortion. It had to do with me, with wanting someone who was mine, completely mine. Megan. Red-haired, impish features. She'd just lost two more teeth. And when she smiled. Oh, *God!* When she smiled.

For some reason her mind suddenly switched tracks. She found herself thinking of that dark, angry man. Wondering. Is his anger from pain or loss? Or is he simply angry? A man with gray starting in his hair and a mouth that, in repose, looks so soft. Perhaps misleadingly soft. Thinking of kisses, that man's kisses. Slipping down into a kind of hungry lassitude. Mouths, tongues. Moving hands. Urgent bodies. I must get out, she thought. Out of the house, away for a bit. For some fresh air. Clear my head.

She drank the wine rather quickly, trying not to appear in a hurry to get away, but in a hurry to get away. She needed time, space. To think about what was happening here. With Jenny pregnant, about to move in with Pat. An apartment that would be needing new tenants. A life that kept on and on when she wished over and over it would simply end. The loneliness eating away at her bones, at her brain.

She bade them both good night and returned downstairs to her apartment, in a fever now to get out. If she didn't go, she'd start to feel as if she were drowning. Hastily drank another glass of wine, feeling it spreading inside, everything easing, loosening. Pulling on her coat, a pair of comfortable shoes. She went out.

The air striking her face with the chill edge of autumn. Walking with no idea where she was going. Just walking. Cutting across toward Old Street, thinking it would be nice to lose herself in the crowd of people there always seemed to be here. Moving up and down in perpetual motion on Old Street. She walked, heading downtown, letting herself float mentally, thinking it would be nice to have another glass of wine. To sit somewhere quiet, dark, with a glass of wine. Anonymous, alone.

But you know what will happen, she told herself. What always happens. And I didn't want to start all that here. Promised myself. Keeping away from it all this time. Telling myself this way is better. But it isn't. Not better at all. Alone in bed. I feel so desperate afterward, hating my hands, keeping them away, out of sight, tucked under the pillow. So awful. Finished when it could all just be beginning. That marvelous feeling, wanting more, more. Not the other. That's for the last, the end. When they've given you all the other and have to come into you. But all the rest. Eighteen months. I've never been with a man here. Perhaps they're different. One glass of wine, then I'll go directly home. Take the bus. Not even walk.

Thinking about Jane. Asking would she consider taking driving lessons. She'd wanted to say, I have a driving license. I did drive once upon a time. Mother let me take the Rover. Megan and I would go off. To Windsor Castle. Or Stratford. It's just that I can't anymore.

She was passing a restaurant and bar. A pleasant-looking place. Advertising a singer-guitarist in the bar. That would be nice. A glass of wine, listen to some music, and then straight home.

She pushed through the door and climbed the stairs to the bar. Dark, quiet. Good, she thought. Good. Just what's needed. And found a table in the corner where she could clearly see the singer, who was sitting there looking so preoccupied strumming his guitar, adjusting his microphones, his amplifiers. Ordering a glass of white wine, lighting a cigarette. Something so familiar and reassuring about darkness, the smell of smoke and drinks. The music a bonus. The waitress stood the glass of wine down on the table in front of her. She unbuttoned her coat, shrugged it off, keeping it around her shoulders; eyes on the singer, tasting the wine, the cigarette, perfect. Perfect. Spreading all through her now, unsnapping the edges of her tension, releasing it. Her chest starting to feel fuller, lighter.

Halfway through the wine the waitress returned, smiling, setting down a second glass. Bending down to whisper confidentially, "That gentleman there, at the bar."

Gillian whispered, "Thank you." It was happening. It always happened just this way. So many pubs. She'd gone through all the locals. They'd been beginning to know her. So she'd had to go farther afield. No, no. I'll just finish this one and go. He was looking at her, wanting to be invited over. Waiting. She looked down at the second glass. Unable to tell what he looked like. Just someone in a suit, with a tie. She finished the first glass, lit another cigarette. Get up and go home now, Gillian. Now! This is going backward, not anything good.

"May I join you?" he asked.

She looked up at him. About thirty-five. Pleasant-looking. Well dressed. A businessman. With a wedding ring. Good. She preferred them married. It meant there'd be no calls, no invitations out for a second or third round. She said nothing. He sat down beside her on the banquette.

She started the second glass, keeping her eyes on the singer, heat building, the feeling her bones were bending. Wanting to laugh. Or cry. Mother, you'd be so angry with me. I can hear you, see you. I am angry with me. But I can't help myself. Can't.

"My name's Michael," he said, looking not in the least uncomfortable. As if this was something he, too, did very regularly. "Michael Zawicky."

She looked at his mouth as he talked. Always able to tell from the shape of the mouth, the way it moved, the sort of man behind the face and clothes. Still she said nothing, just sat steadily drinking the wine. The waitress came by. Michael ordered another round. He was drinking vodka martinis. Straight up. Ordered them sounding self-assured. Effortless in his moves, gestures. The drinks came. His arm went out along the back of the banquette, slowly descending onto her shoulders. When it made contact, her insides contracted pleasurably.

"What's your name?" he asked, looking at her face, watching her lift the glass to her mouth.

"No names," she whispered, shaking her head.

They went in a taxi to his hotel.

He put her coat over the back of one of the armchairs, hung up his own. She stood perfectly still, watching him.

"I like to take my time," he said, loosening his tie as

he came across the room. "So I hope you're not in a hurry."

She shook her head. He flipped the tie onto the dressing table, put an arm around her waist, and kissed her. Slowly, searchingly. So she could pretend. Good. With her eyes closed, pretending. His hands skimming over her, his breath suddenly indrawn as he brought his hands to a halt on her buttocks.

"I want to undress you. I'd like to," he said quietly. "Okay?"

She stood, waiting. He smiled and reached around in back of her to unzip her dress. She was already wet. It was seeping down into her tights.

"What do you do?" he asked, the dress following the coat to the armchair. "Model, actress?" He unhooked her brassiere, let it drop; covered her breasts with his hands, fingers splayed; murmuring, "Mmmm."

"Secretary," she lied as she always did. "And you?"

"Salesman. You're beautiful." He smiled more widely, his palms chafing her nipples, kissed her again. Then put his mouth to her breast. When he lifted his head, she smiled at him and began unbuttoning his shirt.

"Live in town?" he asked, pulling the shirttails out of his trousers, unbuckling his belt. She watched, captivated.

"No," she lied again. "Do you?"

"Buffalo," he said, then carried her down onto the cold hotel sheets, efficiently disposing of the remainder of her clothes. "I want to eat you. Let me, okay?"

She said nothing. He smiled again. And said, "You've done this a lot, haven't you? Don't have to say a word, honey. That's fine with me. Christ, you're beautiful! And wild!" he exclaimed, thrilled by the direct responses he got touching her.

Closing her eyes once more, caressing his hair, his ears, his eyes. Letting her fingertips tell lies. Thinking, Oh, yes, I love that. Yes. The wine rubbing the edges of her vision, making them blurry. A lovely humming buzz. His fingers probing, she opened her thighs more. Letting her hands move over him. Opening her eyes for just a moment as his head moved down. Then closed them. His tongue darting against her, the pleasure twisting.

While he was in the bathroom showering she quickly dressed and slipped out. Waved down a taxi and went home. To run a hot tub—no bloody bath cubes—and sink into the water, a last glass of wine sitting on the side of the tub. Exhausted. Depressed. But grateful he was just another of the ones she wouldn't have to see again. And grateful, in a remote way, for his insistence. He'd gone on and on until she'd started feeling raw. Holding her against the wall. Then over the chair. The bed. Everywhere in the room. Seeing the two of them now. Like rutting animals. Panting, gasping. But finally eased. For a while.

I will not do that again, she swore to herself. I vowed I wouldn't.

The tears started. She slipped lower in the water, took a sip of wine. Mother saying, "Give it up, Gillian. You don't have to *do* these things. It's so demeaning. And please don't lie to me anymore, either. I *know* you. I wish I could understand. You've the morals of a bloody alley cat. How *can* you? By the time you're thirty you'll have worn yourself out, used yourself up. It's no way for you to live, Gillie. Can't you see that, darling? You're a beautiful woman. You could have any number of men. You're talented, young. You surely don't still believe that man's coming to get you? You *can't* believe that. Isn't it obvious he didn't care? Oh, I know what it is. I do

72

know. And I'm sorry. I'd kill that bloody man if I could get my hands on him. How *can* you go on believing?"

I'm sorry. I did try. I won't do it again. You were right. You were always right.

She sat up and poured the wine into the sink. I won't do it again.

She turned over on her stomach and held herself, facedown, under the water until her lungs felt on the verge of bursting. Stayed down a little longer. Then came up gasping, gulping air down into her straining lungs. Then turned on the shower, stood up, and began painstakingly washing it all away.

Once Jenny was moved in with her, Pat seemed very happy. Bustling about buying groceries, cooking elaborate meals. Looking so happy, Gillian was bemused. Had she been this way with her own children—fussing, doting? Well, no matter. They both seemed well satisfied with the arrangements. So fine. One problem solved. For the moment.

At the office they started her on a second project. Working with Carl—whom she did like, very much—on a house. He was soft-spoken, infinitely patient, and very gifted. His preliminary design, the model, were breathtaking. Vast open areas, an entire wall of glass, a wonderfully natural flow from one room to the next. She started work on the drawings, enjoying the change, much preferring work on the house to work on the school.

She went up to take a look at the apartment after Jenny moved downstairs, touched to see Jenny had left the place spotless. She'd even cleaned the oven and the windows, scrubbed out the bathroom. There was nothing that needed doing. So she placed an ad in the evening paper and the calls began to come in almost at once. The telephone was ringing when she came through the front door the same evening the ad appeared. And that same night let the apartment to a retired businessman and his wife, who told her, "We go to Florida for the winters. Six months of the year we're here. You wouldn't mind keeping an eye on things?" They signed a two-year lease, gave her two months' rent, one month's security. They'd move in in two weeks' time. Leave for Florida directly after Christmas. Fine. For three twenty-five a month. They didn't think the price at all high. And complimented her enthusiastically on everything from the front entrance hall to the closet space.

Two or three times a week one or another of the staff drove her out to visit the job site. And each time she went she found herself wondering about Gabe Hadley, expecting him to be there, something akin to disappointed when he wasn't. But the work was progressing well, smoothly, with few problems. Minor disputes among the subcontractors. All to be expected. Occasional calls about matters easily settled over the telephone. She could, at last, remember all the names.

Carl stopped by her cubicle one morning after she'd been there a month to say, "Everybody's happy. The job's moving beautifully, we should bring it in right on schedule. How're you enjoying it here?"

"Oh, fine," the color flooding into her face. "Just fine."

"Good. No problems?"

"No, none at all."

"Okay, good. We're happy you're here, Gillian. Anything you want, anything crops up you can't handle, let us know."

"Yes, all right. Thank you very much."

He returned to his own office smiling, again seeing her face turning crimson. Poor woman, he thought. It must be murder finding yourself out in the world every day.

And that evening commented to Jane, "You were right, you know. She is unbelievably shy. I know exactly what you meant, saying you want to help her get the words out. But her work's exceptional, the best. And the school's really moving. You should see the way those men fall all over themselves when she goes up to the site. Six hands shooting out to light her cigarettes. All of them wanting to help her through the mud."

"Don't you wonder about her, though?" Jane said, mechanically cutting Lissa's meat. "I mean, even shy, you'd think she'd have at least one male friend."

"How do you know she doesn't?"

"I don't. It's just the feeling I get. You know Gabe Hadley actually *talked* to her. Now, that's really something."

"Maybe he felt safe talking to her," Carl said. "It isn't hard to talk *to* her. It's hard getting her to talk *back*."

"God, what I wouldn't give to look like that. I mean, she's even got a great figure. It isn't fair."

"She'd probably give it to you to have your ease with people."

"You think so?"

"I think so."

There was something so nice, so sort of peaceful being with Pat. Especially after Sandy. Even the old-timey furniture was nice. She liked looking at it. Didn't even mind sleeping in the twin bed, in the same bedroom. Pat was so quiet half the time she forgot all about her. And when she was being mad as hell about Sandy, Pat listened without putting her down. And, boy, was she ever excited about the baby. I wish I could get that excited about it, she thought, touching her belly. Just the slightest little bit of a bulge and she was already in the fourth month. Wishing it was already over.

She'd never get that promotion now. Not having to leave in a few months to have the baby. And they were really watching her, too. She got the feeling they were, anyhow, even if maybe they weren't. She'd have to stop her night classes soon, as well. Which would mean losing the credits. Damn it! How the hell had she ever let this happen? Listening to that idiot saying he didn't like the foam and hated the stinking rubbers, so why didn't she just play it brave and forget it for once. And look! Pregnant and the son of a bitch did a split. Probably making it with some other chick already, too. All because she wouldn't sit around and listen to him down Gillian. Well, not just because of that. But she couldn't hack the way he was always downing people. Women mostly. You'd say you really liked, say, Sarah Caldwell or Gloria Steinem or Margaret Trudeau, Betty Ford. Any woman. And Sandy would make some imbecilic remark about their just being women, not so damned special. If you happened to disagree, well, boy oh boy, Fuck you, turkey. You're dumb. You don't know shit. Well, I *do* know. And *you're* the dumb, fucking turkey.

But, damn it! What in the hell'm I going to do with a baby? I don't *want* a baby. I'll have to give it away to be adopted. To some folks who really want a baby. I wonder what happened to Gillian's kid. Did she maybe give her away to some folks who wanted one? Sad. That's sad. Why is the idea of giving babies away so stinking *sad?* Mine. Or maybe Gillian's. She never talks

76

about personal stuff. But it doesn't matter. She's so nice.
I never knew such nice people. Telling me I'd better
sign on with an obstetrician. Thinking it was like the
National Health or something here. And drink a good
deal of milk, Jenny. Pat was into that, too. The two of
them looking after her.

What am I going to do?

Pat felt worthwhile, purposeful for the first time in
years. Years. So glad of Jenny's presence. Glad to have
someone to feed, look after. So touched when the child
offered to pay half the rent. Sweet child. There's no
need for that, she'd told her. Well, then, she said, I'll
pay for the groceries. And Pat could see her wanting to
pay her way, not wishing to find herself beholden.
Settling on twenty dollars a week. Jenny didn't eat half
that. *When* she ate.

Lord, a baby! Won't that be grand?

She could almost reach out and touch the baby it was
so real to her. And felt very protective of Jenny because
of this longing inside herself for the baby. But Jenny
didn't want to keep it. Still, perhaps she'd change her
mind once the baby was born and she got the feel of it.
Nothing in the world lovelier than a new baby. Nothing.
The sweet softness of them. Lovely.

Dr. Peter Flannigan whispering into her ear. The
words sending heat into her face, turning the folds of
her ear to fire. I want to put my hands to you hold your
breasts in my hands rub my cheek against your belly
your thighs Pat come out with me come away with me
I'll go mad wanting you Pat.

Inexplicably, she started to cry. A terrible anger inside. Terrible.

77

He didn't really have to go out there. But he was curious. Well, maybe not curious. He wanted to look at her again, see if she really was as beautiful as she'd seemed that first time, wanted to see if something he'd say would send the color into her cheeks. Offer her a cigarette, see how the job was coming along. Satisfy the board with a progress report that everything was going along well. They'd be into the damned place by early spring.

It was sure as hell getting cold. Her hair. What hair! Soft, thick-looking. The color of sunshine on a cold day. He turned the heater on high. Another five or six weeks and it'd be Christmas. Hated Christmas. Maybe he'd take off that week, head somewhere warm. Hell, he'd left it far too late. He'd be lucky to get a seat on a bus into town, let alone a reservation on a flight to anywhere south. Stupid. Shouldn't have left it so late. Now he'd be stuck in town for ten days.

He thought of Penny. Didn't want to think of her but couldn't help himself. Thinking of her leaving, the way she'd left, taking Craig. Going off to California. I can't take any more of this. Nothing's happening for me here. And this marriage is a bad joke. I'm taking Craig and we're going to California. Okay, fine. You go to California, but leave Craig here, with me. You know you don't want to take him. Maybe I don't. But I'm *taking* him.

Out of spite, stupidity. Whatever. God damn it! You fool, you moronic, childish fool. Parking Craig with sitters so you could go out looking for exotic routes to stardom, jobs that never materialized, never could. Leaving him with a teenager with the mentality of a toilet seat.

Penny's voice on the telephone. Thinned by hysteria.

Craig had an accident. He died, Gabe. I'm so sorry, Gabe. You were right. I shouldn't have taken him. I'm sorry, Gabe. Gabe?

Stop thinking about it! Just stop!

What the hell am I doing going to the site? There's not one legitimate reason for my going out there today. Except to see her. See her face and the color of her hair. Going up like the flag on Memorial Day just thinking about her.

Craig. You'd have been eight this year. I shouldn't have let her take you, should have stood my ground, said no. No way. No. Damned stupid Penny. Getting cold. It'll probably snow. And the mud out there'll turn hard as rocks, wreck the car's undercarriage. Why am I bothering?

The nightmare again. She had to get up. And walk and smoke her way through the balance of the night, trying to get some work done but unable to concentrate. Gave it up and sat on the sofa staring at the room, listening for the sound of Pat's footsteps overhead. Sat on the sofa in her nightgown with her knees drawn up and the perspiration drying, the panic receding, heartbeat slowing down, down.

Alone. So alone. Loving this house but feeling the walls were holding her in. Captive. Hurting inside. Eyes moving slowly over the walls. Wall to wall to wall. The ceiling, the floor. So desperately alone. Her head filled with echoes. No.

Thinking about having to go out to the site in the morning. Hating disrupting one of the others to have a ride out. I should apply for a driving license here. There's no reason for all this. It's irrational. It would so simplify matters if I started driving again. They must

think me odd, eccentric. Like the man who came in response to the ad about Mother's Rover. Looking at me
as if I was quite, quite crazy, being willing to let the car
go at such a price. And the woman who eagerly paid out
the cash in five-pound notes, all the while clutching
Mother's mink to her breast. As if thinking I'd change
my mind. It doesn't matter. God! Yes, it matters.

Trying to get Hugh to take back all the jewelry. His
eyes, his expression of horror. Insisting he couldn't
possibly. Not possibly, Gillian. Tactless, unwise of me.
But I couldn't bring myself to sell them. Not those. Not
gifts of love. In another box on the shelf in the closet.
Rings and a locket, diamond earrings. Words engraved
by someone in a shop, someone who couldn't know.
Don't go on this way!

Wondering if this time that strange, angry man would
be at the site. When he'd smiled, he'd changed so utterly. Just for a few moments. Is it the way I am when a
few glasses of wine start me talking? The way it was
when he smiled. People see the change, must think me
an alcoholic because of the change. But I don't drink all
that much. It's simply something to ease it all, lighten it.
One has to have something. And drink is so socially ac-
ceptable, a matter of course. Could I be alcoholic? No,
no. There's no craving, none of that.

It's the other. *That* craving. When I think I'll go mad
and have to get out, go out, find someone. Shameful.
Mother was right. I could get myself murdered.
Complete madness, taking such risks. But what does one
do? I do love this place. I do. This room. The windows,
the floor. But the walls again start moving closer,
pressing against me, and I must get out, must. But I'll
not do it again. She was right. I'm back at work now. I
have this house, certain responsibilities. Keep going. I

must. For what, though? If I could just know for what. *Why* is he so angry? Puzzling, that anger. Yet I do envy him. He's able to show it. What have I ever done with my anger—any of the feelings—but push it down inside me, hold it down? It's no good, simply gets all tangled up with everything else pushed down in there. All of it building, becoming so frightfully *heavy*. It's that that sends me out. For air. Pat must be sleeping late this morning.

Six-fifteen. She got up and went into the bathroom to shower. Thinking, I must go down to Hamilton's, find some more bath cubes. Bloody silly, being fixated on bath cubes. Under the shower, soaping herself. Hate my legs! Look at them! How I'd love fine, slender ankles. So many things one can have done surgically. But nothing to be done about one's ankles. I'll fix an omelet. With the cheddar. Must shop for groceries. It's my Wednesday this week. Perhaps I'll do a lamb roast.

Watching Mother pushing cloves of garlic into the roast, readying it for the oven. Megan sitting at the counter, leaning on her elbows watching the two of us, asking, "What's a bastard, Mummy? Alison said her mummy said I'm one. Is it bad?"

Mother's hand shooting out to grip my elbow. A look in her eyes that surely was duplicated in mine. And a pain so intense.

No, no, no! I'll do a lamb roast, after all.

Pierce drove her out this time. She liked Pierce very much. He was so serene, his smiles so beatific, his voice so soothingly low, gentle.

"How're you liking it working with the Downtown Irregulars?" he asked, laughter floating on the edges of his words. So that she laughed, answering, "Are we irregulars?"

"In a certain sense, oh, yes, we are." He glanced over at her. "We have a very fine collection of outrageous people doing an assortment of projects that about runs the gamut. Schools, houses, churches. You want a doghouse, sir? Oh, yes, indeedy! We'll be happy to have one of our juniors do you up a fine old doghouse." He laughed.

"But you enjoy it."

"The best," he said. "Do you?"

"Very much. Everyone's so relaxed."

"Except for the famous Renée. Who is with us to remind us of our government's requirements having to do with income tax, Social Security, and sundry other nondelights. And her frequent states of panic illustrate how perfectly under control the rest of us are."

She looked at him to see if he was serious. He was smiling at her. She laughed. "You're very droll, Pierce."

"Oh, I like that." He chuckled. "Droll. You, on the other hand, are exceedingly understated. For a former Miss Universe."

"Oh, never." She flushed hotly. "That's such rubbish."

"You think so, huh?"

"Of course it is. I'm just muddling through, trying to get the jobs done one at a time. Any number of women far more beautiful than I."

"Not in the Downtown Irregulars. So, if you don't mind, we'll all go on sitting around, enjoying the privilege."

"Is that what you do?"

"No, not all the time."

"You're having me on," she accused.

He glanced over again. "A little. But I like the way

you laugh. I've got it pegged now, see. A bit of flattery, a touch of whimsy, and you laugh like a champ. And bingo, no more problems getting the words out. Makes me think I've got a little of the magic touch, getting you to talk, making you laugh."

"You're very nice, Pierce."

"So're you. But you don't think so, do you?"

"Why do you say that?"

"'Cause it's true. Isn't it?"

"I suppose. Do you think you're very nice?"

"Nope," he said. "I plain don't think about it. And neither should you. Did you always stutter like that?"

"Not always, no."

"Since when, then? Am I bugging you?" His eyes looked concerned.

"No," she answered, surprised to find it was true. He was so forthright she felt quite free with him. "Since three years ago."

"Mind if I ask what happened?"

"I'm afraid I do mind, yes."

"Okay, Miss U, we'll drop it. What d'you think of our man Hadley?"

"I think he's very angry."

"He is very, very angry, Gabe is. I'd be, too, my twenty-five-year-old child-bride wife with the intelligence of a grapefruit took off with my three-year-old son and the son got killed as a result."

"Is that what happened?"

"Not too many people know that," he said soberly. Silently telling her this story wasn't for public consumption. "But Gabe and I are old drinking buddies. Went to high school together. Been friends a whole lot of years. We got very very drunk together a lot that year."

"When was it?" she asked, her heartbeat turning erratic.

"Must be five years now. Has to be rough as hell on him out there every day with all those kids. He loves them all, you know. Knows the name of every last one of them, too. It put him down on his knees when it happened."

"What happened to the boy?"

"One of those stupid freak accidents. Could I have one of those while you're lighting up? Thanks. What happened was Penny would go off days and leave Craig with some girl. A sitter. They were at the park one afternoon and this girl was diddling around with some dude, not paying attention to Craig. Craig tried to get himself a drink from a water fountain. Climbed up and fell, hit his head on the concrete, and died that same night."

She was shaking her head. Back and forth, back and forth. Telling herself, I won't cry. I won't.

"Hey!" Pierce said softly. "Man, I *really* brought you down with that. I'm sorry. Are you okay?"

"I'm fine," she said thickly.

"Come have dinner one night," he said, smiling gently. "With Amy, my wife, and me, our kids. Come. It'd be good." Impulsively he took hold of her hand, squeezed it. "Come."

"Yes. I'd like that."

He smiled and the panic inside her started to dissolve.

"Okay," he said, releasing her hand. "O-kay."

5.

She was just concluding her conversation with the electrical contractor when she saw him. Standing looking out at the oak tree, the walkway. A cigarette between his fingers. An aura of intense concentration about him. And seeing him, was mortified by the heat surging into her face and neck, her sudden stammering so that the contractor looked at her with lifted eyebrows. She lit a cigarette to try to calm herself, wondering why she was reacting so strongly to his being there, knowing it was because of what Pierce had told her. She managed to finish with the contractor, who nonchalantly returned his hard hat to his head, told her to have a good day, and went on his way. She wasn't quite sure what to do next. Then Hadley came down the corridor, smiling. His smile sending the color right back into her face. So that she wanted the floor to open and swallow her. Or a dark curtain to drop between them.

"It's really coming along," he said. "You seem to be keeping everybody moving."

"Yes, well . . ." She wet her lips, looking down at the tips of her boots. Then cleared her throat and tried to think of something, anything, to say.

"Getting damned cold," he said. Was it just him or did everybody affect her this way? "I see you've got boots this time."

"Oh. Yes. I r̄ . . . ruined my sh . . . shoes the l . . . l . . . last time." Please, let me speak. Just let me get the words out.

"Do I bother ȳou?" he asked bluntly, his eyes boring into hers when she finally dared look at him.

"No." She shook her head, lying outrageously. You bother me dreadfully. But not in the way you think. I'm not sure in what way you bother me. But you do, yes. Bother me.

"I do bother you," he argued. "Look, I'm sorry about coming on strong that time. I was angry. About the tree. They dump it all on me when the slightest little thing goes wrong out here."

"It's all right," she said, unable to look away. His eyes were odd, unmatched. One green. One blue. How odd, she thought. How very odd. And his mouth. It did look soft.

"I want you to know I'm sorry," he said. "Look, how about lunch? Let me buy you lunch."

"I don't drive, you see. What I me . . . mean. I haven't a license. Pierce br . . . brought me. And well . . . well, I haven't any way to get back."

"Wait a minute. Let me make sure I'm getting this right. You don't have a license, so you don't drive. Right?"

"Yes."

"So you can't have lunch with me because Pierce

86

brought you and if you come out to lunch with me, you won't be able to get back to the office. Right?"

"Yes."

"*Why* don't you drive?"

"I simply don't."

"Well, that's ridiculous. You should know how to drive. Especially in a city this size. And most especially if you have to make job-site visits all the time. Do you want to learn how to drive?"

She could do no more than stare at him. Was he being angry with her now for not being able to drive? She had an overwhelming desire to strike him, make him stop leaping at her.

"How about this?" he said, awaiting her response and getting none. "We'll *all* go to lunch. Okay? You and me and Pierce. I haven't seen him in ages. I didn't know he was here today. Okay?"

"Yes, all right."

"Good. Let's go find Pierce. You're finished here for now?"

"Yes." Bloody agony. If she could just leave with Pierce, go back to the office. She couldn't speak at all with this man. Something about him turned her tongue to stone. She walked along the corridor beside him, the palms of her hands wet, her throat pulsing hurtfully, eyes down.

And stopped in surprise as Pierce and Gabe threw their arms around each other, pounding each other on the back, grinning.

"How the hell are you, man?" Pierce laughed. "God-damned good to see you!"

"The old philosopher." Gabe laughed. "We're going to buy the woman some lunch."

Gabe turned to look at her, his face transformed by

the obvious pleasure he derived from being in Pierce's company. So that she smiled, still mute, and went with them.

"Let's take my car," Gabe said, his arm around Pierce's shoulders. "That is, if you're still driving that Rolls Canardly."

"Your car." Pierce laughed. "Same old stinking jokes, I see."

An ancient Jaguar sedan. Gabe held the door open for her and she got in, passing so close to him he could smell her hair. He wanted to reach out and bury his hand in her hair. Just close his eyes and breathe in the smell of her hair.

Pierce caught the flicker in Gabe's eyes and thought, You're going to try again. You're finally going to try again. And felt oddly elated and a little choked up.

She excused herself to go to the ladies' room and Pierce leaned across the table, saying, "Don't come on too strong with her, Gabe. She's very fragile, very good quality."

Gabe looked surprised.

"That's all," Pierce said. "Just a word."

"You haven't changed one bit." Gabe's face relaxed into a smile. "It is really great to see you, you know."

"You, too, man. You splitting as usual over Christmas?"

"I left it too damned late."

"Well, okay. We'll get together. I'll get you put on the list."

"Surprise me," Gabe said. "Don't tell me about the list."

"Okay, I'll surprise you. She's beautiful, eh?"

"She's very beautiful," Gabe agreed.

"She's good, too, Gabe. Carl says her work is the best. Strange, sweet lady. You should hear her laugh."

"You have your eye on her?"

"No, no. She moves me. You know? Not a whole lot of women look that way and don't have a printed set of rules they give out. She's a *friend*."

She washed her hands, then looked at herself in the streaky mirror, trying to understand why she was here, having lunch with him. One moment seeming so angry, apologetic the next. It kept her riding on a fine tension wire. Vibrating. She wished he was nothing more than one of *them*. Someone she'd meet over a drink. They'd go to a hotel together, make love, never see each other again. Would he, she wondered, be as angry in his love-making as he was at so much else? He wouldn't. She knew.

Only once had she gone with an angry man. A mistake. A dangerous mistake. He'd used her so badly, so hard there'd been nothing for her but pain. Frightened her, so that she'd stayed to herself for almost five months after, nightly nursing the memory of his insane anger. And how he'd used her. Warning herself away from the pubs with the memory. How she'd stared at the bruises, wincing with the pain every time she sat down for days after. But that anger had been different, having had something to do with women, his hatred of them. This man had other reasons, different causes. But still he might seek to inflict injuries. And she wanted to have the question answered, wished he was one of *them* so that they'd drink together and later go somewhere anonymous. Then have it ended, done with. She couldn't do any of that with someone she'd have to see many more times. Until the school was completed. She brushed her hair and returned to the table.

"We'd better start heading back," Pierce said. He and Gabe had carried the conversation while she'd sat silent, listening, picking at her food. Aware of Gabe's eyes on her. Not the ominous, intense way Sandy had stared. Not so blatant. Simply studying her.

He was looking at her now and blinked, refocusing on Pierce with a smile, saying, "Let's do it again soon. No more of this years-on-end business."

"Right."

And the three of them again sat in the front seat of Gabe's white Jaguar, driving back to the site to collect Pierce's car. Close together in the front seat so that Gabe's thigh moved alongside hers as he moved his foot from the brake to the accelerator. And she was acutely aware of the contact, of the molten sensation it created low inside her. Overheated inside her coat and very aware of her breasts, her thighs, her belly. Keeping her face perfectly blank, staring straight ahead through the windshield while the occasional movements of his leg alongside hers turned her insides to jelly.

Back at the site, the two men embraced once more, pounding each other on the back. Then Pierce waited over by his car while Gabe shook her hand—short and hard, his eyes searching hers for something—saying, "Thanks for coming. I just wanted you to know I'm sorry if we got off on the wrong foot." Ask her out. Go ahead. Ask her.

"That's all right. Thank you very much for the meal." She turned, took a step, tripped, and nearly fell in the ruts of frozen mud. And miserably embarrassed, climbed into Pierce's car, once more wishing she could disappear,

90

vanish. Chain-smoking all the way back to town until Pierce said, "Come down, sweet lady. We all love you. And everybody trips in the mud one time or another. It doesn't *matter*."

Which made her cry behind her hands so that Pierce pulled over, opened her handbag, fished out some tissues, and pressed them into her hands, saying, "Don't do that, Miss U. None of it matters."

"I'm sorry," she said, wiping her eyes and nose. "It's just that he makes me so nervous."

"He knows it and it bothers him."

"What makes you say that?"

"Because I know Gabe. We go back a long, long way. Been through the wars together, me and Gabe. And underneath all the anger is one very decent guy who wouldn't hurt anybody. No one. It's just that we've all got things inside we can't handle all that well. And don't be sorry. It's cool. Okay now?"

"Pierce, you *are* nice."

"So're you." He smiled. "Just think of me as a sister."

She laughed.

"Should we put Gabe down, too?" Jane asked.

"Sure. Why not? We need a few extras."

"Okay. Who else?"

"I think that's about it," Carl said. "How many does that give us?"

"Fifty-six."

"Jesus! We'll have to take out everything but the rugs."

"I think a big ham. And a lot of cheeses, breads."

"Okay."

"D'you think she'll come?"

"A toss-up," he said. "Maybe. If she says no, try to persuade her. It'll be a good one."

There were three invitations in the mail that week. One from the Bradleys upstairs. For cocktails on the evening of the twenty-second. One from Jane and Carl for Christmas Eve. And one from Pierce and Amy for Christmas night. She pinned all three to the cork square on the wall beside her drawing board at home and sat looking at them trying to get herself to respond to the RSVPs.

I should go, she told herself. The Bradleys are very nice. And they'd be leaving for Florida the twenty-sixth, not returning until May. She'd have to go. And she'd most likely know the majority of people at Jane and Carl's party. Christmas night. With Pierce and his wife, others. I'll go, she decided. To all three. And telephoned her acceptances.

Friday evening, as she was letting herself into the apartment, the telephone was ringing. Gabe. She heard his voice, was able to respond to his hello, then listened—frozen—as he said, "I know it's kind of late in the day. But I thought if you weren't doing anything this evening you might like to come out for dinner."

She couldn't think of one decent alibi. Nothing that would allow her to turn him down without feeling guilty. So, not without reluctance, she agreed.

"I'll pick you up," he said.

"No, no." She didn't want him to come there. No idea why. She simply didn't want that. "I've got to go out for a bit. Some errands. I'll meet you."

"You're sure? I don't mind. I mean, I'll be happy to come by for you." He was beginning to think calling her ranked as one of his better mistakes. She wasn't interested. What was he trying to prove?

"That's all right, really. I'll meet you."

He gave her the name of the first restaurant that came to his mind and arranged to meet her there at seven-thirty. Then hung up feeling kind of down. Annoyed with himself for having started any of this. It couldn't work.

She put down the receiver and hurried to look through her closet, deliberating over what to wear. She didn't want to go. He was so angry. So unpredictable. Why couldn't she lie effortlessly, convincingly? Why couldn't she just say no and save both of them the embarrassment?

Too late to do anything about it now. She couldn't ring him back if she wanted to. Well, she could. Simply look him up in the telephone directory. But that would only serve to make her look more ridiculous. She'd have to go. But what to wear? Trousers. To cover up her legs. And a top. She went through the chest of drawers looking for a sweater. If she wore the black trousers, she could wear the black turtleneck. But that would be too funereal. With the navy trousers she could wear the blue angora Mother had bought her. The one she'd never worn. She removed it from its plastic bag and spread it out on the bed. Creased. From being packed away for more than three years. Seeing Mother's smile as she watched the package being opened. Saying, "I thought you'd enjoy that. When I saw it, it brought you to my mind. Do you like it, darling?"

My mother. The softness of your face against mine, the infinite tenderness of your hand stroking my arm. Sending love through your hand to my arm, fanning out through every part of me. Your hands speaking love to

93

any part of me you might touch. Able to say with just a hand what my mouth couldn't say in days of trying. I want you need you nothing makes sense how could anything make sense when you and Megan . . .

She glanced over at the clock. Less than an hour in which to shower, dress, and get to the restaurant. She'd have to wear the sweater as it was, creases and all.

He was waiting just inside the restaurant. And when she saw him, her stomach lurched. He was so very nice-looking. If only he didn't make her so nervous. Smiling when he caught sight of her, saying, "Right on time. That's great. I can't stand waiting for people." Which made her more nervous. As if he was telling her one of his rules and warning her how close she'd come to breaking it.

"Hungry?" he asked, helping her out of her coat, handing both their coats to the checkroom attendant.

"Yes," she answered, thinking she should have kept her coat. It was cold in here.

"Crazy about your sweater," he said, running his hand down her sleeve. "It really takes me back. High school and all those cute girls in sexy angora sweaters." Noticing how every single guy at the bar swiveled round to look at her. Their eyes going wide.

She smiled stiffly, her arm feeling paralyzed where he'd touched her. Both of them following along after the headwaiter to a table in the very rear of the restaurant.

"Ever had Mexican food?" he asked when they were seated.

"No, I haven't."

"It's my weakness," he said, scanning the menu. "The special combination's really the best. You get to sample just about everything that way."

"All right." She put down her menu.

94

"How about a margarita?"

"What is it?"

"Tequila, lemon juice, salt, triple sec. Or is it dry sack? I don't remember exactly. But they're delicious."

"Thank you, but I think I'll just have something soft."

The waiter was standing by Gabe's elbow, pencil poised.

"Coke?" Gabe asked her.

"Yes, please."

"Okay. Coke and a margarita. Two special combinations."

The waiter scribbled it down, went away. Gabe took out a pack of cigarettes, lit one, thinking, This is going to be murder. Offered her one. She took it and as she bent forward to his lighter he noticed how her hands trembled and felt something. What? Sorry for her? Something. Wishing he knew the right things to say and do to relax her.

"I make you nervous, don't I?" he said.

"I'm sorry." She risked looking at him. "You do, actually."

"Anything specific?"

"No, no. It's just me. I'm not terribly good company."

"You would be if you could relax." Oh, great, Gabe. Two or three more backhanded compliments that sound like insults and you'll really win her over.

"Yes," she said distantly, looking away at the people at other tables. All of them conversing so easily, laughing. The noise level high. Good-smelling food.

She was starting to make *him* nervous, anxious to get a conversation started but unable to think of very much to say.

"How are you liking working with Jane and Carl?" he asked, thinking how lame he sounded.

"Oh, very much." She looked at his mouth, crossed her legs. His mouth so appealing.

"That's good. Given any more thought to learning how to drive? It'd sure as hell make your life a lot easier."

"N . . . no." Don't start in at me, she thought. Please. "I . . . um . . . no."

"Are you afraid of cars?"

"I'd really rather not dis . . . discuss it."

"Okay."

The waiter came with the drinks. Gabe licked some of the salt from the rim, then took a swallow of the margarita. He felt like getting plastered, bombed out of his head. What a stupid idea this was. She obviously wasn't going to unbend and start talking. He watched her take a sip of Coke, then carefully set the glass down on the cocktail napkin.

"This is a very charming place," she said. Then blushed. As if she'd said something utterly outrageous. I want to go home, she thought. I shouldn't have accepted this invitation.

"I've been coming here for years. It was the first Mexican restaurant in town. There are three or four others now." What was he saying and doing to make her so uncomfortable? "Do you have a favorite kind of food?"

"I like all sorts, really."

"I like to cook." He tried out a smile. Got no results. She merely looked more ill at ease. "Italian food's my specialty. But I make pretty good Chinese. And spareribs. I'm crazy about spareribs." Why don't I shut up? "Sloppy Joes, too."

"What is that?"

"A mess you make with ground beef, onions, this, that, and the other." He smiled again. She nodded soberly. As if he'd just given her Charpentier's original recipe for crepes Suzette. Another silence. It made him feel as if he was trying to tow a stalled-out car with his bare hands.

"D'you cook?" he asked, making one more try.

"When I have time."

"What's your specialty?"

"I haven't one, actually." You *do*. All sorts of things. What's the matter with you? You're making him dreadfully uncomfortable. Why can't you simply *talk*?

He drained the margarita, waved down the waiter, and ordered another. Then sat back and looked at her. Large brown eyes, high cheekbones, a perfect nose, perfect skin. Absolutely gorgeous. And the shyest, most nervous woman he'd ever encountered. A disaster. The whole evening was bound to be. He'd drop her home after dinner. And that'd be that. Forget it. Chalk it off to bad impulses, lousy readings.

The waiter brought the second margarita, went off, and immediately returned with two huge pewter platters. "These are very hot," he said, sliding the platters down onto the table. "Very hot," he warned, removing his oven mitts. "Everything okay here?"

"Oh, fine, fine," Gabe said.

"What is all this?" she asked, staring down at the large quantity of food.

"That's guacamole," he pointed. "Made with avocado. That's an enchilada. Cheese inside. That's a taco, with beef. That's . . . I forget. What the hell is that? A burrito or something. I can't remember. That's rice, of course. And that is frijoles, refried beans. Eat up. It's great stuff."

He picked up his fork and began eating very quickly. She looked about for a knife, saw there were none on the table, wanted to ask for one but couldn't. Made the mistake of putting her fingertips on the edge of the

97

platter and burned herself. So that tears leaped into her eyes and she shoved her hand underneath her, sat on it, feeling her whole hand going numb. She could scarcely swallow, had no idea what the food tasted like. The avocado—what was it he'd called it?—cold, the rest of the food varying degrees of hot. She was hungry. But she couldn't eat.

"What's the matter?" he asked. "Don't like it?"

"Oh, I do. It's very good." She took several small forkfuls very quickly, hoping to force his attention away from her. If she didn't move her hand, it might go dead. She withdrew it from beneath her and at once felt the stinging in her fingertips, so wrapped her hand around the Coke glass, letting its coolness ease the burns. She wished she could close her eyes, open them, and find herself at home. She looked over to see he'd almost finished eating. So fast. She ate a bit more. Getting stomach cramps.

"You don't like it," he said. "Don't eat it if you don't like it."

"I'm sorry." She set down her fork. "It isn't that I'm not hungry. I . . . I . . . um . . . I'm afraid I f . . . feel r . . . rather ill. Ill. Would you forgive me if I went along home? I'm terribly sorry. Really. But I've a dreadful stomach ache and I think it might be best if I go home."

"That's too bad," he said, looking disappointed. "I'll take you."

"No, no. That's quite all right. I'm so sorry to spoil your evening. But I do feel ill. I'll just take a taxi."

"Come on," he said, plainly put off. "I'll get your coat, put you in a cab."

"I'm so sorry," she said again, hating herself. "I do feel badly about this."

"It's okay." He beckoned to the waiter, telling him, "I'll be back in a couple of minutes. Leave my drink."

She got up, then remembered her bag, bent down to retrieve it, straightened, and knocked over her water glass. Started to try to clean up the mess but the waiter smiled, saying, "Just leave it, miss. I'll take care of it."

Her face on fire, she walked with Gabe through to the checkroom, where he got her coat from the attendant, helped her on with it, then held open the front door, following her out into the street coatless. Flagged down a passing cab, held the door while she got in—all the while stammering out apologies—carefully closed the door, handed the driver a bill, and, without one further word, returned to the restaurant.

She bit the insides of her cheeks. So hard she could taste blood. And the instant she was back in the apartment, burst into tears. Sat down on the sofa still in her coat and cried until there were no tears left and her chest was aching. Then she got up, hung away her coat, and went to the bedroom to undress and put away the blue angora sweater, the trousers. Her chest still heaving with residual sobs.

He went back to the table to light a cigarette and finish his drink. Feeling positively rotten. He hadn't had a date go so wrong since high school. Depressing. He took another drag, stubbed out the cigarette, left the unfinished drink, put a twenty and a five on the check, and went home. Driving like a teenage hot-rodder. So angry, disappointed, depressed.

"I've definitely decided I'm not going to keep it," Jenny said. "Definitely. It's impossible."

"It's your decision to make, dear," Pat said tactfully. "No one can tell you what to do. Whatever you think's best." She'd never felt so profound a sense of pending loss. It was so deep, so total her body felt hollowed out by it, emptied, sucked dry. And had to force herself back into optimism, hopeful Jenny would change her mind once she saw the baby.

"I thought we might do up a Christmas dinner," Gillian was saying. "I'll do the turkey and I thought perhaps you'd do your marvelous stuffing, Pat. And the roast potatoes. Jenny could do the salad and perhaps the dessert."

"That's a fine idea," Pat said. "Shall we have the meal midday or evening?"

"Why don't we compromise?" Gillian said. "Let's plan to eat at three. That way we can take the rest of the afternoon to recover from all the overeating we're bound to do."

"You don't have a tree," Jenny said. "You've got to have a tree. Somebody has to. It's not Christmas if nobody has a tree."

"I hadn't thought about it." Gillian looked around the room. "But I could rig up some decorations."

"You *have* to have a tree," Jenny insisted. "Otherwise where'll you put your presents?"

Gillian laughed. "You're quite right. I'll see to a tree."

"Will you let me help you decorate it?" Jenny asked eagerly. "I love to do the tree."

"Of course. We'll all do it."

"This will be fun!" Pat said. "I'm quite looking forward to the day now."

"Me, too," Jenny concurred.

Gillian was thinking she'd have to go downtown, do some shopping. She hadn't given any thought at all to

100

gifts. As if Christmas had gone out of existence three year earlier. Three seasons she'd missed somehow.

On the evening of the twenty-second, still depressed by her failed evening with Gabe, feeling now as if she was about to attend her own ceremonial execution, she went woodenly up the stairs to attend the Bradleys' cocktail party. People had been arriving for close to an hour. Gillian had sat inside her apartment made up, dressed, and ready to go, listening to the front door open and close, the footsteps on the stairs. Wishing Pat and Jenny were going to be there. But Pat had taken Jenny to the ballet, to see the *Nutcracker*. Besides, they'd not been invited. So she sat waiting until she couldn't delay any longer. And went up.

She knocked at the door, waited, and plastered a smile to her mouth when Mrs. Bradley swung open the door, smiling, saying, "Come in, come in!" Mrs. Bradley in something yellow that was either a most peculair dress or a strange two-piece outfit. And Mr. Bradley looking well on his way to being drunk, coming over to take Gillian by the arm, insisting she have something to drink.

"Some Coca-Cola would be fine," she told him.

"Oh, come *on*," he urged. "Have something a little stronger. It's Christmas!"

"Really, Coca-Cola would be perfect."

"Okay," he said, giving her a look that plainly stated he thought she was out of her mind to turn down free booze. "One Coke coming up."

About thirty people. All couples. All sitting. No music. Just the sound of very muted conversations. People talking in twos and threes. About their children mainly. And football scores. Mr. Bradley brought her her Coke and she found an isolated spot near the fire. Sat down and stared into the fireplace, chain-smoking, waiting it out. Listening to the people nearest talking about how awful teenagers were nowadays, how disrespectful, not like when *they* were young. And three men sitting off on the other side discussing some football game they wished they were watching, debating whether they dared switch on the set. She drank some of the Coke, smoked, wished she wasn't there, hadn't felt obligated to come. Achingly alone, separate.

Mrs. Bradley came over and perched on the arm of Gillian's chair. Smiling. Saying, "You must eat something. There's tons of food. Don't you look pretty! Have you met everyone?" Asked all her questions, patted Gillian on the arm, didn't wait for any answers, and went off to sit on the edge of the sofa beside three women crowded together there, jumping into the middle of their conversation.

Gillian got up, walked over to the buffet, dipped a carrot stick into a bowl of something brown. Ate the carrot. It lumped in her throat. Returned to her chair, drank some more Coke, lit another cigarette, resumed staring into the fire. And when the fire began dying down, put the screen to one side, added two more pieces of wood from the supply in the brass log holder, and sat down again. If the fire were to go out, what would she look at?

It dragged on forever. They were nice people, the Bradleys, she thought. But she just didn't belong here with all these sedate, middle-aged couples. The only unattached person in the place. And such a quiet, toned-down party. Without any music. How could one give a party and not have music? Looking around, it seemed the only two people who were high and having a good time were the Bradleys. But they were working awfully hard at it, perhaps realizing the party wasn't quite the success they'd been hoping it'd be.

She looked at her watch. And couldn't believe it. She'd been there only an hour. If felt like three in the morning. But it was only seven-fifteen. She'd have to stay at least another half hour. Her eyes were smarting from staring so fixedly into the fire and she longed for a real drink or some wine but knew she wouldn't. Would not. So sat on, periodically attending to the fire, enisled in the middle of the party.

And finally, at seven-forty-five, got up, carried her empty glass back to the bar, then looked about for the Bradleys. To say goodnight. They came rushing over, saying, "You can't go *yet*." But she was able to lie, claiming another commitment for the balance of the evening. And Mrs. Bradley said, "Of course, of course," and shooed Mr. Bradley back to the other guests, walking with Gillian to the door.

"You have a good Christmas, now. And we'll see you when we get back. Hope your evening is pleasant."

"Thank you very much. Really a lovely party."

The door closed and it was over. Feeling a fool standing out in the hall all made up, dressed up. Going nowhere. The party over. She turned and went downstairs. Hating parties, dates, all of it. Determined to learn to say no. She sat up and watched a late film on television, thinking with dread of the office party there'd be the next afternoon. And after that, Jane and Carl's party, then Pierce's. She should have said no to the lot of them. Even the film wasn't very good. But at least she was able to have several glasses of wine and relax while she watched.

Near midday, Renée discreetly distributed envelopes. Then Jane and Carl, with the help of Renée and Lucy, the secretary, began setting up a bar in the conference room. In her envelope Gillian found a check for three hundred dollars. A week's salary. A Christmas bonus. She was sitting staring at it when Pierce leaned around the end of the partition, saying, "Time to join the festivities, Miss U."

"Yes, I'm coming." She tucked the envelope into her bag. "They're very generous, aren't they?"

"A little matter of recognizing ability. Come on, woman! I've got a terrible thirst working here."

The radio was turned on loud to a rock station. Everyone was drinking, dancing, eating the abundant food. Gillian sat on the receptionist's desk drinking tonic, watching, smiling. This was certainly more like a party. And she knew everyone. Jane and Carl dancing wildly, Carl's hair flying all over the place. He had a very sweet face, Gillian thought. The two of them went so well together, he and Jane. Pierce slid onto the desk beside her, saying, "Good time, huh?"

"It's wonderful. They're all having such fun."

"Don't you dance, Miss U?"

"Oh, no. I'm shocking. Dreadful."

"I'll bet you're not. What's that you're drinking?"

"Quinine water."

"Tonic?" He made a face. "Come *on*, sweet lady. It's not allowed, drinking tonic at an office party."

"No, really. I don't fancy a drink."

"Well, dance at least. Come on. I insist."

He tugged at her hand and she stood up, setting down her drink. "I really am not any good. Honestly."

"Come dance." He laughed. "Let me disprove the old

104

maxim that all black folks have rhythm. If you're worse than I am, we'll quit."

Laughing, she allowed him to draw her into the group. And feeling hopelessly clumsy, tried to find the beat of the music.

"You see?" she laughed, knowing her face was bright red. "Didn't I tell you? Bloody awful."

"Shush, shush. You're doing just fine. Keep moving."

Fortunately the music ended and she was able to escape back to her perch on the desk, Pierce returning to stand in front of her.

"You're going to the party tomorrow night?" he asked.

"I'll be there, yes."

"Good."

He stood a moment longer smiling at her, then drifted off to dance with one of the juniors.

After the party she went downtown to do some last-minute shopping. The store was jammed, noisy. She made her way along the main floor in search of bath cubes, wanting to smile. Such a long time since she'd done this. Pleasure shopping. For herself. And gifts. It was fun. She found the bath cubes. Imported, of course, from England. She paid for them and continued on her way, hoping to spot something Pat might like.

As she was coming out of the store she saw a taxi discharging a fare and managed to get there before another woman.

"Have you any idea," she asked the driver, "where I might get a tree?"

"A Christmas tree, you mean?"

"Yes, that's right."

"Sure. A coupla blocks over. You wanna go get a tree?"

"I do, yes."

"Okay, lady." He pushed down the flag.

She found one small enough to fit in the trunk of the taxi. Then gave the driver her address. At the house the driver helped her with the tree and she gave him two dollars saying, "Thank you so much."

"Thank *you*, miss. And have a nice Christmas."

She managed to find half a dozen decent-sized rocks in the garden, an old plastic outsized flower pot in the cellar, and with the rocks wedged the tree in the pot before half filling it with water, finally standing back to admire her efforts. A rather dreary little tree, a bit lopsided. But, still, a tree.

After washing the resin and dirt from her hands, she sat down on the sofa to look through her purchases. A scarf and a bottle of Blue Grass for Pat, some scented sachets. A pretty shirt for Jenny, some L'Air du Temps cologne. A book of poems for Pierce. A large scented candle to take along tomorrow evening for Jane and Carl. The bath cubes. Some tissue and ribbons, a pack of stickers, and some gift cards. It didn't seem like very much. In fact, spread out on the rug, it looked meager. She left it all there on the rug, pulled on her coat, and went out to do a little more shopping. Before the shops closed.

It occurred to her as she was coming out of the last of the stores that she was having a very happy day. And wondered what Gabe was doing, if he was enjoying himself. Yet, thinking of him, felt mildly agitated. And slowly started descending from the day's pleasure, wishing she hadn't thought of him. She felt so badly at the way that evening had gone. Very badly.

She returned home to put everything away in the bedroom closet—she'd wrap the gifts later—thinking she ought to eat but not in the least tempted by anything in the refrigerator or the cupboards. So she poured a glass of wine instead and got a fire going, then sat down on the rug, gazing into the fire. A gradual constricting sensation in her chest, thinking about Brooke. Bloody stupid of me to go on year after year, wondering. Thinking about Christmas, a residue of the day's elation still clinging, decided it was high time she wrote her father, let him know where she was. Break the long silence. Ask about Brooke in the course of the letter. Settle the matter once and for all.

She got up and went into the bedroom to sit down at the drawing board, drawing a fresh sheet of airmail paper over in front of her.

It's thirteen years after the fact and time to put paid to all this. Walking about imagining myself coming face to face with Brooke on some street or in some department store. When I know it's impossible. But I must know. Must.

And began to write.

6.

He told himself it was a hell of a lot better to go out to a party than sit home alone, trying to watch television, killing time. Putting in appearances at a few school-related functions. Trying to forget about Christmas altogether, bothered by the decorations, the lights. By all of it. Because there was such an absence of feeling inside about it.

Not like that first Christmas when he'd surrounded Craig with stuffed toys, a squeezy Santa that said ho-ho-ho when you pulled the string. Ho-ho-ho and Merry Christmas, boys and girls. But Penny had to move all the toys. Saying, "He's too little, for God's sake, Gabe! You'll smother him."

Not like that second Christmas when he'd taken Craig downtown to see the parade, and Hamilton's windows, up to the toy department to sit on Santa's lap. Craig had been scared, started to cry. So that Gabe had had to carry him around for a good half hour before Craig calmed down. Then wanted to go back, see Santa again.

Getting home to find Penny all pissed off because they were late and she'd had to miss her dancing lesson.

"Why the hell didn't you just go?" he'd wanted to know, confounded as always by her complete lack of logic.

"Well, how could I?" she'd asked, standing hands on hips in her tights and leotard. Capezio. The bill for her dancing outfits a tidy hundred and twenty-six dollars. While she went thrift-shopping for castoffs for Craig. Which made him so furious he'd had to go out and buy Craig's clothes himself. Decent stuff. Not some garbage somebody'd given away. Not for Craig.

He should've known better. Going on that way, believing there had to be some kind of mother love somewhere inside her. Believing just enough to allow her to take Craig in spite of the considerable misgivings. Believing just enough to let her take him. Sending him back four months later in a little crated pine coffin. To be buried beside his grandparents. And let her go ahead and divorce him, glad never to have to see her again. Because the sight of her might have moved him to commit murder. Hers.

The pleasure in life seemed all gone. Except for a few friends. Old friends. Like Pierce. Who went the rounds of the bars with him for a solid month. The two of them on an epic drunk. Pierce the Prophet. Pierce the Philosopher. Pierce liked her, too. But not in the same way. What does that *mean?* Not in the same way. What do I mean? *How* do I like her in the way that Pierce doesn't? I don't know that I like her. Yes, I like her. Something about her that's so damned fragile. Pierce, right again. A fragility that doesn't go with the looks or the height. But does go with the stuttering, the blushes. She is sweet. I never met a truly sweet woman before.

Apologizing, saying how sorry she was. Really sorry. I should've been the one apologizing to her for coming on so strong. Trying to force the tempo instead of just allowing things to happen in their own time. Wrong of me.

Stretched out on the sofa, with his arms folded behind his head, his eyes closed, thinking about her. Never mind the reality, the colossal fuck-up it had turned out to be. Imagining her on the sofa with him, lying on top of him. Just this way. Her skin creamy, that thick hair touching his chin. He sat up abruptly, reaching for a cigarette.

It all comes to nothing. Always. Right back to zero. There's nothing left here for the giving. It's the truth. It's dried up, gone.

She spent the morning wrapping all the gifts. Then went through the apartment in the afternoon cleaning, dusting, refusing to allow herself to think about what sort of party it might or might not be. Not thinking at all. Just getting on with it. Cleaning up for tomorrow. Keeping on until she looked over at the domed clock on the mantel and realized she'd worked far later than she'd intended. She'd have to hurry and start getting ready.

She changed her clothes three times before finally settling on a rose-colored caftan of soft wool. Tried on the caftan, then took it off to have a second look at her underwear. Thinking, This is absurd. Not a soul's going to see or care what I have on under my dress. But she didn't like what her brassiere did to the smooth lines of the dress and went looking through the chest of drawers and then the closet for the long silk slip she knew she'd put away somewhere. But where? When she was at the point of tearing her hair, she remembered having

110

wrapped it in tissue along with several other items she wore only rarely, placing all of it in a flat, lidded wicker basket she kept under the bed. And dragged the basket out to find the slip hopelessly wrinkled and in need of ironing. Which meant she had to go to the kitchen, set up the ironing board, and spend twenty-five minutes cautiously ironing out the wrinkles with a cool iron.

That done, she was so overheated she had to go back to the bathroom, run a tub, and bathe a second time. All the while thinking, I'll never get there. I'm already late. The invitation said seven-thirty and it's gone eight.

She spilled the entire box of hairpins and spent another ten minutes on her hands and knees on the bathroom floor picking them all up. Then she couldn't get her hair to go the way she wanted. Trying for a loose knot on top with a few wisps in front of the ears. But her hair was too soft from the washing and wouldn't stay up. Until her third—and she told herself, the last—try. Pushing the pins in so hard she was quite sure she'd drawn blood.

By the time she was finally dressed it occurred to her she couldn't possibly walk to the bus stop. She'd ruin her shoes. And if she wore boots the outfit would look idiotic. So she rang for a taxi and was told she'd have to wait half an hour, Christmas Eve, you know. Everybody wants a cab, lady.

Bloody hell! She collapsed on the sofa with a cigarette to wait. Her coat, the candle, the gift-wrapped book, and her bag at the ready. And now all dressed, made up, her hair finally done right, she felt just as she had the other evening while she'd sat waiting to go up to the Bradleys' party. She didn't feel like going. There were bound to be any number of people she didn't know. And what if Pierce wasn't there? Or any of the others? She'd

111

stand the entire evening in some corner, waiting it out until it was time to go home. One or two people might approach to talk to her. But they'd give up—as they always did—after a few minutes. While she groped about frantically trying to think of something to say.

The book. Perhaps he'd already read it. And it was impolite to give a gift to the husband without having one for the wife as well. Pierce's wife would be there if he was. And the candle. A stupid gift. A bottle of wine would've been more appropriate. Or some flowers. Anything but a candle.

A car honked three times outside. She ran to the window, saw it was the taxi, ran back, snatched up her coat, the candle, the book, and her bag, and went flying out. To sit in the rear of the taxi realizing she'd not only forgotten her earrings—she'd planned to wear the diamond ones Hugh had given Mother—but her necklace as well. And, tentatively touching the back of her hair, felt certain it would all come tumbling down if the wind caught it or if she moved her head abruptly.

She paid the driver and stepped out of the taxi directly into a snowbank that served, instantly, to turn her foot numb to the ankle. She managed to extricate herself and stood on the cleared sidewalk in front of the three-story house shaking her foot to get the snow off, looking in dismay at her saturated shoe.

"Sod it!" she swore aloud, rearranging her parcels, making her way up the front steps to ring the bell.

Through the wavy glass of the front door she saw Carl come skipping down the stairs to open the door.

Beaming, he said, "Hi. Wow, you look fantastic. Come on in, you can park your coat in here."

"I'm terribly late," she apologized. "I had to wait half an hour for a taxi."

"Hey, that's okay. Come on. It's a great party."

He took her hand and led her up to the second floor, where the noise level was just shy of deafening so that she wanted to stop but his hand kept her moving, right along to the kitchen, where Jane was working at the counter. She said, "Hi!" with a smile, waving a long-bladed knife. "Glad you're here. Get in there and get yourself a drink, something to eat. Terrific dress. You look sensational."

"I brought you a small gift," Gillian said, setting the wrapped candle down on the counter.

"Oh, that's really nice. What is it?"

"Nothing very inspired, I'm afraid. A candle."

"You didn't have to do that, Gillian," Carl said, beside her. "Thanks a lot. Come on, I'll get you a drink. What'll you have?"

"Have you anything soft?" she asked, going along with him past the kitchen to the dining area.

"Coke, Seven-Up."

"Coke would be lovely, thank you."

He handed her a glass, then vanished. And she was left standing there surrounded by groups of people all talking, laughing loudly, some dancing. People wall to wall. She turned to look behind her at the buffet that had been set up in front of the windows, then turned again to look through the wide archway and beyond into the living room. Music was roaring out of two very large speakers and Carl was down at the far end stacking more records on the turntable. She took a sip of the Coke, then opened her bag for a cigarette. No one she recognized. She saw no one she knew and felt the weight of hours stretching on into the night, the hours when she'd stand first in one corner and then in another, drinking the same glass of Coke until she'd put in her

113

time and could safely say thank you and good night, go home, take off the dress, the foolish fussy underwear, take down her hair, take off her face, and go wearily to bed. With another night gone. Another party done with, ended.

Carl had changed the record. Something sweet. A painfully pure voice singing about clowns, send in the clowns and suddenly it was all too much all the years and the flushes and stuttering, stammering down through the days; without words or thoughts to think quickly enough to get them said before the audience of one or two grew bored and impatient and went on their way to someone less tongue-tied, someone with flash. She looked over at the bar, at the bottles, set down her Coke, and poured some wine into a glass, took a long swallow, then again looked at the room, the people assembled. The high, perfect voice cutting into her with its sad clown philosophy having to do with perfect entrances and pratfalls in style, all of it cutting like a fine diamond on glass, like paper slicing so easily through skin and the surprise seeing the blood when surely flesh had more substance than paper, how could paper draw blood?

"You really are beautiful," he said, right beside her, pouring himself a drink. "I go away thinking you're not, that it's something in my head that does it. But every time I see you again, I'm surprised because you really are. Beautiful." He picked up his drink and turned, smiling at her, and she thought, *No!* Why didn't I wait? Why did I take this? I shouldn't have risked a drink but I thought no one was here; that damned record.

"Thank you." Her voice smoothed out already, so quickly it worked. Just a little and it nicely browned the edges, making everything rise. Like yeast. Remembering

114

the book under her arm, the one she'd brought for Pierce, but thought perhaps it was impolite after all to offer gifts to married men and the wine was boldness by the bottle, any number of things. "I thought I'd bring this along in case I saw you." Giving him the package, seeing the surprise of the totally unexpected doing startling things to his face. Turning it soft and vulnerable, his mouth. Oh, God! I didn't want this to happen. You're not one of *them*. You won't you'll never understand when I say no the next time when I won't see you or answer your calls you'll think it's you something you said or did never knowing all the time it was me.

"Did you know I'd be coming?" he asked; even his voice turned soft with the surprise as he accepted the package and turned it over in his hands.

"No." She told the truth. "But I saw it and thought of you." And that, too, was the truth. "I thought you might like it." Rilke. I like Rilke.

"Come over here," he said, taking her arm, drawing her into a quiet corner by the fireplace, away from the bar, setting his drink down on the mantel. Asking her, "Who are you tonight?"

She couldn't stop looking at his mouth, not even when she took another swallow of wine before answering, "Someone else."

He looked at her face, then down at the glass, and did something no one else but Mother had ever done: instantly added it up. Correctly. "Dutch courage," he said. "When you drink, you don't blush, you don't stutter. Should I keep you bombed?"

Yes, she thought. Yes, if you ever want to see me again. She drank some more.

"Should I open this now?" he asked, bemused, looking down at the gift she'd given him.

115

"Yes, if you like." Oh, my God. Look at me. Smiling. Surely I must smell of it. *They* always know. Do you know? Can you sense how readily I'll bend?

She watched him tear off the wrappings, toss them into the fire, then turn the book right side up, studying the jacket before opening the cover.

"I'm . . ." He looked at her. "Thank you. I haven't got anything for you."

"I wasn't expecting anything. It was an impulse."

His hand reached out and slid past her ear onto her hair and he smiled. It *was* soft. "This is an impulse, too," he said, his eyes open as he kissed her on the mouth, then lifted his head, his eyes investigating the depths of hers. Thinking, thinking; so many thoughts all at once. None of them making very much sense. But the way she looked, the scent and touch of her, her hair.

"Is your proper name Gabriel?" she asked, holding her glass in both hands.

He nodded, retrieving his drink from the mantel. "Have you got a habit?" he asked. "Don't get angry with me. I know I'm blunt as hell. And forceful. I've never been good at playing social games. A lot of questions I want to ask need direct answers. Do you need that"—he nodded at her drink—"to get you through?"

She, too, looked down at her drink. Then back up at him. "Not to get me through. To get me *out*."

"Okay. Did you come with someone?"

"No." I never see my "someones" more than once. I shouldn't be doing any of this. I'll hate you in the morning. And by afternoon, you'll be hating me.

"Well, now you're with me." He smiled suddenly, dazzingly, so that she had to smile and wanted him to kiss her again, hold her, hold her.

"Hey! Look at that spread. Hungry?"

116

"Yes, very."

"Then let's eat." He took her bag and set it and the book on the mantel, then started to lead her toward the buffet, then stopped. "I'll take you home later. All right?"

"Gabe, wait!" What was she going to say. "I'm going to have to talk with you. While I can. You understand? Because if I don't . . . that is, I know what will happen . . . . It has to do with me."

"Okay. Let's get some food and find someplace on the quiet side. And we'll talk. I just want to tell you one thing."

"What?"

"I don't know who you brought that book for. But I'm glad you gave it to me."

"But . . ."

"No. It's okay." He laid his forefinger against her lips. "It's really okay. Now let's grab a couple of plates and we'll go talk. All right?"

Godgodgod*god!* Why tonight? Why? I'll despise him, come the morning. I always do.

"I don't believe it!" Jane whispered to Carl in the kitchen. "Gabe and Gillian?"

"Why not?" he said, nibbling on a sliver of ham.

"The four of them sitting there on the stairs laughing it up, talking away. I don't recognize either one of them. It's like two entirely different people came to the party. And Pierce sitting there looking like the Messiah or something. It's too much. Amy looks as if she's having the time of her life. Too much!"

"Let's dance," he said. "I *feel* like *dancing*."

She laughed. "First slice some more ham. Then we'll dance."

117

Carl picked up the carving set and went out to the buffet. Jane stood a moment longer in the kitchen doorway watching the four on the stairs. Pierce and Amy. Gillian and Gabe. A nice contrast, the two of them. Gillian so many tones of silver and gold, highlights of pink. And Gabe. Dark accentuated by a black cashmere turtleneck, black trousers. It was the first time she could recall seeing him smile for longer than five seconds. The first time she'd seen Gillian effortlessly laughing and talking. Too much!

She would have told him. Something. She wasn't sure what. But some explanation, something. It was too late now. Pierce and Amy sitting on the step above and all the soft laughter, the talking, it was too late. Far too late. Her third glass of wine and all her signals were sending themselves out their thighs touching his hand twice more reaching out to stroke her hair looking into her eyes from moment to moment as if awaiting the stroke of midnight and her evolution into six white mice or a large very orange pumpkin. Or perhaps some other, shadier form of herself. Because unlike those others, he'd seen her before, knew her in the daytimes and might not understand. Frightened, too. Because she wasn't sure if it was the drink or if this was the second time in her life when someone's voice and gestures, the eyes and the shape of the mouth, the words and slight touches, unlocked something inside her that was completely receptive, compliant.

Had Brooke known? Or had he merely been very clever, practiced? Random caresses, innocent enough, superficial, applied over a period of days, weeks, leading her into an expectation of a continuation of those lazy, apparently unpremeditated signs of affection. So that the first kiss was like punctuation and the first time one of his caresses was direct and obviously planned she accepted both because she'd been waiting, expecting anything, everything.

Perhaps he'd thought her simple-minded, a bit of a fool. Is that what you thought of me? So willing he had to stop and say, "What's happened to your shyness, then?" Which at once brought it all back so that he'd known after that not to give voice to his thoughts but simply to avail himself of what was plainly his for the taking. She'd thought him beautiful. All of him. And accepted the brief pain as a matter of course because the other feelings, the emotional responses, were there, gratified. He'd been exultant, jubilant, an avid adventurer. Starting her off down a road that had no ending. Sending her on her way with a glass of wine in her hand and an itching need inside. Along with a baby. Saying, "I'll come to you directly." A tale in a child's book of fables.

Oh, God! That song again. Couldn't they play another, something less directly intended to find its target inside her? How old had she been? Eleven, twelve perhaps. They'd been on holiday in Devon. Twelve. The summer after the divorce. A small circus came to town. Mother took her. And pushed her to her feet when the ringmaster called for a flock of children to come be lowered onto a horse's back, to be trussed into a stiff leather harness and swung through the air before being deposited with a dreadful bump onto the broad sweating back of that horse. She'd screamed, terrified. And when they'd released her from the harness, everyone had laughed. She'd wet herself and had to go back, dripping, miserable, to sit out the rest of the show while Mother, refusing to allow her to make more of a fool of herself than she'd already done, sat with her arm around her, whispering, "It's nothing, nothing. You'll be back at the hotel shortly and we'll get you changed into fresh clothes. Look at the clowns, Gillie! Aren't they funny, darling?" But no. They were sad with their grotesquely downturned painted mouths, rhinestone-studded teardrops gracing their cheeks. The clowns broke her heart, had her turn her face into the warmth of her mother's breast, crying silently.

"What's wrong?" Gabe asked, his hand on her knee.

"It's that song," she whispered, "I can't bear that song."

"You don't like it?"

"I do. But it's too true, you see."

His hand stayed on her knee as his head lifted. Listening while she suffered through it, watching his face, waiting, curious to hear what he'd say.

I don't know, he thought, what I thought you were. But you're more than I guessed and victim to something I know too well, wish I didn't. And he had this image of the two of them playing at therapeutics, doctoring old injuries. An image containing mixed pleasures. Because the idea of unburdening, freeing his head of old thoughts, old sorrows, was one that might offer great relief. But also a possible dependency he wasn't sure he wanted. What in hell do I want? he wondered. Are we all clowns? Is that the point? Does it matter if we are if we all know it?

He turned to look up at Pierce, then at Amy, and again at Pierce. They, too, were listening.

You two, he thought. Do you think of yourselves as clowns because you've grown together, made children, have happiness, pleasure as a routine in your lives? Are you inhibited by the possibility of people nearby hearing parts of your more intimate conversations? Finding yourselves feeling suddenly foolish because what you're saying, all you've said, has been said and said and said for so many thousands of years and you're suddenly presented with a sickening image of your own banality because some people over there are listening in on words you'd intended seriously? You don't. I can see you don't. It has to do with not caring about the externals, about appearances, or eavesdroppers. And I don't give a damn about any of that either. But no more Pennys. And no more of those willing victims with the desperate eyes and the insouciance that comes out in the indifferent ambience of bars, vanishes in the dim light of bedrooms, and becomes a little-girl tenacity, a truly dreadful need to offer reluctant access in exchange for something that might magically turn into real contact. I can't do that anymore. That was the anger. Moving me into bars, into the bodies of women who made me both sadder and angrier because there was nothing there for me or for them and none of it was real and had little if anything to do with genuine feelings or desire. I was a clown, have been a clown. But Gillian. Who am I when I'm with you?

"You think you're a clown, man?" Pierce asked softly, leaning fractionally closer to Gabe. "D'you think it?"

"Pierce, don't," Amy said, a little chilled by what the song had done to the other three. "Don't."

"It's cool," he said even more softly, stilling her with his hand. The signals there, always. "Tell me. I've been wondering about it."

"Sometimes," Gabe admitted. "Don't you?" His hand tightened on Gillian's knee. She felt it in her groin.

Pierce threw back his head and laughed, then looked at Gillian. "How about you?"

She smiled. "Oh, yes," she said. "Very definitely. I'm not sure that it matters. Do you think it matters?"

"Hell, it doesn't *matter*. You tell yourself inside there"—he pointed to her head—"tell yourself it doesn't matter, Miss U. Then get in the ring and do your stuff. Fuck 'em! It don't *matter*."

"Pierce," Gabe said to her, "is a philosopher. You may have noticed."

"Yes. And I know he's right. *Tonight* I know he is. *Tomorrow* I'll be a clown again."

"Don't be," Amy said, her hand falling lightly onto Gillian's shoulder. "Don't even think about it. It's only inside. And we all feel it at times."

Gillian looked at her. A tiny, red-haired woman with delicate features and a very sensuous mouth; almost frail-looking, yet somehow very strong, enviably strong. She took hold of Amy's hand and held it against her cheek.

I've had too much to drink. And tomorrow evening they'll expect this of me, expect me to be able to display my feelings, respond truthfully. But unless I drink again, they won't be there. Perhaps I do have a habit. Is that what it is? I don't know. But how do you get past being a sad-faced clown and become the high-wire act without the wine to get you there? I wish I knew. God, I wish I knew. Tonight I love these people. Tomorrow I'll cringe inside at the sight of them. Knowing their expectations.

The record ended at last and something loud and mechanical-sounding replaced it.

Pierce said, "Let's dance," and drew Amy up, away. Her hand slipping out of Gillian's grasp. Away.

Leaving the two of them still on the stairs, staring, trying to read messages in each other's eyes.

The drumming inside, all awareness, thinking of her

silk underthings, the silk against her skin like hands lightly skimming caresses. You can have me, I'm readily had. Do you know that, can you see? I don't want to be. Not this way. I want to be all one thing all of the time but I've never learned how or perhaps it's simply that I can't, there's no continuity.

"Do you dance?" he asked.

Only lying down, she thought. And laughed aloud. "I'm a shockingly bad dancer."

"Good." He smiled. "So am I."

I can't tell you I live out of town, I'm a secretary. None of those things. What will I *tell* you? Is there anything it's safe to tell you? Will you, like that man in the bar, know that this is something I do a lot? Will it matter?

"Have you ever been married?" he asked.

"No."

"I was."

"Yes, I know that."

He looked at her questioningly for a moment, then said, "Pierce."

"Yes."

"Did he tell you all of it?"

"The pertinent details."

Another questioning look. Don't feel sorry for me, he thought. I can handle a lot of things. But not that. That's not something I've ever needed.

"What was your little boy's name?" she asked.

"Craig."

She wanted to say, My daughter's name was Megan. But of course she couldn't say that. Telling him that would mean having to tell him all the rest of it. And she couldn't talk to anyone about that. Not anyone. The newspaper people, the television people, the radio

123

people, the foreign-press people. Please send them away please. Finally hiding in the closet. The hall closet. Crouching beside the hot-water tank, the linens airing on the shelf above her. Mother had folded them, put them there the day before. Crouched in there, resting her head against the wall. Make them go please please.

"What?" he asked, touching her hair.

"It's nothing. Listen, there's a slow number. I'm not quite so shocking at slow numbers." And I want you to hold me hold me.

"Me neither." He smiled, extending his hand, suddenly wanting more than anything else to feel her moving inside the circle of his arm.

There was an awkward moment while they stood looking at each other, both of them listening for the beat, trying to locate it. Then, did she go close against him or did he bring her close? She couldn't tell. He simply fit so well it was difficult to tell which of them was doing what. But close to him, she had to stop smiling and look at him. He was hard against her thighs and the pleasure was dizzying, the response within her making it difficult to breathe. His eyes questioning hers again. She let her head rest against his shoulder and moved closer still.

He wouldn't have believed it, could scarcely believe what was happening. This woman. This woman, who'd turned scarlet and gone almost incoherent the last time they'd met, was all at once very much present, of the earth, exquisitely acquiescent. And so good in his arms. Her scent mesmerizing, her softness compelling. No bra. Her breasts pressing against his chest. They might have been wearing nothing at all.

She felt so very aware of everything. The smallest gestures. The flex of his shoulder muscles, the restraint he was exercising; but still hard against her. So gratifying. And exciting.

Is this it isn't is it it feels like it is oh oh I'm falling in love am I?

7.

It was freezing in the car. He started the motor, then turned to look at her, extended his arm, and pulled her over against him. Her hair cold.

"It'll warm up in a minute. This car warms up fast."

"Good," she murmured, warm where he held her.

He'd kiss her. She knew he would. And if he did, when he did, it wouldn't end. She'd dissolve, spinning. And tomorrow evening, at Pierce's party when she saw him again, it would be more and then more. Because she'd have to have something to drink. But in the next daylight encounter—whenever that might be—he'd be confused, angered by the way she'd be. His hand on her throat, tilting her head back. His eyes of odd unmatched colors studying her face so thoughtfully.

"How the hell did this happen?" he whispered, her throat cool satin, her scent suddenly more pronounced. Perfume. He wanted to cry. The damnedest feeling that the whole thing was a dream, something taking place in his mind, he was still on the sofa with his shoes off, arms folded behind his head, dreaming the most impossible dream of this beautiful woman with the glowing skin and large brown eyes, eyebrows so fair they almost weren't there, gleaming skin and a mouth so perfectly sculpted. Perfect. All of it. Her face. He didn't want to trust how she looked, how he felt, wanting her. The car beginning to warm up, the windows misting over inside. This silent conversation. Keeping his arm around her, he turned, released the brake, then said, "I don't know where you live."

"Pleasant Avenue," she said lazily, so content inside his arm. A catlike sinuosity overtaking her limbs.

"How far up?"

"Just past Remington Park, on the north side."

"Okay." Putting the car into gear, saying her name over and over again in his mind. Gillian. With the soft G. Dzh Dzh Dzh Dzhillian. Jill Jill Jillian. I can't have to stop have to.

He pulled the car over to the side of the road and wrapped his arms around her. So suddenly, her hair came undone, some of it falling against his face, the rest staying up where she'd pinned it.

His mouth so sweet the taste of tobacco on his tongue sweet delicately probing the inside of her mouth she couldn't breathe her head filled with air all light urgent her arms trapped so she couldn't touch him desperate to touch him open his coat put her hands up inside the soft sweater feel his skin but couldn't trapped his mouth moving on hers his lips soft inside smooth his breathing as painful-sounding as hers what is it what's happening all of it silently breaking shattering inside like ice sliding down a window pane.

"No!" She pushed him away, sitting with her hands on his chest. The both of them gasping. "I can't," she whispered feverishly. "I can't do this to you. Oh, God. How do I explain to you? Where are the bloody words? *Come on!*" She looked up at the roof of the car, as if the words she needed might be up there waiting for her to pluck them down. "How? Gabe, I . . ." *Help!* She prayed. Tell me what to say to him I want him so much but tomorrow? "I'm frightened," she said helplessly, hearing how inadequate an explanation that was for anything.

He stared at her, feeling it all quickly subsiding, looking at her wet mouth, the look of sheer panic in her eyes.

"What is it?" he asked, tracing her mouth with his fingertips so that her eyelids fluttered and she looked as if he was torturing her.

Tell him the truth he'll take you home you'll never see him again it'll be over. She closed her eyes. "Gabe, I'm someone who frequents pubs, tells tales. No, I'm not from here. I'm a secretary. Yes, thank you very much, I would like another glass of wine. No, no names. None of that. I don't know why. It's all so bloody desperate and they're never ones I have to see again but I'll see you again and it's years and years of all that. . . ." She opened her eyes, positive he'd say any number of cruel, angry things.

He hadn't had any idea what was coming. Instantly geared himself up for frigidity or virginity or some wild story. But this. This was the refrain of an old song he'd sung so many times he knew the lyrics backward.

"Gillian, so what? I'm from out of town myself and I sell aluminum siding. And could I get you a refill on that? Waiter, same again."

"You don't!" she whispered, wide-eyed.

"The hell I don't! Well, maybe not lately. But like for three or four years, sure. Jesus, Gillian. It's the goddamned way of life. What else do you do? I'm not some wet-eared kid that I don't know how it all goes around. And Jesus! Who the hell am I to pass judgment on you? If you've been around a few times, good. Good! I don't want to have to teach when I'm not at school. The way that sounds. It's not what I mean. It's just that I'm in no position to be judging anybody, let alone you."

"But it's so bloody shabby, such a mockery of everything. You're not bothered?"

"I think I'd be bothered a lot if this whole preamble tonight had been a con, some sort of prelude to a put-down. I'd be bothered by that. Jesus! Can you really be this naive?"

"Most likely."

"I want you," he said quietly. "I want to take you home, take you to bed. And it's what you want, isn't it?"

She nodded.

"Would you prefer to go to my apartment?"

"No. I'd like you to see my house."

"Oh, Jesus." He laughed, putting his arms around her again. "You're crazy."

"I know it." She started to laugh. And he thought, Pierce was right again. Elated by the sound of her laughter. "But I do like you so much," she went on, "and it's never happened to me quite this way before. I'm not sure ..."

"What?"

"I don't know. How one ... You'll ... I can't say."

"I'll take you home." He smiled, keeping his arm around her as he pulled away from the curb.

Jenny couldn't sleep. She got up, put on her robe, and walked barefoot through to the kitchen to get a glass of milk, then stood drinking it, looking out the window. Thinking how pretty the snow looked, loving the snow.

The streetlight making a nice circle of light. Her toes cold. She stood with one foot on top of the other in the dark, enjoying the milk, touching her belly inside the robe. Getting bigger. It was happening faster and faster. Watching as a car pulled up across the road. What kind of car was that? Something foreign. Seeing the man at the wheel turn, a woman sliding over close to him, the two of them kissing. The streetlight catching her hair. Gillian. With a guy! She moved closer to the window. Getting the weirdest feeling watching. Gillian and a man sitting down there in the car kissing each other. Then breaking apart, the car engine turned off, the doors opening and the two of them getting out. Wow! Gillian going right down in the snow. She could hear them laughing. It sounded so loud, the night was so quiet. She looked quickly at the other houses, expecting to see lights start to go on all over the place. But no. Nothing happening. He was picking her up, brushing off the snow, putting his arms around her with his head way back, laughing. Then the two of them running across the street. The sound of the front door opening, closing. The door to her apartment opening, closing.

Boyoboy! How about that! She looked at the glass of milk in her hand, took a drink, looked out again at the street. Why was she so surprised? No big deal seeing Gillian with a guy. But it was. It really was. And she couldn't figure out why. A kind of gassy feeling in her belly. Gas? She spread her hand out over her belly, her head cocked to one side. Feeling it. Starting to laugh. She put the glass of milk down and went running to the bedroom to sit on the side of Pat's bed, saying, "Pat, wake up. Come on, wake up! Guess what! *Guess what*!"

"What?" Pat alarmed out of her sleep. "What is it, dear? What's happened?"

"The baby" Jenny laughed, grabbing Pat's hand, holding it on her belly. "D'you feel that? It's *moving!* Can you feel it? It's really *in* there."

Pat sat up and put her arms around her, laughing, saying, "Of course it is, dear. Of course." And felt hope surging back into her.

"This is great," he said, meaning it, admiring the room while she hung away the coats, then knelt down to light the fire. "This is your house, Gillian?"

"Mine, yes. I have tenants on the two floors above."

"And you did all this work yourself?"

"I like carpentry," she said, holding a match to the newspaper she'd bunched up and pushed under the grate. "Not the cabinet making sort. The house-building sort."

"And the plastering, too? The floors?"

"All of it but the plumbing. I subcontracted for that." She laughed. "There's wine on the counter in the kitchen if you'd like some."

"D'you want a glass?"

"Why not? The damage is already done."

"Okay." He got up and went into the kitchen and started opening cupboards, looking for glasses, found them and poured the wine. When he returned, she was still sitting on her knees, gazing into the fire. He sat down on the rug beside her, handing her a glass.

"I'm doing Christmas dinner tomorrow," she said. "Pat and Jenny and me." Her eyes captured by the fire. "Have you somewhere to be tomorrow?" Stop, Gillian. You're going too far, too fast. It's wrong of you to say whatever's in your mind.

"No."

"You'll come, then?" she turned to look at him.

131

"Who are Pat and Jenny?"

"Pat's my tenant directly above. A very dear lady." She pointed at the ceiling. "And Jenny was one of my third-floor tenants. But she and her boyfriend rowed and he's gone off." Thank God! "So she's moved in with Pat. It's a bit complicated. Jenny's pregnant, you see."

"And how old is Jenny?"

"Nineteen."

"And how old is Pat?"

"Seventy-one, I think."

"And Pat's looking after Jenny?"

"That's about right," she said, looking into the fire again. Her hair half up, half down.

"Let's fix that," he said, sitting up on his knees, feeling around in her hair for the pins, pulling them out one by one, dropping them on the coffee table, then smoothing her hair down.

"That feels much better," she said dreamily, hypnotized by the fire and the soothing gentle motion of his hands on her hair. "I've never had a man into my home," she said, thinking about it. "Not ever." She turned her head slowly, her cheeks warm from the fire. "I used to imagine, when I was young, having someone with me. Things are never quite as one imagines."

"How is it?" he asked, picking up his glass.

"I'm not sure." I do so like looking at you, she thought. I find you beautiful. How will you be without your clothes? Will you think my legs dreadful? I wish you didn't have to see my legs.

"Would you like me to drink up and run along?" he offered.

"You haven't said if you'll come tomorrow."

"I thought I said yes."

"Oh. Good!"

132

"You haven't answered my question," he said.

"Do I want you to run along?"

"Do you?"

A whisper. So bold. "No."

His eyes on her face. He returned his hand to her hair, spreading his fingers, letting it slide silken through, around, over his hand. Then he took her wineglass and set it beside his on the coffee table. While she watched, everything drumming inside. Both of them on their knees, eyes reconnecting. His hands on her face drawing her forward to his mouth the heat from the fire the wine his closeness so stimulating, thrilling his mouth persuasive, not hard; her arms not trapped this time so she could hold him, slip her hands up inside the back of his sweater, feeling the smoothness of his skin, the tightness of his flesh over ribs and chest his hands behind her unzipping her dress while she pushed the sweater up baring his chest to stroke him wanting to close her eyes with the pleasure swimming into the pleasure. He broke away for a moment to remove his sweater, pulling it off over his head, dropping it to the floor all serious-eyed looking at the way the caftan was puddling around her hips, her nipples showing through the silk slip. A finger each side of her shoulders dropping the straps uncovering her breasts. She couldn't breathe with his eyes on her, studying her, then his hands and the soft sound of his sigh as he held her to his chest his hand sliding down her back down, bringing her to her feet, his hand going down the slip sliding down around her feet, down, his hands taking down the tights standing near naked against him, shivering everything caught at her feet he knelt down took it all away, drawing his hands up the length of her thighs, over her hips leading her forward by the hips his mouth on her

133

breast, closing on her nipple she made a sound it simply came, clasping his head in both hands holding him there. His head in her hands. His mouth leaving her breast so he could quickly throw off the rest of his clothes, then open and close his arms around her the length of his body full against hers she'd fall surely she'd fall was falling but no taking her down on the rug the fire hotter now.

"You are so beautiful," he whispered, on top of her. The weight so substantial, welcome. "Your skin, beautiful. Here. And here, here. Your breasts."

I love you, she thought, stunned. I love you. I didn't know I could. Love you. How you feel. Please be good know me know the feelings what feels so good touch me everything everywhere I want to put my mouth to you God so much know the feel of you in my mouth.

His kisses breaking her bones creating an ache inside his hands in her hair on her face her shoulders his mouth leaving hers to find her breast again so that she arched closer. He knows, he knows. His lips, tongue. Teeth just lightly. The flush in her throat, chest a darting spasm, contracting she'd come with his mouth on her breasts so wild excited. Her hand moving between them to direct him down between her thighs, closing her legs to hold him there moving against him his head moving on the other breast his fingers circling circling his mouth teasing the pressure building intensifying the ache moving up and down the counterrhythm, opening her mouth, gasping for air. Do you know can you feel me I'm going to . . .

He lifted his head to look at her, thinking. It can't be but no, yes, her eyes glassy, fixed and his mouth again closed over her nipple silently saying, Go ahead I'll make you never had a woman come this way just from

134

this moving with her against her, biting gently she was going tight under him going rigid her hands on his head urging his mouth hard against her suddenly still, unmoving he nudged open her thighs, slipped his hand down to touch her and she cried out, bolting against his hand, her body convulsed, shuddering a rush of heated warmth pulling his fingers into her her thighs clamped around his hand, pulsing inside as that sound, cries coming from her mouth and her body jerking, jolted against him; finally falling, her face damp, eyes unfocused, feverishly kissing his mouth, her hands gliding up and down his back.

Only just beginning and I knew how you'd be. Her heartbeat slowing, the hunger quickly climbing again. Smiling seeing his face above hers so close, reaching down to put her hand on him, shivering with the enormous craving. Awed. Do I love you is this the way it is? The way I felt about Brooke so different, not the same. Love? I wish I could know.

Unsteadily finding her way to her feet, taking him by the hand, the air moving through the air cold. Tearing away the bedclothes, all of them. Out of the way. To lie with him, spread beneath him, blind with the hunger, wanting.

"I've never known a woman who could ..."

"I know," she whispered, mystifying him. A flash of hair as she slid away, went past him, her hands whispering down the length of his body, curling reversed against his side, her hands cool, her mouth.

Please don't let me hate you in the morning when I love you so much tonight wanting to do this love this loving this how you feel taste all of you.

He had that nagging sensation again that none of this was real but something part of that same fantastic

135

dream, being in her bedroom—as cool and beautiful as she was—unable to connect the thinking rational part of himself to the emotional responding one. His thoughts all too effectively scattered by her by her potent mouth, her tender hands and the sight of her, watching her giving him the profoundest pleasure until watching seemed some sort of serious omission when the pleasure might be returned, become doubled. He reached for her, eased her over and down and felt her surprise, delighting in it, in her, in his suddenly enormous appetite.

Something none of *them* had ever done. But then she'd only ever done this for Brooke, couldn't somehow put her mouth to any of the others it had seemed so wrong. The mixed sensations so strong, his head between her thighs, his touch piercing. Not like the other she couldn't recall his name but he'd been busy as if it'd been some sort of game this didn't feel like a game it felt . . . like love. Yes. Love in his mouth. Taking so little to make her forget everything what she was doing everything forget, her arms closed around him securing him to her mouth, going mad lifting closer extending her legs until they'd snap or break surely they'd break writhing wildly under his mouth until he held her down, held her fast, both of them moving moving the harder faster dance, holding her mouth closed around him while he lit the fuse tended to it making sure it caught burned ran its course exploded. Then lay at her side making patterns on her belly, kissing her inner thigh, then suddenly starting again so that she'd only just begun to return when he was sending her back once more. At last, sitting up, smiling, to kiss her mouth, his lips slick cool, his hands skimming over her, then closing on her breasts so that she knew he wanted to come into her now. And she went down, over, holding still to take him in, so glad to hold him, surround him, watch his face, mouth, eyes as he moved in her; keeping herself quiescent, the tempo elusive, hard to locate she found it willing him to come. Come into me a strange benediction.

"What's the best way for you?" he asked her after, holding her cradled against his chest, caressing her hair, smoothing it. Succeeding as no one else ever had in making her feel tiny, delicate.

"Inside, you mean?"

He nodded.

"With me on top. I never come the other way. On top I can."

"Is it good?"

"Not the same as the other. Diffused somehow, duller. But very good. You're wonderful."

"Why aren't you shy about this?"

"I'm never shy once I've taken my clothes off with a man."

He had to pause, think about that.

"That's a hell of a thing to tell me." He laughed. "I'll keep you locked up in here for the next thirty years."

"Are you thirsty? I am. Very."

"I'll get the wine."

He walked unselfconsciously out of the bedroom, returning with a glass in each hand, smiling as he handed one to her.

"How old are you?" she asked.

"Thirty-seven. You?"

"Twenty-nine. Near to thirty."

"How near?" He looked amused.

"May."

"That's not all that near."

"Near enough." She sipped the wine, then felt about on the night table for the cigarette box, found it, took out two, lit them both, and handed him one, setting the ashtray down on the bed between them. "I don't fancy going to sleep just yet." I'm afraid to go to sleep because I'm afraid to wake up and find myself hating the sight of you.

"I'd like to stay," he said.

"Yes." She'd known he would.

"And in the morning, with the cold, killing light of day, you'll be back to blushing, stammering."

"I am afraid so, yes."

"Would you rather I go?"

"No." You'll have to find out sooner or later. We might as well both find out. In the morning. But before then, just once more. Once more. I want you and want you and want you can't stop wanting to touch you hold you kiss you.

"If you ever get a vacancy, will you let me know? I'd love one of these apartments."

"I'll put you down on the list." She turned slightly more toward him, smiling.

"How many others on the list?"

"Only you. It shouldn't be longer than two years."

"Is that the john?" He indicated one of the doors.

"That's the closet." She laughed softly. "That's the loo."

"May I?"

"By all means."

He got up and went into the bathroom, quietly closing the door. In an astonished state. In what looked to be a night-long aroused state. Failing to understand this woman and that other one.

She sat back against the pillows, enjoying the cigarette, waiting. Once more. And then they'd sleep. But once more. Once more.

Is this really you? he wondered. Or the other one? This one urgently moving, reversed in his arms, the weight of her head on his thigh, her mouth slowly steadily taking him past control this time. Reading the flow of her motions, the tensing of her thigh muscles under his cheek. Wanting to have her come again so sweetly hear her cry out that strange startled cry. Holding her harder, feeling her going rigid. Losing himself to her. Wanting to wait just long enough to stay aware know her in that moment closer, approaching. Closing his eyes, her body completely impaled on his hand his mouth feeling her inside outside part of her having her here part of him just a little longer holding back her mouth still around him motionless dependent. Yes yes yes oh how you are how you go. Stopping only long enough to drag air into her lungs before insistently directing him up forcing him up taking him into it taking him.

She plummeted into it, distantly aware of his arranging the blankets over both of them; down, gone. And dreamed she was atop the number 73 bus, screaming. Woke up panting, drenched, to find him lying quietly at her side, looking at her.

"That was one hell of a nightmare you were having," he said softly. "I was just about to wake you."

"I'm so . . . sorry," she whispered, struggling for air. "Pl . . . please g . . . g. . . go back to sl . . . sleep. I'll j . . . just wa . . . walk it off. Off."

"Do you want to tell me about it?"

"No, no! I c . . . *can't!*" Her eyes panic-filled. She got out of bed and went into the bathroom. He'll think me insane, she thought, fumbling with the faucets, getting the shower started. Perhaps I am. Oh, God! When does it end? I can't bear it. Over and over and over. Always the same, the same. Please let it end.

He was sitting up, smoking a cigarette, when she came out.

"Come back to bed," he said, lifting the bedclothes. "We'll talk it out or walk it out, whatever you like. Maybe get a little more sleep."

"No." She shook her head. "I n . . . never do af . . . after. I'm up for the n . . . night."

"Well, maybe we can break the pattern," he said, holding his hand out to her. "At least come and let me hold you."

Yes, hold me.

She took off her robe and climbed in beside him, at once on her way to being lulled by his warmth, shuddering as she came up against his body, then subsiding.

"Want any of this?" he asked, holding up the cigarette.

"No, thank you."

"Okay."

She could feel him twisting, turning to put it out; then he was moving down, settling her into his arms. Caressing her. Her hair. Her shoulder, her arm. Her breasts. Lovingly. "I'm happy holding you," he whispered. "Are you happy being held?"

"Oh, yes." She shuddered again, his arms tightened, his legs wrapped around hers. Securing her. His hand stroking, stroking.

"Close your eyes," he murmured, his thumb lightly grazing her eyelids. "Close your eyes, love."

Love. She fought against it but her eyelids felt so suddenly heavy. He smelled so good, felt so fine, secure. Strong. His warmth. His voice whispering. You've done it, she thought. I'm falling asleep. Yes.

8.

To wake up, see him sitting beside her drinking orange juice. The irrational fear sitting right there between them.

"I got you some, too," he said.

She looked. A glass of orange juice on the table beside the bed. She couldn't speak. The fear had frozen her interior. Shakily, without looking at him again, she got up, grabbed her robe, and fled to the bathroom. To stand with her hands gripping the sides of the sink, head bowed, heart pounding so hard it was like marching footsteps inside her skull.

What will I do? I can't look at him. Don't want him to touch me. Don't want to hurt him. Asked him to come back. To dinner this afternoon. How? Why?

She ran the cold water, opened the medicine cabinet, and shook two aspirin out of the bottle. Her head didn't hurt but perhaps the aspirin would slow down her heart, cut through the fear. Brushed her teeth, washed her face, used the toilet, then filled the basin and washed

141

under her arms, her breasts, between her legs. Pulled on her nightgown, put her robe back on, belting it tight, tight; it might hold her together. She couldn't stay all day in the bathroom. Opened the door, went slowly out, unable to look at him. How could she look at him?

"You're shy again," he said.

She glanced up. He wasn't smiling, didn't look smug. Does he know? He seems to. She walked over to pick up the glass of juice. He watched her. Then he got up and she thought, If he's undressed I can't bear it what will I do? Saw he had on his shorts and let out her breath she'd been holding it so hard it hurt exhaling.

This isn't a typical case of "morning after," he thought, studying her. It's something else. Something that's part of the nightmare, the stuttering, all of that. And when she had a drink or two, he went on, adding the pieces together, it *does* get her out. But more than that, it somehow makes her forget. But what?

"Do you have that nightmare often?" he asked, stopping a few feet away.

"Quite often," she admitted, holding the glass in both hands, eyeing him.

"And you don't want to talk about it."

"I can't." I wish to God I could. How I wish it.

"Am I still invited to the turkey party?" Venturing to risk a small smile.

She nodded.

"Good." His smile widening. "Was it true what you told me last night?"

"What . . . what did I t . . . t . . . tell you?"

He moved fractionally closer. "You say you're never shy once you've taken your clothes off with a man."

She flushed, unable to answer. He came closer still.

"Shall we just see if the theory holds?" He extended

142

his hand. It went past the robe, past the nightgown, covering her breast. She began to tremble, her lips parting, knees unlocking.

"You're warm," he said, her breast so soft under his palm. Soft and perfectly fitted to his hand. "Do you want me to stop?"

She stared at him, her nipples going hard, her belly quivering.

"You're going to spill that," he said, taking the glass from her, reaching past her to set it down.

"Wh . . . why are you do . . . doing this?" she asked unsteadily.

"Because I want you to want me to come back after today."

"You w . . . want to co . . . come back?"

"I. Want. To. Come. Back." He brushed his mouth against hers, his hand gently shaping her breast.

She could hear Pat and Jenny moving about upstairs. Her eyes going automatically to the ceiling.

"No, down here," he said, his hand under her hair on the back of her neck. "Was I wrong for you last night?"

"No."

"Hate making love in the morning?"

"I . . . I don't know."

"Never done it?"

She shook her head.

His hand left her breast. Half of her felt suddenly cold.

"You've got this knotted. I can't undo it."

She looked down. Lifted her hands, untied the belt. Her hands once more falling.

"Thank you." He smiled. Coaxingly now. "May I?" He held his hands out to remove the robe. She didn't say anything, so, feeling decidedly tentative, he eased it off her, laid it carefully at the foot of the bed.

Hands on her shoulders, he put his mouth to hers. Softly. She couldn't respond. He turned her. They were falling together. Backward under him on the bed, his mouth on her throat, her ear, the side of her neck. His hands easing the nightgown down, around her waist. She felt so frightened watching him stroking her breasts, telling her, "I like your breasts. Love your breasts," going round and round her breasts with his fingers, again again until the feeling began to slowly come into her as if he was unwrapping her, peeling off some invisible protective skin. Pressed his mouth down between her breasts, into her belly, his tongue dipping into her navel. She felt it. Twitched. He was inching the nightgown down over her hips, collecting it up in his hands, dropping it over the side of the bed before leaning on his elbow at her side, his hand traveling back and forth up and down her thighs as he, smiling, dropped a kiss onto her mouth, then another, another. Little kisses, smiles, his eyes turning from moment to moment to look at her, at where his hand was going. Her knees hurting from holding her legs pressed so tightly together. His hand rounding her kneecaps so that her legs relaxed, opened slightly. Hand moving lazily up and down the inside of her thighs now. Feeling her eyes growing round. More kisses. On her mouth, the base of her throat, each nipple, her belly again. Then he swooped down, spread her legs with the palms of his hands flat at the apex of her thighs, and opened his mouth on her, his tongue curling against her. Strange, different in daylight with the sun catching the gray in his hair she had to watch feeling so peculiar, removed, but he was reconnecting her, her thigh muscles relaxing. Good, he wasn't forcing, simply kissing. Gently, delicately. Her back suddenly untensing, the muscles in her belly going tight.

I can't do this not in broad daylight seeing us both it's ludicrous look at us we look absurd here with my legs wide open your head there your tongue lapping at me absurd but I don't care don't care. Her eyelids drooping, his hand covering her breast. She let her hand fall over the top of his, both their hands stroking her breast: she sighed. He kept going until he'd succeeded in building that aching emptiness inside her. Then he sat up, saying, "Shall we try it the way that's best for you?" His fingers continuing to move on her.

Dizzy, sunspots dancing, seeing him kick off his shorts, looked at him, looking, wanting. Climbing over on top of him, holding him in her hand, easing herself down very slowly. Burning inside, aching. Taking him in, in, in. Then arching herself back, her hands either side of his ankles. He lifted, saw her eyes widen, then slid his fingers down her belly and began rubbing, pressing. Generating the response so quickly it took her by surprise. Quietly. Shaking her, slight tremors. Then she came forward, her hair hanging down over her face, their eyes locked, her belly quivering again, riding him. His one hand on her shoulder, the other on her breast, his face changing, smoothed out, his eyes round as surely hers must have been, she lifted and fell, matching thrusts until his hands flew to her hips, holding her steady, hard, reaching higher into her, harder. Until it ended and he drew her down on his chest, his mouth against her ear, whispering. She couldn't decipher his words. Holding her, stroking her spine, her buttocks. She kept her face hidden against his neck.

145

They lay, still joined, for a very long time. She felt very safe. Even loved.

Then they started again.

"I'll go home, shower, shave, and change and come right back. Okay?"

"Yes. Okay."

"You're all right? Everything's all right?"

"Yes. Yes."

"Okay."

He gathered her against him and kissed the top of her head, then released her.

"I'll be back in a couple of hours," he said, happily smiling. Then let himself out.

She stood there by the door, trying to understand what had happened, was still happening. Everything looked different, felt different. The living room suddenly larger, brighter, even prettier. And hungry. I'm hungry. She went into the kitchen. Feeling madly like dancing. Set the thawed turkey on the counter. Made herself toast, an egg, coffee. Moving around the kitchen, feeling the wetness drying at the tops of her thighs. Wanting it there as long as possible. I've finally gone completely mad, she thought. All alone in the kitchen smiling at the turkey. She turned on the radio. Christmas music filling the apartment.

Humming along to the music while she stripped the bed, pushed the linens into the hamper, then debated over which set of sheets to put on. The new ones, she decided. The lovely new Christian Dior sheets she'd bought because Father had so liked pontificating, declaring, Life is not, dear child, a bed of roses. And she'd wanted so to go to sleep on a bed of roses. So she would.

Tonight. They smelled so new. Would he stay the night again, make morning love to her?

Into the bathroom for a quick shower. No time for a lovely long soak with the new bath cubes. The bird had to go into the oven. What to wear? Something pretty. He liked it that I wasn't wearing a brassiere. I'll leave it off. Brown trousers, a flowered shirt open at the throat. Mother's gold chain. No need to bother with shoes. She waltzed into the kitchen to push Pat's stuffing into the turkey, brush the breast with butter, a sprinkle of paprika—for the color—then into the oven. Done.

"He just left," Jenny said, grinning impishly.

"You are a one." Pat smiled, shaking her head. "Stop spying out that window and come help me take this load of wash down."

"Oh, I'll take it. I don't mind."

"Well, if you're sure. Careful as you go, mind. We can't have you falling."

"I'm not going to fall. You don't suppose she went ahead and did the tree without me?"

"Gillian wouldn't. Not if she said you could do it."

"You really like her, don't you?" Jenny stopped in the doorway with the basket of laundry.

"And so do you"

"I know. But I just wondered why you do."

"She's a lovely woman. Kind and generous, thoughtful." And I hope she has the wits not to send away a young man who cares for her. Seeing Peter Flannigan going down the front steps.

"I wonder if she's invited him to dinner," Jenny speculated, continuing on her way. "I'm dying to see what he looks like. He stayed all night, you know."

"Go on with you." Pat laughed. "You're worse than an old lady."

"You're not an old lady," Jenny said seriously. "You're not at all."

"Go on," Pat said softly. "And mind how you go."

Watched Jenny go on her way, then stood gazing into space, thinking about Walter Meyers. Her lawyer's father. Introducing himself to her at the office. An expression in his eyes. One she could still recognize all these years later. Changing her back to someone young again, someone still desirable. Inviting her to come out for coffee. And over the coffee, having declared himself a widower and available and not in the least deflected by her four-year advantage in age, invited her to come out to dinner. She'd had to refuse, of course. But came away astonished at the response inside herself. A completely sexual response. At seventy-one. Impossible, of course. But for a few minutes, over coffee, she'd been young again. Indulging in a delightful flirtation.

Smiling, thinking of Gillian's having found herself a young man. Don't let him go if there's anything there, she thought. Don't be a fool. As I was. As I continue to be.

He drove home with the radio blasting Christmas music into the car, the heaters going full blast too, and the window open, smoking a cigarette that tasted better than any cigarette he ever had, his chest feeling huge, expanded. Passing the shopping center a couple of miles from his place, wondering if anything might be open. Drove in and saw the drugstore had a half-day sign on the door. Open. Parked and went in, emerging twenty minutes later with a huge bag and a tube of wrapping paper.

Singing in the shower, then going through his closet, deciding that since they'd probably go directly from her house to the party, he'd better wear something in between. And settled on the blue cords and navy cashmere turtleneck.

While he was wrapping the packages he stopped, telling himself, Wait a minute. Slow down, here. You're going too fast. Sat down and saw her above him, her eyes partially hidden by her hair. Her eyes, the way she'd looked at him. Something he perhaps hadn't wanted to see because he was so bowled over by the suddenly different woman she'd been. Her long, angular body, her breasts. Large, but not too large. Full and soft. Smooth, flat belly, hard prominent hips, her thighs muscular, long. They were almost the same height. He had maybe an inch on her. Which made her just under six feet. Fantastic! And that hair. Thick, thick, soft. But her eyes. He kept coming back to her eyes, the way she'd looked at him. With her hair that way, falling across her face. Like someone in a cage, behind her hair. Her eyes wild, dark. Tortured. Only a moment. And being inside her, being so close he hadn't been able to stop, more closely examine what was there.

And last night. The way she'd come that first time. Stroking her breasts, gently teasing, sucking, and she'd come. He'd never known a woman like her. How many times? Six, seven? At least. He'd wanted to keep her there for days, seeing her turn on so hard. Everything. Except being inside her. Then it all changed, closed down somehow.

What're you into? he asked himself. The first time and it was sensational and you want it all one hundred percent? Give her some time, yourself, too.

So goddamned painful when she starts that business.

Knotting her hands together, stumbling over every word. Wanting to tell her, Calm down. Take it easy. Take your time. I'll wait. I'll be glad to wait to hear what you want to say. And that nightmare.

It *had* been one hell of a nightmare. Does she know she screams? he wondered. Maybe she doesn't know. Should I tell her? Scared the hell out of him. Waking up to see her head turning back and forth back and forth, screaming, NOOOOOO! Sweat pouring off her. Her eyes shifting wildly under her eyelids. Seeing something. Something terrible.

He looked over at the window. Thinking, I want to be with you. Want to be with you more than I ever wanted to be with anyone in my life except for Craig. My son. Oh, Jesus! Close my eyes and I can see you, hear you laughing. And want to kill her. I'd kill you, Penny. But what the fuck would it prove? My anger? How much I loved that boy? I want another kid. A whole goddamned school full of kids, seeing them every damned day of my life, looking at them, hearing the ridiculous, terrific things they say, seeing how beautiful they are, how goddamned clean, fresh, and beautiful, and thinking which class Craig would've been in now. Heading on down the hall to his classroom, carrying his books. Losing teeth, getting new ones. We'd have gone ice-skating Sunday afternoons, out for bike rides. Talked. I want another kid. I want this woman. Scared shitless wanting this woman. Why scared? What's she going to do? Not what *she's* going to do. What I might do. I don't know. Scare her off again with being angry, forcing. I don't want to scare her, have her run. Finish wrapping the stuff and let's go, Hadley.

With a little less enthusiasm than he'd had initially, he finished wrapping the packages, returned everything to the paper bag, picked up his hat, gloves, coat, pulled on his boots. Telling himself, She's beautiful. Go with it. See what happens. Go with it.

Jenny flitted around the room, making sure the tree looked good from every angle before picking up another something—a piece of tinsel or one of the gold balls—and placing it on the tree. Having a wonderful time.

Pat was in the kitchen with Gillian, the two of them cooking, getting the table ready. Pat in a long velvet skirt with a white silk shirt and a Christmas-tree pin on her lapel. Jenny thought she really looked beautiful. For somebody who thought of herself as old. Maybe she was, but she sure didn't think or act old.

They'd come in with presents to put under the tree.

Gillian had been so surprised.

In the kitchen, Pat said, "I think it's time we had some of the eggnog. Jenny, you have some, dear. It's good for you. For baby, too."

"I hate eggs right now."

"You won't even taste them," Pat coaxed. "Come along, now. We'll have a toast."

Gillian got glasses and the three of them stood admiring the tree, their glasses raised.

"To Christmas," Pat said. "And to good friends. Happy day to you both."

"You, too," Jenny said, turning to see Gillian staring at the tree.

Her eyes were caught. Seeing Megan with an entire packet of tinsel draped across her forearm, prancing about hurling the tinsel a strip at a time at the tree. And Mother sitting in the armchair, drinking gin and bitters, smiling at Megan's antics. Slender legs crossed, legs looking shimmery in stockings she always bought at

Harrod's. "She's quite mad, is your child," Mother had said. "Quite mad!" And Gillian had stood there looking at her mother, thinking, You're so beautiful, *so* beautiful. "I love you both," she'd said, thick-throated. "You're *both* of you quite mad." Oh, the laughter. Megan's laughter. Like silvery music. Tall, freckle-faced girl with plaits. And dresses always too short, she grew so quickly. Mother had bought her a red Christmas dress. With white collar, cuffs. And little Father Christmas buttons Mother had sewn on to replace the very ordinary white ones it had come with. Always surprising she'd do the things she would. Sitting down, looking so unbelievably elegant. With needle and thread to change all the buttons on Megan's dress. I want you back need you want you here.

"Are you all right, dear?" Pat asked. "You've gone off dreaming."

"Sorry. I was admiring the tree. It's lovely, Jenny. I've invited along another friend for dinner," she told them both.

"Your new boyfriend," Jenny laughed. "Tell us. What's he like? Who is he?"

Gillian blushing, smiling. "He's very nice. You'll see for yourself. I'm hopeless telling one person about another. I'd better see to the vegetables."

Pat returned to the kitchen with her, busying herself at the sink peeling potatoes. Remembering in a kind of silent agony. The night of Father's first stroke. Summoning Peter Flannigan. He'd arrived at the front door. Looking not in the least altered. And had hurried upstairs to attend to Da. While Pat hovered in the corridor, a shawl wrapped over her nightgown. Fearful of waking the others. But they slept right the way through it. And at last Peter had come out into the corridor, quietly closing the door behind him, saying, "Come along in here, now, Pat," steering her into her bedroom. "We must talk." Warming his hands at what remained of the coal fire, telling her what had happened, what would happen, that it had been just a small stroke and there was no need for her to be fearful. Then lifting his head, looking at her in that same way. The same, the same. Taking hold of her by the upper arms, whispering, "You're even lovelier, Pat." So that she'd trembled, very aware of her body naked under the shawl, the nightgown. Pressing kisses on her mouth that made her weak, dizzy. Sitting with her on the side of the bed, ignoring her whispers. More kisses, his hands on her breasts burning through the shawl, the nightgown. Feverishly whispering, "No. We mustn't, no." His hand going up under the nightgown, moving up between her legs. Kissing her into silence, filling her with a terrible guilt. "Let me love you, Pat. You know I love you, Pat." His fingers slowly moving up into her, meeting resistance, removing all her resistance. His mouth. Kisses, delirium. Making something happen inside her. So exquisitely violent what happened inside her. And then his small, sad smile when she held him away, shook her head, saying, "I must not. Must not." So that he'd released her at last, whispering, "If I've nothing else, at least there's the satisfaction of knowing it was I who opened you, Pat. And no other man will ever be able to make that claim." The realization spiraling through her brain, leaving her stricken. What he'd done. And followed her wishes, never again returned. Whispering, "You're a fool to do it, Pat. There'll be no reward in heaven. One last time, come away with me." No, no. And he'd gone.

"I am happy for you, Gillian," she said. "My girls, you know, were very lucky. Married fine young men. Only one of my lads left not married. The one in the Middle East. All the others married, with children."

"You must miss them."

"Oh, I'll go on a round of visits this coming year."

"Quite a trip that must be. Vancouver, was it? And Scotland, Wales, the Middle East?"

"And Manchester," Pat added. "Well, now, what've we left needs doing?"

"Let me think." Gillian looked around the room, then at the table. "The serving spoons. Where have I put them?" She began opening drawers, seeing in her mind the silver serving spoons in their soft blue bag. "What did I do with them?" she wondered aloud, completely unable to remember anything about where she'd put the spoons. She had brought them, she was certain of that. Surely she'd brought them. She couldn't have forgotten the spoons. Not Mother's spoons.

Seeing her becoming upset, Pat said, "They'll get themselves found, my dear. Why not let me have a look round? A new pair of eyes sometimes sees what's been overlooked."

"No, I know they're here. I'm sure they are."

Opening and closing drawers, cupboards, moving from one end of the kitchen to the other until Pat stopped her. Putting her hand on Gillian's wrist, saying, "You're getting yourself awfully het up over these spoons, Gillian."

"They were my mother's, you see. I couldn't have I . . . left them be . . . behind. I *know*. Know I didn't."

"Steady, now, we'll find them. Just sit yourself down there and have a bit of your drink while I take a look."

"In a blue bag," Gillian said anxiously.

Pat opened the cutlery drawer, lifted out the divided

box of knives and forks, and bent to look into the rear of the drawer. "Here we are," she said, extricating the bag.

"Oh, *thank you,*" she cried as Pat set the bag down on the table. "I'm sorry. I shouldn't have carried on so. But ... I'm sorry."

"That's all right, dear. I understand."

Gillian took hold of her hand. "You're very patient. Thank you for being so patient with me."

Pat leaned down and kissed her on the forehead. Gillian closed her eyes, holding hard to Pat's hand. "You're just a little girl right now," Pat said, "aren't you? We all have those moments. Lord only knows, I have enough of them. Drink your drink now."

"Hey, somebody's at the door," Jenny called.

Gillian held on to Pat's hand a moment longer, then let go, got up, and went to the door, out into the hallway.

He stepped inside, saying, "Pretty heavy security you've got here. Hey, don't rush off. Wait a minute." He grabbed hold of her hand. "I want to tell you something," he said, detaining her.

She couldn't speak. Could only stand there, waiting. Pleased by the sight of him but frightened again.

"First of all"—he smiled—"Merry Christmas. And second of all"—he kissed her lightly on the lips—"hello."

"Hello," she whispered, the blood flooding into her face.

"Okay. Now"—he straightened his shoulders dramatically—"lead me unto the breach, dear friend." And succeeded in making her laugh.

"You're a bit daft," she said.

"All the best people are."

"Meet Pat, Mrs. O'Brian. And Jenny," she said, stepping away from him into the room.

155

"Merry Christmas to you, ladies." He removed his hat with a flourish.

Jenny said, "Hi," and Pat came forward to shake hands with him, asking "Will you have some eggnog, Mr. . . .? Gillian, you haven't told us his name."

"Gabe," he answered. "Love some. It's cold as hell out there." Thinking, What a great-looking woman. Gillian must've made a mistake. This woman couldn't be seventy-one.

"Now, isn't that interesting?" Pat said. "I've never considered hell a cold place."

"It probably is," he said, removing his coat, hat, and gloves. Passing them over to Gillian, who was standing, waiting to take them. Smiling at her and then at Jenny. Smiling happily. Three beautiful women. Fantastic.

Jenny stood by the tree, thinking, He's gorgeous. How about that! Absolutely gorgeous. And nice. Really nice.

"I have a few packages to add to the collection," he told Gillian. "Okay?"

"You needn't have . . ."

"I'm doing Santa today," he said playfully.

Pat went off to get the eggnog and refilled Gillian's glass while she was about it. Very impressed by Gabe, by his good looks and easy manner. It was bound to be a lovely afternoon.

Gillian accepted the refilled glass from Pat, continuing to stand by the door, watching Gabe push a number of packages under the tree, then get to his feet, balling up the paper bag, tossing it into the fire. Turning to see Pat waiting with his drink.

"Happy days," he said, looking from Gillian to Pat to Jenny, then back at Gillian, thinking how well the colors of her shirt point up the brown of her eyes. He caught

156

her eye. She blinked and looked down at her glass, then up again at him.

"Do all of you sit down," she said. "I'll just check the turkey. It shouldn't be more than another half hour."

Jenny was remembering the last Christmas with Gran. She hadn't even looked sick or anything. Not one bit different. Gran sitting in the old rocker by the fire. With the Christmas tree right behind her. So that Gran had seemed like a part of the decorations. Calling Jenny over, patting her hair. Her face like a dried-apple doll. Saying, "What'll you do, Jen, after your old gran's gone? Where will you go?" Knowing her so well, knowing how trapped she felt in the house with all the others. Nobody with any time to talk or listen. "That's not going to be for a while yet, Gran," she'd said, scared by the conversation. "Maybe so, maybe not. But you be thinking on it, Jen. 'Cause I know my girl and I know you'll take it into your head to run with nothing holding you here. Don't go running off with no plans in mind, no set ideas for where you want to go and how you want it all to end up. Bide your time, awhile. Then, when you know, you make your move." Gran giving her the scarf she'd knitted with those bent old hands. Resting her head on Gran's knee, feeling Gran's hand patting her hair.

If you were there, Gran, I'd come home to you. I would.

"We need music," she said. "Okay with everybody if I turn on the radio?"

Gabe had lit a cigarette and was sitting on the sofa, smiling over at Pat, who smiled back at him before setting her glass down on the coffee table and said, "Something I've forgotten to do. I'll be back in a few minutes." and went out, up the stairs. Jenny turned on the radio, fiddled with the dials.

Gillian stood by the stove. Thinking. Trying to. Do I hate him? I don't hate him but what is it? My mood changing from one moment to the next how I feel don't feel like dislike want not want and that shocking display about the spoons. What's wrong with me?

She could close her eyes, see him, feel his hands on her, and the heat flew into her face, all through her. I don't hate him at all. And I shouldn't have carried on so about the spoons. Pat knew. I was being a little girl. But I'm not. Far from it. I don't know what to do. Listen, he and Jenny talking, laughing. Shouldn't I be able to sit myself down, talk and laugh, too?

She opened the oven door and looked in, knowing perfectly well the turkey didn't need seeing to. It was ninety-five percent done. Jenny had done the salad. The potatoes roasting in the pan. All the trimmings done, the table set. Wine at the ready. I'll have a glass. No. I won't. There comes a time. I have to know how I feel.

"Gillian?" He was standing in the doorway. "Are you hiding out in here?"

"I believe I am."

He laughed. And relaxed. "Any particular reason why?"

"Sheer bloody stupidity. I can't seem to get myself started."

He was so glad he'd come back. So glad.

"Come on," he said quietly, holding out his hand. "We'll get you started."

She put her hand on his, then went close to him, dropping her head down on his shoulder. "How can you bother, Gabe? I'm such a twit. I'll walk into a wall or trip in the mud, fall flat on my face in the snow. I always do."

"So, I'll pick you up, wipe you off, and point you in the right direction."

"Why?" she asked, soothed by his hand playing over her hair.

"I don't know. Just that it makes me feel good being with you. I love making love with you. I'm crazy about your hair. Enough? Or do you want more?"

"I loved making love with *you*."

"Lucky me."

She lifted her head. "Do you mean that?"

"No."

"But you do mean it." She could feel a smile forming on her mouth, the tension easing away out of her limbs. "You do, don't you?"

"We're starting to get a little repetitive. And your cute little friend in there's going to think we're in here playing doctor."

"Doctor?" She laughed. "You'll have to explain that to me."

"I'll do better than that," he said, giving her a hug. "I'll *show* you. Later."

She took a deep breath, looking into his eyes. "I am glad you're here," she said. "I am."

9.

"I do envy her," Pat said.

"Why?" Jenny asked. "Because of Gabe?"

"Oh, being young, having a young man, fine times." I must be more careful in what I say, she thought. Unwise to speak without thinking.

"That was so nice of him to bring presents for everybody when he didn't even know us."

"He's a *very* nice young man," Pat agreed.

"You call everybody young. He's pretty old. Forty, I'll bet."

"That is *not* old." Pat smiled. "Seventy-one, now, is a bit on the old side."

"You always say that. But you don't seem old to me. At all."

"I can promise you I feel it right about now. I'm off to bed."

"Okay. I'm going to watch the movie. I'll keep it low."

"Jenny, you haven't changed your mind about the baby, have you?"

160

"Oh, I don't know. Maybe. I don't know. Now that it's kicking around in there and everything I'd kind of like to see it. You know? But I don't know. You must think I'm really stupid."

"No," Pat said sagely. "You're young. It sometimes does seem unfair we have to make the decisions we do when we're young. Enjoy your film, now. I'll see you in the morning."

"Okay. Sleep tight."

The telephone rang. They looked at each other.

"Now, who might that be?" Pat said.

"I'll get it," Jenny said, and went over to answer the phone. Then held out the receiver, saying, "It's for you."

"For me?" Pat came across the room, took the receiver from Jenny, and said hello. To hear a deep voice on the other end saying, "You're a very hard woman to get hold of, you know that?" Walter Meyers. She glanced over at Jenny, who was already engrossed in the movie.

"How are you?" she asked, feeling all at once overheated.

"Fine. Just fine. I wanted to call you up to wish you a happy Christmas. Did you have a nice day?"

"Oh, lovely, thank you. And did you?"

"A nice day with the kids, the grandchildren. Nice. But I've been thinking about you. So I figured, why not? I'd call you. So here we are."

"Well, that's very nice of you."

"Listen, Pat, are you free for New Year's Eve?"

"Am I free?"

"I thought maybe we'd go out, have dinner. Celebrate a little. What d'you say?"

"Well, I . . ." She looked over again at Jenny.

"You have another engagement?" he asked, his deep voice magnetic.

161

"No, I haven't."

"Okay, then." He laughed. "Eight o'clock. If the weather's bad, I'll pick you up in a cab."

"Yes, all right . . ."

"Was that one of your kids, answered the phone?"

"No, not one of mine. That was Jenny."

"You don't want to tell me over the phone because she's there in the room, right?"

She smiled, pleased. "Yes, that's right."

"Okay, Pat. I've got the message. I'll see you next week."

"Yes. Fine."

She put down the telephone, asking herself, What do you think you're doing? Creating further complications. Jenny looked over, curious.

"It seems I have a date for New Year's Eve," Pat said, flustered.

"Hey! No kidding? Who with?"

"The father of my lawyer." She laughed.

"Boy, oh boy!" Jenny laughed. "Don't you tell me anymore about how *old* you are. How about that? What'll you wear?"

"Lord! I haven't any idea. Tomorrow you'll help me decide. I'm off now. Good night, dear."

"Night. See you in the morning."

I should have refused, Pat thought, carrying Gabe's gift of dusting powder along with her into the bedroom. Setting it down on the dresser beside the cologne Gillian had given her, the sachets. Standing looking at the gifts these children had given her. Jenny's tiny crystal owl. Partly excited at the prospect of an evening out with a man. Partly frightened at the new complications to her life.

162

Bubble bath. Jenny smiled. Sitting in the armchair with her legs over the arm, the box on her lap. Bubbling bath crystals. Sandy would never have thought of doing anything that nice, that thoughtful. That rotten creep. The whole thing made her feel like such a dumb sucker. Gran would've told her how dumb she was.

Pat going out on a date for New Year's Eve. Gillian would probably be going out with Gabe. Which left her the only one who'd be staying home. With her belly.

Wondering what the family would be doing now. Probably sitting around the kitchen table playing rummy, eating turkey sandwiches. Boy, if they ever knew. They'd throw her right out on her ass. Never mind waiting to hear what she had to say or anything. Just out. Peasants. Stupid peasants. The only sensible one had been Gran. If she was still around, there at the farm, I'd go live with her, keep the baby, too. What the hell'm I going to do *here* with a baby? I can't stay here forever, living off Pat. Not with a baby. *If* I keep it. I sure would like to know if it's a boy or a girl. It kicks like a football player.

The commercial was ending, the movie starting again. Pat going out on a date. How about that? That was really something.

"We don't want to get there too early," Gabe said, stretched contentedly in front of the fire. "Nine-thirty, ten. That'll be time enough."

"It was so generous of you to bring gifts for Pat and Jenny. Really a lovely thing for you to do."

"How would it look, Santa arriving without goodies? That wouldn't look good."

She looked down at her hands, then at the fire. He'd been so relaxed, so easy with Pat and Jenny. Me, too, she thought. "I didn't know . . . how did you . . . Thank you very much for all these things, Gabe. I feel badly I haven't anything for you."

"You're forgetting the book."

"But there should have been something for you under the tree."

Smiling, thinking about how he'd played Santa Claus, distributing the packages. Jenny giving her a crepe cookery book and oven mitts. Pat going to all the trouble to find the book on Le Corbusier. And Gabe. The bath powder, a marvelous make up mirror, a super hairbrush, packets of sweets. She'd never known anyone so generous. Except Megan. Saving her money. Fivepence here, fivepence there, buying little things. Loads of little things. Marks & Spencer's panties, Boots' notebooks and diaries, sugar mice. So many, many things. Wrapping each item carefully, then printing out little notes to go with every one.

"Where do you go when you go off that way?" he asked, tapping the back of her hand to get her attention.

"Sorry. My . . . sorry."

"Why don't you come sit over here with me?"

I am perfectly sober, didn't even drink the wine with the meal. It's just gone eight. In an hour and a half we're to be at the party. If I move over next to you, what will happen?

"You have my word of honor I don't attack before midnight," he said, straight-faced.

"You have to think me mad. Perhaps I am, finally."

"I think you're—different. Definitely something. But not mad. Come on, I want to put my arm around you."

Oh, yes, put your arm around me. I know what will happen.

She sat down in front of him, looking at his mouth,

studying its shape, put out her forefinger to trace his lips, know their texture. How strange, his being here. Strange having someone else here with her. Not being alone.

"You look so serious," he said, catching hold of her finger, taking it into his mouth, one by one sucking each of her fingers so that she shivered. Incredibly arousing, having him do that. She took hold of his hand and began doing the same. Until they were sitting facing each other, their hands locked wetly together, and he was urging her closer, whispering, "Come here, come here. Closer." And kissed her so softly, so sweetly it felt like dying, or being born.

"Love your mouth, the way you kiss," he murmured, unlocking one of his hands. Bringing her down on his lap with his arm around her. "The way you look. Why haven't you ever been married?"

"I've never been asked. I'm not the sort who offers a great deal of encouragement. I might like to be. Somehow, even when I think I've all the words prepared and know just what to say, none of it wants to come out. Then I feel so bloody *foolish*."

"It's too bad you feel that way. Because you're not."

"Oh, Gabe, I am. The things I've done. Always, the next morning, telling myself to forget it, it didn't happen. I won't do that anymore. But I feel so—desperate sometimes. I have to get out, breathe; the walls begin crowding me. It's so . . . so . . . *empty* here. I go out, come back, and think perhaps I don't mind the emptiness so much after all. And inside, inside I think how shameful, how shoddy it all is. And I wonder about next year and next year and if it's to be the way it is year after year . . . . I'm going on too much."

"No, you're not. You're making sense."

"I've never really had anyone I could talk with. Mother and me . . . My mother and I would talk. . . . I . . ."

"Tell me about your mother."

"It's very difficult," she said, wondering what it was safe to tell. All of it such dangerous territory. "She, too, was an architect. Beautiful, an exceptional woman. After she and Father divorced, she had a lover. Hugh. He was so very nice. And I couldn't understand why they didn't marry. She said, 'I no longer have that sort of a need, Gillie.' It didn't make very much sense to me. Because I thought if you were fortunate enough to have someone who loved you, surely you'd get married. But at the last I came to see it was much the same as if they had been married. He came round almost every evening. Never stayed right through the night, though. She wouldn't have that. Her ideas were very mixed. It was fine to take a lover, improper to present him at breakfast. Because of me, you see. I was thirteen when she met Hugh. But she did love him. And he was so kind. Hugh." Coming birthdays, Christmasses with gifts, magnums of champagne. Sending away his car. Like a film star. And that time I came upon them in the kitchen. Home early from my job. And Megan was away to a friend's house for the afternoon. Mother with her breasts bared, kissing Hugh in the kitchen. So self-possessed, saying, "Do excuse us, Gillie. We'll be out directly." It made me laugh. She was so lovely.

"You've gone off again." He tugged gently at her hair. "Is she still in England?"

"I thought I'd told you." She looked surprised. "Mother's dead."

"I'm sorry," he said quietly.

"Yes." She looked at his hand on her thigh. Yes, sorry.

166

"Let's change the subject," he said, shifting to distribute her weight on his lap more evenly. "What're you doing New Year's Eve?"

"Not a thing."

"You are now."

"Am I?" She smiled. "What am I to be doing?"

"I'll think of something."

"I always cry at midnight, on the eve."

"You do, huh? Hysterical sobbing or just quiet, melancholy tears?"

"A bit of both."

"Okay, I'll bear that in mind." He kissed her cheek.

"You live in an apartment, do you?" she asked.

"Yup."

"What sort? Is it nice?"

"Angling for an invitation?" He smiled.

"No, really, I'm just curious."

"Typical," he said. "I don't have a nice fireplace. No fireplace at all. Or a bathroom nearly as big as yours. Come to think of it, my whole place would probably fit right in this room. With nice thin walls so every time one of the neighbors uses the toilet, I automatically flush."

She laughed, winding her arms around his neck.

"I was positive if I came to sit over here we'd start making love."

"Oh?" He arched his eyebrows. "You have a little seduction scene in mind?"

"I . . . no." She laughed, feeling his hand creeping up over her ribs. "Oh, *don't* tickle me. Please."

"Just a little." He grinned, keeping on so that she squirmed, protesting, her face turning very red.

"Don't, please. I'm horribly ticklish."

"D'you hate it?"

"Please." She laughed. "I do, I do hate it. You'll make me wet my knickers."

He howled with laughter and rolled over with her on the rug.

"You'll *wet your knickers?*"

"Gabe, truly, I will. Please *stop.*"

"Okay," he said, looking down at her face. "Did you leave off your bra on my account?"

The color remained in her face. "I did, actually, yes."

"Nice of you to be so truthful, so accommodating," he said, beginning unbuttoning her shirt.

"You're welcome." Fun it's fun having fun. Messing his hair, laughing, then suddenly serious as he put his hands, then his mouth, to her breasts.

"Oh." Her voice gone husky. Whispering, "Gabe, that's so good."

He wanted to know if it would happen again. Stroking her breasts, teasing her nipples, one, then the other, feeling the heat emanating from her, breathing in her scent.

She couldn't catch her breath, wanted to rip off his clothes so she could feel his skin, touch him. But he held her hands out to the sides and kept on, going back and forth, what he was doing creating the most maddening sensation inside as if she could tear out her hair, shred her skin, scream.

"Gabe," she whispered frantically. "I'll scream. My God!"

"Go ahead, scream."

"But I want to touch you. I can't ... oh!"

Closing her eyes, moving slowly steadily under him, her hips rolling against him, wanting to feel him so many articles of clothing in the way her trousers getting ruined surely she wouldn't be able to wear them to the party.

"Please, not this way," she whispered. "It's too . . . alone."

He released her hands. She pulled off her clothes, keeping her eyes on him, silently willing him to hurry, hurry. Then on her knees, turning her back to him, taking him in, sitting in his lap, her back against his chest, boldly taking hold of his hand, directing it down, whispering, "Yes, oh yes yes."

No idea what she was doing, none, riding purely on feeling, on pleasure. His mouth moving on her shoulder, the back of her neck, one arm around her, his hand holding her breast, the other slipping sliding over her her fingers digging into his thighs ankles locked behind him. Coming faster and faster and faster. He held her by the hips finally and kept her going, going on on.

She lay on the rug beside him, crying. Just for a moment at the last everything becoming so mixed, so crazily mixed. The Christmas-tree lights, the glitter, pleasure so acute like pain she was there again, the lights. Flashing.

"I didn't hurt you, did I?" he asked, lifting her over against him.

"No, no. You're wonderful, marvelous." She sniffed, wiping her eyes with the back of her hand. "I've never done with anyone the things I've done with you. Not ever."

"I wouldn't want to hurt you." Why do I feel so damned guilty all of a sudden? As if he had hurt her. In some terrible way.

"I know you wouldn't," she whispered, looking into his eyes, her hand on his face. "I think I love you, Gabe."

He closed his eyes, holding her so hard all at once she felt crushed.

I think I love you, too, he thought. Jesus! Does that mean I go through it all again? I don't want to go through all that again. I do but I don't. I can't tell you. I'm too scared to tell you. You're what I want I know you are but commitments get made and then everything starts changing every day changing and at the end it isn't a bit close to the way it was at the beginning. But you. Like one of the kids in the corridor. Someone has to take care of you love you. Maybe somebody ought to take care of me. I don't know. I don't *know.* He lightened his hold on her, pushing her hair back over her shoulder. Her shoulder so smooth, round. I do love you. All of you. Everything. That day you tripped at the job site, I jumped, wanted to rush over and pick you up if you fell, scared to death you'd fall I didn't want you to hurt yourself. Too damned much day after day all the kids looking at their faces, listening to them, hearing them laugh, feeling that shove in the gut over and over remembering Craig how he was wanting him to be here, knowing he'd gone for good not coming back. It never goes away.

"Did you ever think about having kids?" he asked.

"I . . . ah . . . G . . . G . . . I . . I . . ." She couldn't get a word out, not one. Her tongue refusing to function. Her mouth opening, closing, opening.

He thought she might choke, she was struggling so hard to speak. He didn't know what to do. She kept trying to say something, her eyes straining, forehead deeply creased with her efforts.

"Take it easy," he said, his hands on her face. "It's okay. Easy. Go *easy.*"

She shook her head, her hair whipping his face as she

got up, still shaking her head, and went running off to the bathroom. The stuttering turning to gagging, she bent her head over the sink and threw up. Rinsed out her mouth, then slumped down on the floor, her hand over her mouth, seeing the lights, the tremendous flash. Silence. The silence. Oh, God God! Pounding with her fists, her mouth gaping open, knowing she was screaming, screaming, hearing nothing. Silence.

"Gillian, are you all right?"

She lifted her head. He was there, outside the door. I must tell. Someone. Soon. Or I will go mad.

She got up, her midsection hurting. Opening the door to find him standing there, looking so frightened, putting his arms around her. She held on, trying for something to say to him.

"What's wrong, Gillian. Something's so wrong. I can feel it. You go off and don't seem to want to come back. Sometimes you stammer, sometimes you don't. I care. And I'll help you if you need it, want it."

"Gabe, I had a child. She died. Don't ask me about it. I can't tell you, talk about it. Please, don't ask me. *Please.*"

He thought of the crayon drawing.

"You, too," he whispered. "Jesus! You don't have to talk about it. I know how it is. You still want to go to the party?"

She nodded against his chest. "I do want to . . . talk . . . about it. All sorts of things I'd like to tell you, talk about. I simply can't."

"You don't have to. Don't do anything you don't want to do. Or can't. Gillian?" He raised her chin so he could see her eyes. "I don't give a shit about what people think, don't think, what other people think's strange, peculiar, any of that. I'm saying it all wrong. But other people, what they think doesn't mean a good goddamn to me. But you do. *You do.* And I can't talk about what that means—for me—either. But we'll get to it. Okay? We will get to it."

"Yes, okay."

"Okay. Good. Now, how about a bath before we go out?"

"Together?"

"Absolutely."

"Yes, all right. You make me smile, Gabe. Just when I think I've ruined everything, made a complete ass of myself, you make me smile." *I think I do love you. I wish I knew what it was, love.*

10.

He sat on the side of the bed watching her sleep, thinking about the night before. The party. What a good time they'd had. And the good feeling being with someone. Not alone. Then coming home to make love and laugh, whispering. All of it feeling so right, so good. We fit, he thought. We fit so goddamned well together. He reached over to push the hair back from her face. Smiling. She opened her eyes, then closed them. Opened them again.

"You're dressed."

"You're not." He smiled more widely. "I don't have to be back at school until the third," he said. "But the thing is, I've got some paperwork to do. So I thought I'd zip home now and spend today getting it out of the way. Then come back around seven. We'll go out, have dinner. How does that sound.?"

"Fine." She smiled back at him, still on the edge of sleep, ready to slide back down into it.

"Okay." He rested his cheek against hers. "I never felt less like leaving someone in my entire life. But this way, if I get my work out of the way, we'll have tonight and all day tomorrow before you have to be back at work on Monday. And after Monday I don't know how in the hell I'm going to stand it not being with you."

"Hmmm," she murmured, stroking his hair.

"You're not even awake." He laughed, sitting up. "Go on back to sleep and I'll call you later."

She gave him another sleepy smile and closed her eyes.

He sang loudly in the shower, laughing at himself as he toweled dry, shaking his head at his terrible singing. Shaved around the smile that all at once seemed permanently plastered to his face, then put on the coffee and went to his desk to line up the work.

Such a long time since he'd actually enjoyed working. Random moments at school when some kid or another would get sent down to have a talk with him. Such great conversations that sometimes evolved from these meetings. The kids venturing to speak their minds, voice their opinions. Something that sure as hell hadn't been allowed, never mind encouraged, when he'd been a kid. But what they had to say so damned sensible a lot of the time. More sense-making than what half his staff had to say. Maybe eight really good, motivated teachers on the whole staff. The rest of them there because, back in college, teaching had seemed the easiest, quickest route to a decent income or a husband. Not to mention a work year chock-full of holidays, off time. But the husbands didn't materialize. Or something turned sour. So now the kids drove them nuts, got on their nerves, had them demanding pay increases and all kinds of peripherally job-related goodies that might make them feel a little better about having to spend their days doing a job they could

174

barely tolerate, surrounded by kids they half the time viewed as pint-sized enemies. He wished he could fire most of the staff, bring in new people with some motivation, some understanding and enthusiasm. Never happen.

Jesus, but he loved the kids. Sometimes wandered through the school to stand looking in at one or the other of the kindergarten classrooms watching the kids with a pulsing ache in his throat, a painful affection for them, gripped by the sight of their still-round faces and chubby hands. Watching them do their finger paintings, play their learning games. Seeing Craig there in the middle of the group, his head tilted to one side in that listening way he'd had. Or the sudden crystalline laughter spilling from his mouth. Jesus! His laughter.

He chewed on the end of his pen, staring at the wall, the anguish gushing up into his throat. What was the point? He reached for his coffee cup, got up to refill it. Put the cup down on the counter and momentarily forgot why he'd come into the kitchen, his mind still working over images of Craig.

How he'd stood outside the nursery looking at the red, screaming face, thinking about how all the babies looked like Winston Churchill but laughing, thinking, Not my kid. He looks like Joe E. Brown. Standing out there grinning like a fool, looking at Craig, thinking, My son. *My kid.* A moment of undiluted happiness. Complete, total. He could've stayed there forever watching Craig's face settle, the small, waving fists subsiding, sleep smoothing out the creases, taking away the red, turning him beautiful. Christ, what a high. Could've stayed there all day and night. But he'd had to go see Penny.

And he'd gone along to the room filled with love for her. What the two of them had managed to do.

Prepared to embrace her, to spill out all the laughing, happy words. Only to be met with her complaints, her disinterest in embraces. "Don't, Gabe. I really don't feel like it." Her preoccupation with the problem of regaining her figure. So that he'd left the hospital with a lump of resentment in his throat. Only thoughts of the baby serving to ease it all.

The coffee. He poured some into his cup, pulled the plug on the percolator, and went back to the desk. To sit thinking about Gillian. All of him going soft at the thought of her. Thinking of her hands, the way she held him. The caring in her hands transmitting itself through his system like warm oil. No one had ever held him, touched him so caringly. Her hands, her arms holding him, making him so quietly euphoric, speechless with reciprocal caring. So that he wanted to stay with her. Just stay there. Made strong and sane again by her embraces. Love. That's love. Jesus! You know it is. He looked at the telephone, seeing himself dialing her number, hearing her soft, hesitant voice, saying to her, Hey, guess what! I love you. I really do love you.

The doorbell rang, startling him. He got up, went over, opened the door, and there was Penny. His heart convulsed at the sight of her. Standing there in the hall looking at him hopefully. He couldn't even speak.

She said, "Hi," looking and sounding awkward. "I was passing through and I thought I'd stop by, say hi."

"Come on in," he said stiffly, standing well away from the door as if should she accidentally brush against him her touch might turn him to stone. Like the Medusa. A headful of snakes. "On your way to where?" Why wasn't he throwing himself at her throat, ripping out her veins?

"New York. I got fed up with the Coast, so I thought I'd give New York a try."

176

She stood looking at him, waiting for an invitation to sit down.

"You want some coffee?" he asked her, surprising the hell out of himself. What was he doing? Why wasn't he hitting her, knocking her senseless? Beating her brains out? Coffee?

"That'd be nice. It's really cold out."

"Sit down," he said. "I'll get it."

"Place hasn't changed a bit," she said, unbuttoning her coat, sitting down on the edge of the sofa.

He poured some of the still-warm coffee into a cup—no cream, no sugar, he hated himself for remembering something as stupid as the way she took her coffee—returned to put it down on the coffee table in front of her before sitting down in the armchair, staring at her. He'd forgotten what she looked like. With the short, urchin haircut and the big-baby eyes. Forgotten how deceivingly pretty she was, how self-deceived.

"Did you have a nice Christmas?" she asked, warming her hands on the cup.

"All right," he said noncommittally. Thinking, You. With that face. You killed a kid of ours. Killed it through neglect, disinterest, lack of caring. And it doesn't show. Not one fucking thing shows on you. Five years. And you look exactly the same. What the hell's wrong with me? I ought to have my hands wrapped around your neck, watching your eyes bulge, popping. I ought to be breaking your damned stupid neck.

"You look older." She smiled uncertainly.

"You don't. What d'you want, Penny? What're you here for?"

"Don't be mad at me, Gabe," she said childishly, fixing the big-baby eyes on him. Blue as pale as a drop of ink in a quart of water. "I couldn't help it. It wasn't my fault. I told you I was sorry. I wasn't even *there*, Gabe."

"Jesus, Penny," he said tiredly. "Let's not get into that. Okay?"

"But I was. I am. Sorry. You ought to know that, Gabe. I'd never've let anything happen to Craigie. It was an accident." Those eyes begging him to believe her.

"Let's skip it, huh? I'm not up to it. What do you *want?*"

"Well, the thing is, I never took anything from you, you know, Gabe. Never asked for anything. And I could've. The court would've given me something. I know that."

"Come to the point," he said impatiently.

"Well"—looking down at her cup—"if I'm going to be starting all over again in New York, I'm going to need uh a little something to uh tide me over. Until I get a break. You know?"

He couldn't help himself. He laughed. She looked up at him, wide-eyed.

"You're too fucking much." He laughed. "You've got to be kidding. Five years and one dead kid later and you drop by to float a loan? No, wait a minute. Not a loan. You want some money, pure and simple. Right?"

"If you could just let me have a little. I can't ask my folks for anything more, Gabe. You know how they are."

"Oh, sure. And what're you going to do this time? Act, sing, study ballet?"

"Don't make fun of me," she said, looking downcast. "I know you don't think I'm any good. But one day you'll see."

He sat back in the chair and crossed his legs, studying her.

"Thirty years old and you still think you're Shirley Temple." He shook his head sadly. "Other people might be surprised by that, I guess. But I'm not. I'm not."

"I don't need very much," she said, the familiar little whining note in her voice.

"I don't happen to have too much cash on me," he said, trying to think of what there was in his wallet. Thirty, forty dollars. What the *fuck* am I doing? "I could let you have a check, I suppose."

"That'd be great, Gabe. Really. I'd really appreciate it. I'll go and I won't bother you again."

"That's right," he said, getting up to go to his desk for the checkbook. "You won't."

He wrote out a check for two hundred and fifty dollars, signed and folded it, and walked back to put it down on the table.

"Do me a favor," he said quietly, standing on the far side of the table. "Forget where I live. Forget you ever knew me. I don't know why in hell I'm giving you money. Except that for some reason I feel sorry for you. You're never going to change. Or grow up. And that's sad."

She looked at the amount on the check, then opened her bag and put it into her wallet before starting to refasten the buttons on her coat, in a hurry to leave now. So goddamned transparent. All set to go, she stood up and held her hand out to him.

"Thanks a lot, Gabe. I really am very sorry about the way it all turned out. I really am." She looked up at him—a round-eyed child's face sitting incongruously atop the woman's body. He didn't want to take her hand or touch her. But he did. Hugged her hard, his eyes squeezed shut. Then abruptly released her, opened the

179

door, and cleared his throat, saying, "Good luck. Take it easy."

"Thanks an awful lot," she said, then went hurrying off down the hall.

He closed the door, went to sit down in the armchair. Breaking into tears. Sobbing noisily, without control. Mourning the loss of all that anger—what in hell had *happened* to it?—and Craig and a lot of dreams that were all dead now, too.

God damn it. Why did she have to come here? Bringing it all back again. The pain. Too many memories. And some of them good. Some of them containing laughter. Paying her off like some sort of dumb cluck. But she'd always been able to work her way around him. And she'd looked so pathetically young and skinny. A goddamned waif.

He should've given her the thirty or forty in his wallet. But he'd need that. For dinner tonight. With Gillian. Thinking of Gillian. Feeling so rotten. He didn't want to have to talk to anybody. The coffee still sitting there on the table. Seeing Penny sitting there with her hands around the cup, looking over at him with those dumb, watery big-baby eyes. You're a fucking patsy, Hadley. And what're you doing, getting yourself all set to jump right in with another woman. Have to slow down a lot, think about everything.

Why hadn't he beaten her brains out? Giving her money, hugging her. Small, insubstantial in his arms after Gillian. But so deadly familiar. Was everything over now? Did it mean he'd start forgetting Craig? He couldn't forget Craig.

I've got to think, put everything back together. He felt so thrown. Ten minutes and she'd screwed up his head. There she was, all set to go off to a new dreamland, take

180

another shot at the stardom she was convinced was out there waiting for her. She'd probably wind up a topless dancer in some crummy Broadway bar. Or a waitress in some greasy spoon. How did people get such wild illusions about themselves? He'd seen her act in a couple of amateur productions. Awful. Heard her sing. Worse. But she was going to be a star. Spent her entire life dreaming of applause and fawning crowds of autograph seekers. Seeing herself decked out in white satin, fox furs. Not even good in bed. Lying there with about as much animation as a wet towel. Didn't even like making love after the first few times. Just spread herself dutifully, as if that was all she'd had to do. Only good thing she'd ever done in her whole pointless life had been Craig. And she'd managed to kill him.

He lit a cigarette and collapsed back in the chair—eyes stinging, nose blocked—wondering if she felt anything, if she really was sorry about Craig. She'd looked sorry. But it was so damned hard to tell with her. A face as bland and nonrevealing as an egg. And once upon a time he'd found her fascinating. Thinking that inscrutable expression covered a functioning intelligence, interpreting her slight shrugs and meaningful smiles as wise. Wise! How could he have been so incredibly stupid? Suffering through five years of a marriage to that . . . that *marshmallow.*

But Craig. Jesus, Craig. I'd give anything, *anything* to have you here. Sit you on my lap and hold you.

She'd taken it all. He started crying again. She'd even taken his anger.

She woke up at ten-fifteen. And stretched, yawning, feeling wonderful. Lit a cigarette and lay looking at the room, smoking, thinking how different things were suddenly. How quickly life could change when you'd thought nothing could possibly ever change any of it. Gabe would call this afternoon. And this evening they'd go out to dinner. Afterwards they'd come back here, make love. Thinking of making love with him, instantly wanting him.

Is this what love is? I thought I loved Brooke. Poking my way along the beach, waiting down the hours until it would be time to see him. Unable to do anything, think of anything, but him, being with him. Was that love?

Love with Mother, Megan. Something so different. Sitting with Megan on her lap, Megan's head on her shoulder. Megan's clear, sweet voice in her ear. Saying, Could we go to the seaside, Mummy? I do so love the sea. And Uncle Hugh said he'd take us all.

In Hugh's limousine. Megan bouncing eagerly on the seat, looking first out the side window, then out the back, chattering away. The back of the chauffeur's head. His cap. All of it so plainly remembered.

Mother, slender legs crossed, smoking a cigarette, talking quietly with Hugh. The two of them so completely one. Sitting beside Megan, watching her mother in conversation with Hugh, studying the two of them, trying to define the substance of their love. Deciding, Yes, it is love. They do love each other. It's in the way they speak to each other, the way they simply laugh at something they've seen in each other's eyes. Sitting looking at her mother, at the definition of her breasts under her dress, the gold chain around her neck. Her hands. The shape of her mouth. The simple sweep of her hair. Half a dozen pins and it was perfectly coiled at the back of her head.

And Hugh. A very tall man. With thick, graying hair and large features. Large eyes, large nose, wide mouth.

A big, basso voice. Yet so gentle, so infinitely patient. His eyes crinkling with laughter, amusement, indulgence. Suffering Megan's bony elbows, her knees when she'd climb all over him. And he'd turn to look at Mother, the two of them smiling, smiling.

And occasionally, at night, coming in from an encounter with some man she'd allowed to find her in one of the pubs. Tiptoing shoeless down the landing to hear the murmur of their voices behind the bedroom door. Or laughter. Sometimes simply sounds. Sighs. Studying them through the months and years, deciding she could never have the sort of love Mother had with Hugh because she hadn't any of the qualities Mother had. None of the decisiveness, the wisdom, the serenity.

But this, now. This felt like love. It did. And she imagined she knew now some of what Mother had to have known with Hugh. Such tremendous pleasure in simply being together. The lovemaking. Being together. The looks, the laughter, the talk.

And if this was love, then Brooke had been something else, something that was more closely related to what happened when she went to pubs, drank a bit, and accepted caresses, safely hidden behind the shield of her closed eyes. This, though, made all that other even more artificial and unreal. None of that having had anything at all to do with her emotions or with love. They'd had to do with something Brooke had started years before. Something to which she'd become addicted, on which she'd become dependent. Something inside herself she'd feared and disliked.

Now, all that would be different.

She put out the cigarette and got up, pulling on her robe, then hurrying through to the living room to turn up the thermostat. Thinking how extraordinarily well she felt.

The balance of the morning was spent in tidying up the apartment, changing the bed linens, carrying a load of washing down to the cellar. And while the wash was getting done, vacuumed every inch of the apartment, then scrubbed and waxed the kitchen floor. Feeling so energized, strong. She paused midday to nibble some bits of turkey and drink two cups of tea, then folded the laundry, put it away, set up the board to iron the few pieces that needed doing. With the radio playing and the whole place looking and smelling so clean, fresh. Until suddenly it was four o'clock and he hadn't called.

She made a fresh pot of tea and sat down at the kitchen table with a cigarette, trying to remember what he'd said. Just that he'd telephone. She had the cigarette, drank her tea, then went to the bedroom, switching on the light over her board, settling down to do a little work before he phoned.

And when she next looked at the time it was after six. Perhaps he'd just forgotten to call and planned to come directly without bothering. She put her work aside, turned off the light, and started readying herself for their evening out. Wishing he'd telephoned because she wasn't sure what to wear. Staying on the safe side with black trousers, a black and white printed shirt. Her hair down.

She checked the ice-cube trays. In case he wanted a drink before they went out. More than enough ice. But she was running a bit low of drinks after yesterday and jotted down scotch, gin, and vermouth on her running grocery list. Then returned to the living room to sit down, wait.

Darts of alarm shooting into her brain as seven-thirty

came and went, then eight. Where could he be? Perhaps he'd had an accident with the car. At eight-fifteen she walked through to look out the kitchen window. Up and down the street. Her appetite dwindling. By eight-thirty, she decided he wasn't coming. And hadn't any idea what to do. Couldn't understand what could possibly have gone wrong. He'd said they'd go out, that he'd call her. He *had* said that. She was certain.

But he'd left so early. Could she have said or done something to put him off?

She sat in a corner of the sofa, looking at the door, feeling more worried with each passing minute. Watching the hands on the clock making their way around the face. Reaching nine o'clock and then nine-fifteen, nine-thirty. Her appetite completely gone. And she hadn't the energy to get up, go to the refrigerator, prepare something. The feeling that her chest was bruised, hurting. She thought of telephoning him. But surely he'd have called to explain. If she did telephone, he might not answer. Or perhaps he would and it would be embarrassing because he hadn't ever planned on coming back.

She turned off the lights, went into the bedroom, and undressed. Taking great care with her clothes, putting them away. Feeling old and tired but not sleepy. So sad and frightened. *Was* it something she'd done? Carrying on so, rushing off to the bathroom. Or perhaps it was her legs. He didn't like her legs.

Returning to the living room to turn down the thermostat before getting into bed. Lying staring into the darkness. Deciding she'd go out for a good long walk tomorrow. Spend the day out, away from the apartment. Why didn't he call? It was still early. Only just past ten. She listened for the telephone, willing it to ring. Daunted by the silence. Occasional stirrings above. Pat and Jenny up there, readying themselves for bed. Why didn't he telephone? Why hadn't he come?

Had it all been a pretense? He'd never intended to call. Just something he'd said in order to get out, away from her. But surely there was some valid reason why he hadn't telephoned, hadn't kept their date.

Starting to feel ill from the sudden ascent into happiness and the more rapid descent out of it. She chain-smoked, blaming herself for so many inadequacies, failures, her hateful naiveté. To begin thinking about love, willing to believe love had been happening. Such frightful delusions. She'd played the fool again. And he must be laughing at me. He wouldn't. Would he?

Feeling so sad, so unequal to everything. Biting her lip, trying not to cry, but the disappointment was so crushing she turned her face to the pillow and cried and cried. And finally, still listening for the telephone to ring, sank into sleep.

In the morning she couldn't seem to lift her head. It ached. And her joints were stiffened, sore, as if she'd run for miles. A long soak in a very hot tub didn't help at all. She didn't feel like eating, so satisfied herself with several cups of tea, then returned to bed. At once falling into a dizzy semisleep. Her mind skimming over thoughts of Gabe, anxiously—yet distantly—wondering what could have happened. Disappointment a sickness in her chest, her throat, her eyes.

"I think something's wrong," Jenny said.

"Oh? Why do you say that?"

"I don't know. It just doesn't *feel* right. Everything's too quiet. I think I'll go down, see if she's okay."

"All right, dear."

She went down, knocked, and waited a long time, then knocked again, louder.

A different nightmare. Lying naked on a beach, her legs sprawling open. Hundreds of people standing laughing, laughing while she tried to draw her legs closed. Couldn't. Frantically raking the faces, spotting Gabe in the crowd. Laughing with the others. A drum beating somewhere. Beating. Banging.

She lifted her head. The door. Reeling out through the living room to open the door, her heart sinking to see Jenny. "I've flu or something," she said, so dizzy she'd fall down. "Come in, Jenny." Unsteadily making her way back to the bedroom.

"O'you have a fever?" Jenny asked solicitously, tucking in the blankets.

Gillian felt her forehead, cheeks. "I don't know. I haven't a thermometer. I do feel awful, though."

"You feel really hot," Jenny said, laying the back of her hand against Gillian's forehead. "Pat's got a thermometer. I could go get it."

"No, no. Stay for a bit. Keep me company."

"Sure. Okay."

Pat appeared in the doorway, saying, "I thought I'd come down, see how you are."

"I think she's got a fever," Jenny said judiciously.

"I'll fetch the thermometer, shall I?"

"You don't have to, really," Gillian said. Her throat sore. "It's flu, I'm certain."

Pat came over to touch Gillian's cheeks and forehead, pursing her lips. "I'll go up and fix you a good hot bowl of soup. You lie still, rest."

Looking at Jenny sitting on the side of the bed, thinking for the first time how Jenny had to have felt when Sandy left her. Never mind the things she didn't know

187

about him. But how hurt she must have been. The awful disappointment. She hadn't thought about any of that. And felt guilty now, sorry. Not to have considered Jenny's feelings.

"What's the matter?" Jenny asked, touching Gillian's hand.

Her eyes filling with tears at the kindness, the caring.

"Don't cry," Jenny said softly as Gillian turned her face away, trying to hide in the pillow. "You'll feel better."

Helplessly inarticulate, her hand closed around Jenny's small hand, unable to speak, explain the sorrow at her omissions, her losses.

"Have you taken anything?" Jenny asked. "Aspirin or anything?"

Gillian shook her head into the pillow.

"I'll get you some aspirin." Jenny got up and went into the bathroom. Gillian kept her face hidden; ashamed, ill, disappointed, embarrassed. Opening her eyes to see Jenny going out of the bedroom. Closing her eyes for a moment, then feeling the pressure on the bed as Jenny sat down again, saying, "Take these." Sitting holding a glass of orange juice in one hand, two aspirin tablets sitting in the palm of the other. Gillian sat up a little and took the aspirin. Jenny watched, encouraging her to drink the juice.

She shook her head, looking away, over at the windows. The shades drawn, the room dim. Her drawing board, the basket of pencils. Several rolled white-prints. A specification folded over, held open by a rock. Megan had painted it. A ladybug. In red and white enamel. Bringing that rock all the way from London in her handbag. The weight of it constant everywhere she went. Feeling herself being drawn forward, Jenny's hair brushing against her cheek, Jenny's arms, the swell of her belly. Murmuring, "Don't cry. Don't cry." Jenny's small hand stroking her. Crooning, "It's all right. Don't cry."

Pat, returning with the tray, found the moment too fragile to intrude upon. So set the tray down on the edge of the drawing board and withdrew. Going to the living room to take one of the cigarettes from the box on the coffee table. Standing smoking it by the window. Gazing out. Gazing in. Wondering what sort of madness it was to have accepted Walter Meyers' invitation to go out. Experiencing a thrill of mixed anticipation and fear.

Jenny was disconcerted by Gillian's failure to respond. And felt kind of weird sitting there trying to make her feel better, get her to talk when Gillian was stiff inside her arms, her chest heaving up and down. As if it made her suffer, having Jenny there. So she moved to withdraw and Gillian's arms flew around her. Crying, "Stay with me, please."

Jenny sighed and wiped the tears from Gillian's cheek with her fingers. At once caught by the softness of her skin, its texture. She'd never seen or felt skin like it. As pure and poreless as a baby's. My baby will have skin like this, she thought.

The telephone rang and they both jumped.

"D'you want me to answer it?" Jenny asked, leaning away.

"Please," Gillian croaked. It hurt to talk.

Sunday morning he woke up late, miserably hung over. Gingerly climbed out of bed and wove his way through the living room to the kitchen, head throbbing, to fix a pot of coffee. Pausing to pick up the empty bottle—he'd killed the better part of a fifth of scotch—

and the heaped ashtray, the smells of both making his stomach rise as he tossed the bottle into the trash, emptied the ashtray. While the coffee was brewing, he went to the bathroom, gagged down some aspirin, drank two glasses of water.

While he was standing under the shower, his head beginning to clear, he suddenly—with sickening self-disgust—realized he'd not only not called Gillian, he'd stood her up. And groaned, swearing loudly, imagining her waiting for him at the apartment. Picturing her walking up and down, waiting, wondering. Thinking God knew what. She'd think he'd done it intentionally. Jesus. How could he have *done* that? To her, of all people. After that big speech about not hurting her. His fists clenching at the thought of damned Penny and the trouble she caused, kept on causing, interfering, barging in uninvited, crapping things up. Gillian probably wouldn't even talk to him after this.

His head aching worse than before, he tied on his robe and padded through to the living room, trying to think of how he'd put it. God knows she deserved a decent explanation. If she'd be willing to listen to him. Knowing her, knowing she'd gone through all kinds of hell because he hadn't showed up. Oh, God damn it. Damn damn damn! Just let me have a chance to explain. That's all. Just don't slam the phone down. Because I didn't mean this to happen and I know it hurt I know it goddamndamndamn.

His hands trembling as he picked up the receiver. Misdialed and had to start again. In a sweat as he listened to the ringing at the other end.

"Who's that?" a man's voice asked.
"Who's *that*?" Jenny asked back.

"Is Gillian there?"

"Oh." Jenny smiled. "It's you. Gabe."

"Jenny?"

"Hi."

"Where's Gillian?"

"Sick in bed. She's got the flu or something."

"She's *sick*?"

"Uh-huh."

"I'll be there in an hour," he said. And hung up.

"Okay," she said into the buzzing receiver. "Okay."

She went back to the bedroom.

"That was Gabe. He said he'll be here in an hour."

"Oh, no." Gillian's voice thickened to a whisper. What'll I do? What will I say to him? What does he want? Why is he coming *now*?

"I told him you're sick," Jenny said, puzzled by Gillian's reaction. "He sounded really upset."

"He did?" She wet her lips. Hot, so hot. Everything aching, sore.

"Boy, Sandy wouldn't come to see me if I got hit by a truck and was bleeding all over the street. No guy I ever knew would come to see me on a freezing cold day. Sick or not. I mean, I could have gangrene of the arms and legs and go around dropping fingers and toes all over the place and no boyfriend I ever had would even notice." She smiled encouragingly, leaning forward to place her hand again on Gillian's forehead. "You sure are hot." She touched Gillian's throat, then her shoulder. Feeling very motherly. "Hot, hot. I bet if we put you in a whole tubful of ice you'd cool down fast enough."

Gillian smiled weakly.

"Say, Pat left the tray. Why don't you have some of the soup now?" She got up, got the tray, and set it down

191

on Gillian's lap. "Looks good," she said, pushing the spoon into Gillian's hand. "Have some."

"Oh, Jenny," her voice catching, breaking, the spoon jiggling in her hand. "I . . . I . . ."

"Come on," Jenny said gently. "Before it gets cold."

Your eyes, Jenny thought, watching her taste the soup. Your eyes just kill me. I wish I could really *do* something for you. Just to take that look out of your eyes.

Gillian couldn't manage more than a few swallows. She was too apprehensive, felt too ill. Jenny returned the tray to the drawing board as Gillian struggled out of bed and stood wavering for a moment before making her way into the bathroom.

She was so dizzy she could scarcely see. As if there was a film over her eyes. A shimmery heat film so that the outlines of everything were misted and there was a steady, high-pitched whining inside her head. Her nightgown damp with perspiration. She removed it and filled the sink with cool water, sponging herself down with one hand, holding on to the sink for support with the other. The effort exhausting her. And she wanted a fresh nightgown. Stupid. She should have brought one in with her. The idea of walking naked into the bedroom with Jenny there too embarrassing. She wrapped herself in a bath towel, opened the door. Making her way to the chest of drawers. Needing both hands to get the drawer open. The towel fell off, the blood racing to her head. Deeply embarrassed. Keeping her back to Jenny, knowing Jenny was watching, wanting to help. Appalled at the things that were happening.

Jenny stood admiring her, thinking how great it would be to be that tall, have such a dynamite figure, wishing Gillian would let her help. She wanted to help.

She was so dizzy she had to stop, close her eyes,

clutching the sides of the drawers, waiting for the dizziness to go before removing a clean gown, pulling it on, then turning to see Jenny had straightened the bedclothes, the pillows. She wanted very much to thank her but knew if she opened her mouth she'd start crying again. Start and probably never stop. So slid instead into the now cool-feeling sheets.

"You want me to go now?" Jenny asked.

Gillian whispered, "No," taking hold of Jenny's hand. Sliding lower in the bed, letting her head sink into the pillows, closing her eyes. "Stay."

Pat stepped over to the bedroom doorway. Saw Jenny sitting there stroking Gillian's face. The two so peaceful together. She walked in softly, retrieved the tray, let herself out.

He hurried up the front steps, feeling shaky, quivery inside. His insides turned to the consistency of partially set jelly. Greeted Jenny, threw his hat and coat off, kicked off his boots, and turned, ready to face Gillian.

"I'll go on up," Jenny said.

"See you later," he said distractedly, moving toward the bedroom.

To stand in the doorway looking in, seeing she was asleep. Moved into the room feeling so guilty. Looking at the flush of fever on her face, feeling worse minute by minute. Knowing without a doubt just how very much she'd come to mean to him, how much he cared.

"I hate to wake you up," he said, sitting on the side of the bed. "Probably the best thing in the world for you right now, to sleep. But I have some things that really need saying while they're all fresh in my mind. So, wake up, I'll tell you, then you can go right back to sleep."

She blinked several times, then wet her lips. Her mouth so dry. Her head feeling swollen, aching.

"You've got a fever," he said irrelevantly. "I'm sorry. I feel so rotten about yesterday. I did intend to call you, to come. I got drunk instead." He looked past her at the wall, then back at her. "It's a long, stupidly boring story but the thing is it didn't have anything to do with you. You just happened to be the one who wound up getting the dirty end of it all. And I'm sorry. Really sorry."

"I thought . . . it was me."

"Oh, damn it," he said miserably. "It wasn't *you*." So ashamed and guilty. He rested his cheek against hers, feeling the heat from her face. "It wasn't you, Gillian. I care about you. I'd never intentionally do a lousy thing like that to you. To anyone, for that matter. But never to you."

She sobbed explosively, closing her arms around him.

"Could we forget about it?" he whispered, on the verge of tears himself. "I'll tell you what happened, then can we put it behind us?"

"I want to."

Jesus! he thought. Thank you.

11.

"Pat, I was thinking about you. So I thought, better than thinking, I'll call you up. I'm looking forward to Friday night. I can't tell you how much."

"Yes," she said, hearing Jenny moving about in the bedroom.

"What're you doing? Right now, this minute."

"Right now? Nothing at all."

"Come out for a drink. Let's talk. I'd like to see you."

"Walter, it's late."

"It's only seven-thirty. It's not late. Have you had dinner? I'll buy you dinner."

"All right, a drink," she said. "But not for long."

"Wonderful. I'll pick you up in, say, twenty minutes. How's that?"

"Yes, all right. Twenty minutes."

She hung up, her heart beating crazily. Jenny wandered in, munching an apple, asking, "Who was that?"

"Walter Meyers."

"Oh, yeah? What's up?"

"He's coming by. To take me out for a drink."

Jenny looked at the high color in Pat's face and smiled.

"He's really interested," she said. "That's neat."

"I'd better change clothes," Pat said, looking down at herself. Nervous. What was she doing, encouraging this man? This was all wrong, all wrong, could come to no good. Complications piling up one atop the other.

"When's he coming?" Jenny asked, rotating the apple.

"Twenty minutes."

"You'd better step on it, then. What're you going to wear?"

"I haven't any idea." Pat rushed into the bedroom. Jenny sat down to finish her apple.

Twenty minutes on the dot. Jenny got up to open the door.

He introduced himself. This great big silver-haired guy looking like some kind of diplomat. Saying, "You must be Jenny," shaking hands with her. "I've heard all kinds of nice things about you."

"Come on," she said. "What kind of nice things? I like to hear what people have to say about me."

He laughed, looking about the room. "Lovely place," he said, removing his coat, draping it across his arm.

"It's nice, isn't it?" Jenny agreed. "Pat shouldn't be long. Come sit down. Would you like something to drink?"

"No, no, thank you," he said, lowering himself into one of the armchairs.

Jenny couldn't stop staring at him. Silver hair and pink cheeks, gray-silver eyes. In a suit with a vest and a chain—a watch fob?—across his middle. Smiling away, his coat folded across his knee. Pat going out for a date. This was really something.

She heard Jenny letting him in and thought how increasingly awkward things were becoming. How could she? Indulging in romantic escapades at this time of her life, at this time. Smoothing down her dress, fastening on her bracelet. Taking a deep breath, prepared to brave it out. Feeling in every way unequal to this situation she'd created.

He jumped to his feet as soon as Pat appeared in the doorway. The two of them like kids, Jenny thought. All eager and trying hard to behave their best. She got up and got Pat's coat from the closet, surrendering it to Walter, who had his hand out for it.

"Don't you look wonderful, Pat," he exclaimed, helping her into the coat. "I'm so pleased you could make it tonight."

She looked so pretty, Jenny thought. Saying good night, watching the two of them go off down the stairs. Returning inside to turn on *The Hollywood Squares*.

It was so easy to talk to her. Because of her totally attentive manner of listening. He had the singular feeling he was actually being heard. Perhaps for the first time ever in his private life. Professionally, his audience was subject to the political chain of command. His staff listened to him. He, in turn, listened to the school board, the parents' association. But privately, the women he'd encountered in the course of the last five years didn't listen. They simply waited out what he had to say. And while he was attempting to communicate some thought or other they were actively preparing their own monologues. And so what seemed like conversation between consenting adults was, in reality, nothing more than a vaguely connected series of interwoven, nonrelated speeches.

"Once Penny and I were married," he said, "she gave up any pretense of listening and just talked louder and louder until she'd succeeded in talking me down. Rendering her variation on the theme of the moment. 'How it's going to be when I hit the big time,' or 'How I plan to strike it big.' Finally I was as good at tuning her out as she was at cutting me off. At the end we were living inside our silences, hearing other voices, dreaming wildly divergent dreams."

"What did you dream of?" she asked quietly.

"Someone like you," he said, "who'd listen. Not because I've ever thought that what I had to say was of any earth-shattering significance. Because I don't think any of it was or is. But just how nice it would be to *talk* instead of endlessly competing for a chance to get a few words in."

"That seems reasonable."

"I'm talking too goddamned much now," he said with a flustered smile.

"No. I like listening to you. And I'm sorry about what happened yesterday."

"I still should've called you."

"Had it been me, I'd most likely have done what you did. I do understand. Really."

"Feeling any better?" he asked.

"Oh, yes. Much. Perhaps it was one of those twelve-hour viruses."

"Maybe it was. Hungry?"

"Not particularly. Are you?"

"I wouldn't mind something," he said. "Why don't I fix you some tea and a sandwich for me? How would that be?"

"Will she come back again, do you think?"

"Probably not. I hope to hell not."

"Did you love her very much, Gabe?"

"Once," he said, swinging his legs off the bed. "For about three months. I called it love. I think it was really some kind of ninety-day virus."

She laughed. "I hope it didn't make you feel as dreadful as I've felt today."

"Probably worse. It lasted longer."

"I think while you're doing that I'll bathe. I feel so clammy."

"Domestic," he said. "It's all starting to feel very domestic."

"What does that mean?" she asked, feeling about on the floor for her slippers.

"It means I like it." He smiled at her from the doorway, then continued on to the kitchen.

Standing feeling her emotions upswinging again. Life once more assuming optimistic perspectives. Does love mean going up and then down, then up again? Is this how it is? How the bloody hell do people manage to know it's love they're in and not simply the absence of unhappiness? Mother standing in the kitchen spreading Marmite on bread for Megan's tea, saying, "It takes courage to love, to let oneself be loved, Gillie. But very much worth all the risks involved. Be courageous, darling. Things might be better than you expect."

He sat for several minutes studying her eyes, the shape of her mouth. At last saying, "You're a wonderful-looking woman, Pat. It's a pleasure looking at you."

"Oh, nonsense," she said, discomfited. "Old as the hills and gone far past it."

"If I haven't gone past it," he said seriously, "then neither have you. What precisely is it you think you've gone past?"

"Just about everything," she said. Wishing she'd never said any of the things she'd said.

"Not love, surely."

"Love?" She could only stare at him.

"You're not drinking your drink. Is it all right?"

"It's fine, fine."

He reached across the table and took hold of her hand, studying the palm for a moment, then turning her hand over, placing his other hand on top of hers. Her hand trapped between his two. Making her stomach jump about.

"How long have you been a widow?" he asked, his gray eyes, gray hair, wide smile all hypnotic.

"Years," she said, with an indefinite wave of her free hand. "How long have you been a widower?"

"Eight years. Why didn't you remarry?"

"Why didn't you?"

"I've been waiting to meet a woman who interested me." He smiled. "You more than interest me. You have a beautifully shaped mouth. Why have you kept putting me off? I could tell there was something between us at once. Seven weeks to lure you out for a drink. Am I wrong? Is there something about me you don't like?"

"No." He was steadily smoothing the back of her hand, his fingers moving over her wrist, encircling it. She was finding it very hard to concentrate, to think at all, with him doing that.

"There's nothing?" he persisted.

"No," she replied truthfully, wishing he'd stop. All of it. Asking questions, searching her eyes, stroking her hand.

"If there's nothing," he said, "then spend some time with me. A lot of time. Whatever you like. The theater.

200

Concerts. Dinner. Tell me what you like and we'll do it. Have you got family here?"

"No. Not here. Only Jenny. And Gillian."

"What will you do when Jenny has her baby?"

"I don't know."

"I've got a hell of a big house down on the shore," he said leadingly. "You'll have to come see it. Ten rooms. Plenty of room for you and the girl, her baby."

"Lord, Walter! What are you saying? You don't know me. You can't be serious?"

"I'll spend as much time as it takes to convince you," he said, his eyes holding hers. "But I'm going to convince you. I want you, Pat. You're an uncommon woman. Your age is of no consequence to me. None whatsoever. I get the greatest pleasure just in looking at you."

"This is impossible—"

"Nothing's impossible," he interrupted her. "I'm not misreading you. What is it you're not telling me?"

"This *is* impossible."

He shook his head. "I'm not wrong. I fell in love with you the minute I saw you in Matthew's office. It's been a long time. I hate the idea of wasting time alone when I could be with you. We'll go to the theater, the opera. Do you like the opera?"

"Yes." Her voice slowly vanishing. Her powers of thought and concentration draining right out of her and into his two caressing hands. She looked at his hands, feeling his touch spreading heat all through her. Thinking, I must not see you again. Past transgressions and present complications. It's all impossible.

He lifted one hand to pick up his glass. She watched his mouth open on the rim of his glass, watched him swallow, and could almost feel his mouth on her. The

201

madness of it. At her age. He finished the last of his drink, set the glass down, asking, "Would you like another, Pat?"

"Thank you, no."

"Do you mind if I do?"

"I don't mind." If he'd cease questioning her, she'd gladly stay the night watching his eyes and mouth, his hands.

"Good, good." And at last released her hand in order to beckon to the waiter.

"I'd like to stay. Are you up to it?"

"Yes, please."

He laughed. "I like the way you said that. I like sleeping with you."

She smiled down into her teacup. "And I, you."

"I'll leave quietly in the morning so I don't wake you. You're not going to go to the office tomorrow, are you?"

"Not unless I feel a bit better."

The rawness that had been in her throat seemed to have moved down into her chest, creating a heaviness in her lungs, a drag against the deep breaths she tried to take but couldn't quite manage. But she *felt* so much better. Now that he was back with her.

Jenny turned off the television set. Gabe was going to spend the night down there again. And Pat was still out. Probably having a blast with that neat old dude. And here she was with a big belly for company. Trying not to feel sorry for herself. But not making it. Missing her art classes. Wishing things weren't so damned fouled up. Thinking, I ought to work at my drawing, not just let it go altogether because I'm not going to the classes. What good's it going to do me sitting around here being jeal-

ous because somebody's downstairs with Gillian and another somebody's out feeding Pat cocktails? That's nice
for them. But what about me?

Poor you. If Pat hadn't said, Come stay with me,
you'd probably be in some stinking room way
downtown, scared out of your brain worrying about
what's coming next. Not much gratitude showing. You
want to do something, go finish cleaning up the kitchen;
put on Pat's electric blanket so her bed'll be warm when
she comes home. Go make your lunch for tomorrow.
And stop being so jealous. Nobody's going to exactly flip
out over you the way you happen to look at the
moment, kid. So go get stuff done and cool it with the
sorry-for-me number.

Just after nine she started coughing. A spasm that
lasted so long tears were streaming down her face by
the time it ended.

"D'you have any Vicks or anything?" he asked her,
concerned.

"What is it?"

"I'm going to run downtown to the twenty-four-hour
drugstore. Pick up a couple of things. It shouldn't take
me longer than half an hour. You stay tucked up. Okay
if I borrow your keys?"

"Yes, of course. But you really needn't go out."

"Half an hour," he said. "And don't set one foot out of
that bed."

"No, sir." She smiled.

"Riiight!"

"Would you care for something to eat?" he asked her,
once more in possession of her hand.

"I think not. It's getting late."

"I'll see you home."

You could stop all this now, she told herself. Put a stop to it before it goes too far.

But she couldn't. He was too nice to look at, said compellingly outrageous things, talking of love and ten-room houses, making room for Jenny and the baby in his considerations. And allowing herself to slide forward, into an involvement that would not only be all too simple a matter, it would also solve the problem of Jenny's future. But. It was impossible. No one could possibly imagine just how impossible. And never mind that the pressure of his hand made her too readily forgetful—of her age, her presence of mind, of everything, it seemed. He was romantic, insistent. A figure from some fantasy. Someone who'd require explanations. And she couldn't.

In the back of the taxi he gently urged her closer until she was sitting inside his arm and his hand was on her face. His deep voice whispering, "Wear something long and low in the front Friday evening. I'll spend the whole evening enjoying the look of you. We'll have a wonderful dinner. We'll dance and drink champagne. I'll give you the best evening of your life. Beautiful, Pat. You're a beautiful, beautiful woman." His breath hitting her softly, his words like incense filling her nostrils, his mouth closing in on her. Tearing down the wall between what used to be and what was now. So that her breathing turned wildly irregular and her body began generating waves of heat.

"I knew how you'd kiss," he whispered, his arm tight around her, his one hand curved over the back of her neck. "I knew." He smiled in the darkness. And kissed her again, drawing her closer still.

So that when he walked her to the front door, she

knew her face was suffused with color and her eyes not quite in focus. And was so grateful there was no one around at that moment to see.

He said, "Friday. At seven-thirty." Kissed her a last time and went away down the steps and into the taxi. Leaving her in the worst quandary of her life. And so weak in the legs she could scarcely make it up the stairs.

He knelt on the bed and rubbed the Vicks into her chest, then readjusted the nightgown, recapped the jar, and climbed in beside her.

"That ought to help," he said, rubbing the residue into his hands.

She settled herself against him, breathing in the heady aroma, willing herself not to cough.

"Thank you for understanding about yesterday," he said. "You'll never know how scared I was you'd slam down the phone in my ear."

"I wouldn't do that."

"No, you wouldn't. Did you set the alarm?"

"Yes."

"You stay home in bed tomorrow."

"I will."

"I want you better for New Year's Eve. I've got to see your midnight performance."

"Perhaps I won't, this year."

"Maybe *I* will." He chuckled, switching off the light.

12.

"Gabe, I hate the idea of Jenny's staying home alone. It seems wrong somehow, leaving her on her own. I'd be terribly depressed if it was me."

"Okay. Why don't you go ask if she'd like to come out with us?"

"Really? You wouldn't mind?"

"Hell, I don't mind. I could probably even get her a date."

"You're not serious."

"Halfway."

"I think that would embarrass her," she said.

"Go up and ask her."

"Yes, all right."

After two days in bed it was an effort walking. But the cough was going, her chest clearing. She felt tired out simply climbing one flight of stairs and had to stop to catch her breath before going to knock at the door.

Jenny said, "Hi. Are you feeling better? Come on in. Pat's still downtown shopping for a dress."

"I'm a good deal better." She smiled. "Jenny, would you like to come out with us Friday? We'd like you to."

"You mean with you and Gabe?"

"Yes."

"You wouldn't want to do that. A third person tagging along. It'd wreck your whole thing."

"It wouldn't at all. And both of us want you to come."

"Boy! I'd love it. I'd really love it. You honestly wouldn't mind?"

"I promise you. We'd love having you."

Jenny's face fell suddenly. "I can't," she said. "I haven't got one single thing that'll go over this." Standing thrusting out her belly.

"You haven't anything at all?"

"Not unless you want me along in jeans and an old shirt of Sandy's I ripped off. It was really a nice idea but there's no way I can go."

"No, let me think a moment." Mentally going through her wardrobe, trying to locate something that might be hastily altered. "I'm quite sure I've at least one caftan that would do for you if we picked up the hem. I'm sure of it."

"It seems like an awful lot of trouble. . . ."

"No, no." Gillian cut short her argument. "I've a blue dress I think might do for you. I'll go down right now and have a look for it."

"I don't believe any of this. Are you sure?"

"I am absolutely positive. I'll find the dress and you and Pat can come down after dinner and have a trying-on session."

"Boy! Okay. If you're sure."

"I'm *sure*."

Pat came in carrying a large dress box, saying, "What

sort of day did you have, dear? The shops were so crowded. I'm done in."

"But you got a dress. Your friend Walter phoned, by the way. He said he'll call back later."

"I did get a dress," she said. "I'm not certain it's right, though."

"Dinner's ready. And guess what? Gillian and Gabe are taking me with them Friday. Isn't that great? We're going down after dinner to try on a dress she has for me."

"That's fine, dear. I'll just have a wash and we'll eat." She carried the dress box into the bedroom. Wondering what he was calling about. So persistent, so determined to have things go the way he wanted them to. Putting her in such a muddled state with all of it. She opened the box and laid the dress out on the bed. Looking at it with mixed feelings. It would have to do. She dreaded the idea of fighting her way through the crowds in the shops to return this one, try to find another. Why was all this happening? Bound to come to no good. But wasn't it good of the two to invite Jenny out? So very generous of them.

Gillian looked over at Pat. Sitting in the armchair with her legs crossed, taking up the hem of the dress for Jenny. Making her think of Mother, how she'd painstakingly changed all the buttons on Megan's dress. Looking at Jenny and Gabe on the rug in front of the fire, playing dominoes, laughing.

We're all so at ease together, she thought. None of this what she'd expected when she'd started work all those months ago on the house. She pushed off her shoes and tucked her legs under her, returning her attention to the book about Le Corbusier Pat had given her.

In the silence that had fallen Pat could hear the telephone ringing upstairs and forced herself to keep sewing, ignoring it. She'd see him Friday and not again after that. It was too late now to alter the arrangements. But after Friday she'd ask him not to call anymore. Sitting sewing with Peter Flannigan's words ringing in her ears. "You're a fool, Pat. A fool. A fool. *A fool.*" Oh, Lord, I am. Yes. But what's done is done and none of it can be changed. Not now. It's all gone too far. The ringing finally stopping. So that the silence was even more pronounced. Until Jenny and Gabe exclaimed loudly over the end of the game and began turning the tiles to start another. Startling her so that she pricked her finger with the needle and blood blossomed on her fingertip.

"I've stuck myself," she said, setting down the dress. "I'll go up and fetch a plaster for it."

"I'll give you one," Gillian said.

"Not at all. I want my smokes, in any case. I forgot them." She got up and went out.

Gillian looked over to see Gabe looking back at her. His eyes saying, She's very jittery. Her eyes responding, Yes, I know. I wonder what it is. A slight shrug of his shoulders telling her, It's probably nothing. A nod of her head, You're probably right.

Pat lit a cigarette and studied the now-silent telephone, wishing she had the sanity, the courage to tell the truth. All of it. To all of them. Thinking she'd have to have a talk with Matthew. On a day when she'd be certain Walter was not there at the office. Surely there was a certain privileged confidentiality that existed between a lawyer and his client? As there was between a priest and someone in the confessional. A doctor and patient. Were Matthew to engage offhandedly in a discussion of her affairs with his father . . . It couldn't be allowed to happen. She'd speak to Matthew first thing in the morning. Strictly to enlist his assistance. Yes, she'd do that. And felt somewhat better. So that she was able to go smiling back to the children, resume her sewing. With her finger throbbing under the Band-Aid. She'd put it on far too tight in her haste.

At work Friday morning Jenny took a break to go down to the main floor and look around at accessories, wanting something to fancy up the blue caftan. Going down the length of one counter, then up the other, knowing vaguely what she was after, not finding it. So engrossed she collided with one of the store detectives, all dressed up to look like a shopper. Bobby Barrington, who laughed and said, "How's it going? Got six hundred dollars' worth of boosted goodies tucked up under there?"

She had to laugh, jamming her hands into the pockets of her cardigan.

"You look about as much like a store cop as I do. Boy! Are you subtle."

"What's the matter? You don't like the porkpie and the Harris tweed?"

"No, you're gorgeous, Bobby. Flash me your badge." She smiled. "It's a turn-on."

"You mean you can *get* turned on?"

"I'm only pregnant, you know. Not dead."

He laughed, then looked around guiltily.

"They'll have my ass, I start getting too cute with the staff," he said in an undertone.

"Oh, not yours." She laughed. "You're too good."

"So, really," he said. "How's it going?"

"All right. I've still got a ways to go."

"It sure will be dead around here with you gone."

"I'll be back, you know," she said. "Pregnancy isn't terminal."

"I'm glad to hear it. Sandy must be high as hell with all this."

"Oh, sure." She lost her smile. "He split ages ago. I thought everybody knew that."

"He split? That's heavy. I mean, did he know? You know."

"Forget it. It's no big deal."

"Oh, shit!" Bobby muttered. "I've got to cool it. Here comes the floor supervisor. You wanna meet me for lunch later?"

She looked at his boyish face under the silly affectation of the hat and smiled again. "Sure. What time?"

"Make it twelve-thirty. I'll get up there early, grab a table."

"Okay, Bobby. Later."

He strolled off down the aisle, trying hard to look like a nonchalant shopper and, smiling to herself, she returned to looking for the necklace she wanted to go with the blue caftan.

"So, tell me," Bobby said, gesturing with his soupspoon, "what happened?"

"Nothing. He was getting into all kinds of weird numbers and then he split. I moved downstairs with Pat."

"Who's Pat?"

"Pat's this really neat Irish lady. I've been living with her. It's nice, you know? Like home. She fusses over me and makes me drink my milk like a good girl, all that."

"But what're you going to do about the baby?" he asked, putting down his spoon to crumble a pack of crackers into his soup.

"I don't know. I'll have to worry about it later. If I get

211

Charlotte Vale Allen

all psyched up about it now, I'll probably freak out. I just have to wait and see."

"That's rough, man," he said, submerging the bits of floating cracker with the back of his spoon. "That's really rough. When's the baby due?"

"Middle of April." She picked up half of her chicken-salad sandwich.

"Middle of April," he repeated. "Another three and a half months."

"Right."

"You gonna keep it?" he asked.

"I don't know."

"Hope you do," he said, salting and peppering the soup. Doing everything to it, she noticed, but eating it.

"How come?"

"'Cause I like babies," he said, then smiled at her.

"And what's that supposed to mean?"

"I don't know. I'd get off on maybe dropping over, taking you and the kid out. I like babies." He shrugged, took a spoonful of soup, made a face, and put down his spoon. "Shit! I really crapped that up, I was so busy talking."

"You're out of your tree, Bobby."

"Don't you like me?"

"Well, sure I do. I mean, I've been crashing into you every time I turn around for the last year and a half. I don't just crash into anybody, you know."

He laughed. Then started playing with the cellophane from the crackers. "You wouldn't want to go out some night or something?" he said, looking at the red strip, pulling it.

"Are you feeling sorry for me, Bobby?"

His head shot up. He looked offended. "Why should I feel sorry for you? I mean, why should I?"

212

"I don't know. It'd just turn me off if that's where your head was at."

"I've been making a fortune in overtime, double time over the holidays," he said. "Lucked into a dynamite place out near Indian Hill, right near the park."

"That's nice," she said, losing him.

"We could get together one night after work, go to my place, and maybe you'd give me some ideas on how to fix it up. I figured you'd know about that."

"Sure I would," she said. "That'd be neat."

"Hey, great. Okay. Let's do it. Next week."

"Okay. Want half my sandwich? You've got to eat something."

"You sure?"

"Sure. Go on."

"Thanks."

She was ready way before Pat and went to sit in the living room, killing time until Gillian and Gabe were ready to go. Thinking about Bobby Barrington. Really cute with the red hair and all the freckles. Laughing softly to herself, thinking about the way he'd totally wrecked his soup, he'd been so nervous trying to talk to her. But it was nice, the way he was. Not all pushy and hardmouthed like Sandy. It'd really be fun to help him fix up his place. That was a really nice area out by Indian Hill. She wondered what kind of place he had. Laughing again, thinking about that time he'd collared a booster and got so nervous he'd flipped out his badge and thrown it halfway across the store. She'd been sitting in the window working on a mannequin, watching the whole thing. Poor Bobby'd nearly wrecked himself trying to keep hold of the booster and pick up his badge at the same time.

213

Pat came into the living room and Jenny exclaimed, "Wow! Pat, you look *incredible*."

In this long green dress with a low-cut round neckline, long sleeves. Makeup, the whole number.

"You don't think it's too young?" she said, looking doubtful.

"Are you kidding? That's gorgeous. The only thing is you need a necklace or something. Wow! Walter's going to flip out."

Pat smiled, looking embarrassed. "What sort of necklace, do you think?" she asked.

"Come on, I'll help you find one." She returned with Pat to the bedroom and, at Pat's insistence, went through her jewelry box, picking out a thin gold chain. "This," Jenny said. "This is perfect. Want me to put it on for you?"

"Thank you, dear."

Jenny fastened the clasp, stepping back to get the overall picture.

"That's perfect," she stated. "I can't get over it. You just look incredible."

"And you look lovely," Pat said, putting out her hand to touch Jenny's hair, then suddenly folding her into her arms. "You'll have a wonderful evening," Pat said huskily.

"So will you," Jenny said as Pat released her. "What's the matter? Don't you want to go? He's a really nice man. And he really likes you. What's the matter?"

"Oh, nothing. Nothing at all."

"There's the door. It's probably Gabe. Don't forget your perfume," Jenny reminded her, hurrying out. "Drive Walter crazy."

Perfume. She didn't have any desire to drive Walter crazy. He's crazy enough as it is, she thought. But still she dabbed perfume at the base of her throat as Jenny came back, saying, "He's here. Come on. I can't wait to see his face."

Quaking inside. Proceeding ahead of Jenny out of the room. To quake even harder at the sight of Walter Meyers, painfully elegant in a black tuxedo, silk shirt, bow tie. His eyes, his smile brilliant as he held out his hand to her, softly saying, "So beautiful, Pat. Isn't she beautiful, Jenny?"

Tickled to death, Jenny agreeing, saying, "Incredible," standing at the ready with Pat's fur coat. Enjoying the feel of it. So soft.

"Go on, the two of you!" Pat looking even prettier with the color in her face.

"I've hired a car," Walter said, helping her on with the coat. "And a driver. Have a good evening, Jenny." He smiled over at her, purposefully directing Pat away, out the door.

"We can all sit in the front," Gabe said. "There's plenty of room."

"I can sit in the back," Jenny argued. "We don't have to crowd together."

"Come sit up front," Gillian said. "You'll help keep me warm. It's dreadfully cold tonight."

"Oh, okay."

"Where are we going?" Gillian asked for the first time.

"The top." Gabe laughed. "The Imperial."

"You're *kidding*," Jenny said. "The Imperial? You'll go broke."

"Only the best." He smiled. "Everybody all set?"

"You two," he said at the checkroom, pocketing the claim tickets, "are beautiful. Let's go knock 'em all out!"

215

He held an arm out to each of them and they went in.

Settled at the table, Jenny looked around happily. "Boy! This is too much. Hey! Guess what."

"What?" Gabe responded.

"Look. Over there. There's Pat and Walter."

They all three looked. To see Walter holding Pat's hand on top of the table, his head close to hers, talking. Directly opposite them.

"Isn't he a fine-looking man?" Gillian said. Seeing Mother and Hugh in their attitudes, the way they were looking at each other.

"Do you think we should invite them to join us?" Gabe asked.

"I don't know," Gillian said. "Do you think we should?"

Jenny said, "Let's. I'm dying to know what he's really like."

"Perhaps we shouldn't," Gillian said, having second thoughts. "We might be intruding."

"You're right," Gabe decided. "We won't do it."

"Yes," Gillian said, but still unable to stop looking over at them, so caught by the mood of the way they looked.

"Champagne," Gabe announced. "And then I get to dance with both of you."

"Not at the same time." Jenny laughed.

"Maybe." He grinned. "It depends on any number of things."

"Did you buy the dress for me?" he asked, smiling, his hand engulfing hers.

"I bought the dress for myself," she said, unable not to smile. This was all so opulent, lavish.

"You're not telling the truth, Pat. But I won't argue

the point. You look just as I knew you would. Come dance with me. I want to hold you."

"Not just yet." She reached into her bag with her free hand for a cigarette. Stalling.

He lit her cigarette, returned the lighter to his pocket, asking, "Have you ever been to the islands?"

"Which islands?"

"The Caribbean."

"No."

"I'll take you. To Jamaica or Barbados, Eleuthera. Anywhere you'd like to go. Tabago, Tortola, St. Vincent."

"Stop, Walter. You must stop offering me these . . . things."

"I have no intention of stopping. None." He smiled, looking at her breasts, then at her mouth, finally at her eyes. "Tobago is wonderful. You'll like it." Watching her draw deeply on the cigarette. "Magnificent beaches, food."

"Walter, I . . ." Tell him once and for all. Then he'll stop all this, end it.

He took the cigarette from between her fingers, held it to his mouth. Then put it out. "Come dance with me," he said, applying pressure to her hand. "It's a wonderful orchestra." Drawing her up, leading her between the tables, onto the dance floor. Taking her so close to his chest she could scarcely breathe, whispering into her ear, "I wanted to feel your breasts against me." Holding her firmly so that she couldn't move away, guiding her effortlessly, dizzyingly around the dance floor. His hand flat at the base of her spine, turning, turning. His voice filling her head. Whispering, "I love you. I will give you everything, take care of you. I want you in my bed, want you next to me. Wonderful dancer, wonderful. Nobody's too old, Pat. Never."

His body directing her here, there, moving her. Robbing her of her ability to speak. So that she could only go with him, listening, blinded by the images he picked up and cast before her. Knowing unless she exercised her will, he'd succeed in doing everything he proposed. Convincing her of anything, all things.

"You feel wonderful in my arms." His mouth smiling against her ear. "Wonderful. I'll be very gentle with you, Pat. I'll hold you and touch you so gently. How you dance! Your carriage! So proud and happy to be here with you. Anything, Pat. Anything. I want you to have everything you want."

"You can't say these things," she said. "It's . . ." What? What do I think it is? Unseemly. No. Too tempting. Yes.

Her body willingly following his. Around and around and around. Until finally the music ended and his hand, around hers, directed her back once more to the table. Where the waiter poured champagne into their glasses and Walter urged her to drink.

"Drink, Pat darling. It's fine champagne. Fine." His eyes shining, his mouth. And the kisses he'd given her. Wanting to make love to her. To her. She lifted her glass and drank.

"Oh, don't they look neat." Jenny sighed, smiling. "They're so . . . distinguished, the two of them. Look at everybody watching them, nodding away, smiling. They're just gorgeous."

"I think you're in love with them." Gabe teased her.

"I think I am," she agreed. "I'd love to be like that when I'm old. So dignified and beautiful."

"You're beautiful now," Gillian said softly.

"Whose turn is it?" Gabe asked.

"Jenny's," Gillian said. "Go on, the two of you."

The champagne going straight to her head. Staying there. Not even the dinner affecting what the champagne had done to her head. And all the while, Walter was telling about his life, his career, the years alone, interspersing compliments, praise. Finally finishing eating to resume holding her hand, pulling his chair over a little closer to hers so that his knee was against hers under the table. And kept refilling her glass, taking her back out to dance again. And again. Until everything was sparkling, glittery, and her body automatically went close to his and she was going with him in a dreamlike state, entranced. There on the dance floor, when everyone began blowing horns and the band played "Auld Lang Syne," he held her and kissed her. Slowly, deeply. Right the way through till the music ended. Taking all of her away. Even the fading voice that continued to warn her, This is wrong, wrong. Stilling the voice, her uncertainty, her soul.

Jenny and Gabe and Gillian kissed one another. And Gillian forgot to cry. All three of them turned to watch Pat and Walter on the dance floor, their embrace.

Gabe and Jenny smiling happily. Gillian quietly dissolving into the tears that were there, after all. So that Gabe reached for her hand and held it, seeing her eyes go distant, remote.

Walter hurrying her out to the car. The car interior warm, the driver separated from them by a glass partition. Going where? It didn't matter. More kisses colliding with the champagne bubbles still floating at

219

the top of her head. His hands inside her coat, holding her. No idea of where or what or how. Past caring.

Distantly hearing Walter giving instructions to the driver and then they were going down a corridor, into a vast bedroom. All quiet shades of gray, thick carpeting. Walter taking her down, down, down. Their clothes dematerializing. His body, hands, mouth, descending on her. Deep voice whispering, whispering. A moment of terrified sobriety, realizing what he was doing, what was happening. Then starting to lose herself again. One last rational thought. My God, he's done it. I've done it. How can this be? Lifting away, out of herself. Going.

Waking slowly to the delicate touch of his hands, his mouth. And his voice whispering, "I love you, love you."

Going rigid, stopping his hands, his mouth. Saying, "I must go home. Please. Take me home, Walter."

Returning themselves to their finery. Walter beaming at her, looking and talking love at her. Taking her back down the long hallway and into the limousine. Aware of her distress. Holding her hand, telling her, "I'd like to marry you, Pat. Would you marry me?" Sending starbursts of panic detonating in her chest. Her mind recoiling. You damned fool! What have you done?

Rushing away from him, his voice calling after her. "Tomorrow, I'll call you tomorrow. Pat? Pat?"

13.

Gabe called her every afternoon at the office. Unless she was at the site. And then he'd find some way to be there, too. Just to talk for a few minutes, to touch hands covertly. Together each evening. It was tacitly agreed.

He began leaving things. Not artfully, with premeditation. But accidentally at first. And then intentionally, for the sake of convenience. His apartment began taking on the look of an unused motel unit. He regarded the place with growing displeasure, seeing it as an inconvenience, an obstacle. Unable to enjoy any measure of the time he had to spend there, finding the apartment a cheap imitation of a real home. Leaving more and more of his things in Gillian's apartment. Shaving gear, a clean shirt or two, then four, five; extra socks, underwear, the cleaning he'd picked up after school. Some of his books, papers, schoolwork.

She looked at the growing accumulation of his belongings, unsure of her reactions. But she went ahead and cleared out a drawer, put his shirts and socks, other things into it, then stood for several minutes experiencing an infusion of happiness simply from the sight of his possessions there with her own. He wanted to be with her, near to her.

As she'd once upon a time attended classes, taking notes, studying, working in order to attain her degree, arrive at some measure of expertise, she now studied him, noting this and that. The sound of his voice on the telephone rewarding, making something inside her settle contentedly, reassured. And when the nightmares came, he was almost always there to hold her, talk to her, succeeding in luring her back into sleep. And each time she saw him she thought, I'd forgotten how good you look. And was gladdened.

She sat on the side of the tub one morning and watched him shave, fascinated. Something she'd never seen a man do. Witnessing the entire process as he, with a towel tied around his waist, a cup of coffee near to hand, lathered over his face, then began carefully removing both the lather and his incoming growth of beard. She smoked a cigarette, slowly drank her own coffee, watching from start to finish. Then, satisfied, got up, returned to the bedroom, and got dressed. Deciding it was the ordinary things, the everyday things they did together that seemed to have the most meaning.

He was very orderly, always careful to fold his clothes after removing them, always rinsing the sink after he'd shaved, returning his dishes to the sink, his books to the bedside table. Very often she'd find herself watching his hands, profoundly exhilarated by the sight of them. Everything about him entranced her. His skin. The fine line of hair that dissected his belly, running down to his groin. He was very smooth, his skin pleasing to the touch.

And she was surprised when he displayed an equal, if not surpassing, interest in everything about her. Trying not to feel self-conscious when he'd suddenly put the book he'd been reading to one side and take her out of her nightgown, leaning on his elbow examining the size and shape of her breasts and nipples, the surface of her belly, the length of her thighs. Saying he found all of her perfect. Even claiming to like her legs. It didn't make her any fonder of them. She simply believed he wasn't bothered.

When she had her period, he wasn't bothered by that either. And they made love.

"I'm terribly excitable during my periods," she confessed. "But I always thought a man might be put off."

"Nothing about you puts me off. We'll take a shower together after."

He no longer seemed so angry. And in the absence of his anger she felt free to give voice to random thoughts, certain censored memories. Liking the interpretations he lent to her words.

He found some of her observations very amusing. Other things she chanced to say turned his features sober, thoughtful. He grew more increasingly curious about her, about the parts of the story she wouldn't tell.

There were long silences in which they'd move about each other, occupied with their various jobs to be done. And she came to see that silences didn't necessarily require filling. It wasn't mandatory she grope about looking for words to toss into the gaps. They were peaceful times, simply quiet.

They saw a lot of Pat and Jenny. Initially both, but with time, more of Jenny. And several times Bobby Barrington came along, the four of them going out to the movies, with pizza after. Or just staying indoors by the fire, talking, talking. And after an especially pleasant evening with Jenny and Bobby, Gabe ventured to say, "I think she's deciding to keep the baby. Can you feel how her mind's changing?"

"It's Bobby. He's convincing her."

On those occasions when Pat did join them, and the conversation came around to babies, she invariably sailed off into reminiscenses about her five, their infancies, differences of personality. Talking so much of the children that they became very real in the minds of her audience. So that Gillian was prompted to say, "I can almost see them, see Pat chasing about after them."

"She reminds me a bit of my Aunt Dora," Gabe said. "Not in looks or anything. But other things. I was crazy about going to visit my aunt when I was a kid. We'd sit around and she'd give me a midget-sized glass of sherry and ask me what did I think of this and that. Telling me jokes and stories that'd have me rolling around on the floor. A wonderful, crazy lady. I used to tell her that when I grew up, I'd marry her."

"That's lovely."

"You're so sentimental. Which is one of the reasons why . . . " *Maybe I'll marry you when I grow up.*

"Why what?"

"Why I can't stay the hell away from you. Wake up every morning high as a kite knowing I'm going to see you. Go to bed when I'm home wishing I was here and not there."

"Do you really?"

"Really." He smiled, holding his fist under her chin. "Really! It feels so goddamned *right* being with you."

"Do you like living with me?"

224

"I like living with you," he said, pierced by the way certain things she said sounded so innocent.

"Perhaps you'd like to stay. All the time?"

"There's nothing I'd like better."

"I've never lived with a man. But it wouldn't be all that different . . . I mean . . . the way it is now. And I'm able to sleep after. . . ."

"I know."

"I never was able to before."

"Before doesn't count anymore."

"It wouldn't put you in a difficult position, would it? With the school?"

"What I do away from school is *my life*, Gillian. It's nobody's business but mine. And yours."

"Have you a lease on your apartment?"

"I've been running month to month for the last couple of years. That's no problem."

She was all at once very eager to have him there. "Oh, *do* come, then. I'd like it so much."

"What about your tenants?"

"Oh, bother the tenants." She laughed. "I can't believe Pat and Jenny would be in the least upset at your being here. And the Bradleys won't be back for ages. By which time it'll be a fait accompli."

"You're sure?"

"Yes, yes. I'm quite, quite sure."

"Okay. This weekend?"

"Fine."

She lay with her head on his shoulder. Thinking, I feel I love you. But love is something you and I don't speak of. Perhaps we can't. Other things, too. So many other things. But in the night, with you close by me, I feel as if I'm standing on a platform at the very top of the tent. Up there, smiling and confident, knowing I can swing through the air, turn and swoop and fly. And the audience finds me spectacular.

She and Bobby were fixing up his place. It really was a dynamite apartment. "You're really lucky to find a place like this," she told him. "In a neat old building like this one."

"You like it?"

"I love it. I wish I'd been the one to find it."

"You can come here anytime you like, you know, Jen. I'll even give you a key if you like."

"You can't be for real," she said, touched by an increasing number of things about him. "Why would you want to give me a key?"

"Because . . . just because. It's fun having you around. And it's starting to look good, all the work we've been doing. I wouldn't have thought of one-tenth the things you've done."

"It's looking pretty good, isn't it?" she agreed.

"You're so pretty," he said softly, lowering his eyes.

"Bobby, are you trying to make out with me?"

He turned bright red. "No," he said. "No!"

She smiled. Weeks they'd been seeing each other and he hadn't done anything bolder than hold her hand. "Don't you want to?" she said.

"Well, sure. I mean, no. I mean . . . I didn't think. Shit! I don't know what . . . "

"It's okay, you know. I mean, if you're not grossed out by this." She patted her belly. "And it's one hundred percent safe."

"Jenny, I . . . "

"How old are you, Bobby?"

"Twenty-one." He looked agonized.

"Have you ever?"

He just looked at her, the color spreading down into his collar, out to the rims of his ears.

"Do you want to?" she asked.

"I really do. I just didn't think you would. Or want to. I don't know what I'm saying."

"Come on," she said, holding out her hand. "If you can stand it, I can. I just have to borrow your john for a few minutes."

"Pat, I don't understand. You're not *allowing* me to understand."

"Why must you keep calling?" she asked, hating what she was doing.

"You know I'm not going to stop. If you'd just tell me why, I might feel a little better about all this. But it doesn't make any sense, Pat."

"Oh, Walter," she sighed tiredly, "leave me be. I've told you and told you how impossible all this is."

"Fine. But you keep on *not* telling me why. I know you care for me. I know you do. And you know how I feel. Where's the sense to all this, Pat? At least come out for dinner or a drink, even coffee, and talk to me. Just talk to me."

"We're talking now."

"This isn't talking. I don't know what precisely it *is*. But talking it isn't."

"Please, Walter. This is doing neither of us any good."

"Coffee. Just a cup of coffee. I have to see you. We have to talk."

"It's not possible."

"It was wonderful, Pat," he said sounding so sad it wrenched her insides. "The most wonderful thing that's happened to me in years. Come out for one cup of coffee. How can it hurt you?"

"No."

"Four weeks of this," he said. "My calling, your telling me it's all impossible. But not one reason why. And I *know*, I can hear it in your voice you want to be with me as much as I want to be with you. So why won't you tell me and give us *both* a break?"

"I'm going to put down the phone now, Walter."

"Okay, okay. I'll phone you tomorrow. Maybe tomorrow you'll have something different to tell me. Pat, I love you."

"Good-bye. I must go. Good-bye."

"All right," he sighed. "Go."

She was trembling as she put down the receiver. Quickly lit another cigarette and went to the kitchen to put on the kettle. Stopped with her hand on the faucet, staring. Devoutly wishing she'd never left Ireland, never come to this city, this house. That she'd never started any of it. Utterly intimidated by Walter's persistence. And the knowledge that he was slowly, steadily grinding her down.

"Don't be uptight," Jenny said softly. "The first couple of times are always pretty lousy. We'll both get better."

"I like your big belly." He smiled, stroking it, looking up in startled surprise as the baby kicked under his hand. "Holy hell! That kid's got some right hook."

"Want to try again?" She smiled, directing his hand up over her breast. "A different way?" Sitting up beside him.

"You're too much," he said. "I can't believe it."

"You're so sweet," she murmured, kissing him. "*I* can't believe how sweet you are. Mmmm, that's nice. Don't stop."

This is actually happening, Gillian told herself. To-morrow morning he's going to come here with all his belongings. To live with me here. Gabe. Thinking about his face when he was inside her. His face transformed. As if being contained within her body was miraculous. She'd watch him as he moved in her and wonder why having him inside her was nowhere near the pleasure for her it was for him. A fine feeling of closeness, warmth. But nothing like the panic of pleasure it so evidently was for him. But then she wondered if perhaps he didn't feel this same curiously distant excitement when he put his mouth to her. Because those times for her were exquisite. Making love seeming to be an exchange of gifts, of pleasures. From a distance, she was bemused. Within touching range, she couldn't think at all.

She drove herself into a state akin to distraction, thinking of this, of that. And slept badly that night. A sleep riddled with nightmares. Old ones, new ones. One that brought her awake laughing. So that she got up and went into the bathroom with her mouth curved into a smile, then returned to bed—it wasn't yet five—trying to remember what she'd dreamed that so amused her. Slept again and awakened just over an hour later with perspiration streaming down her temples, the back of her neck, both hands cramped and useless because she'd lain upon them.

Once the sensation had returned to her hands, she decided it was pointless to try for more sleep and got up to start the day. Putting the kettle on to boil. Making up the bed. Setting a pot of tea on the table to brew while she brushed her teeth, washed her face. Then to the kitchen once more to pour her tea. Pausing to listen for sounds overhead. Silence. She'd hoped Pat might be stirring. But nothing above.

He would come. There was no reason not to believe he wouldn't. But, unreasonably, she wanted him to come right at that moment. To put an end to her uneasiness. Wondering, How did I get to be almost thirty without ridding myself of that fearful child inside? When does she leave me? Isn't it time I put all that in back of me? It is time. It is.

He would come. She rinsed her fears down the drain with the tea leaves from the bottom of her cup. Rinsed it all away and went to dress in readiness for his arrival. Of course he'd come.

And when he arrived, watched him carry in the first box, quite unable to move, immobilized by gladness. He put the box down on the floor and hugged her, swinging her around. Then set her down, examining her eyes, saying, "You make me so goddamned happy. And I'm so rotten when it comes to getting important things said. This is important. It's the most important moment I've had in years. And I want to tell you but it's so goddamned *hard*. It shouldn't be. I should be able to just open my mouth and say all the things I want to say to you."

"It's equally difficult for me. We're a pair, aren't we? Both of us tongue-tied when it come to feelings."

"We're damned well going to get past this," he said firmly. "I mean it."

"Come on, I'll help you bring in the rest of your gear."

He caught hold of her hand as she started to move away. "I need you, Gillian. In all kinds of ways."

"Yes. Me, too."

"*He's moving in!* Come see. I knew it. Didn't I *tell* you? Come look."

Pat came to stand beside her at the kitchen window,

looking down, seeing Gabe and Gillian carrying boxes in from his car.

"It seems you were right," she said.

Jenny looked at her, seeing a strange mix of sadness and pleasure on her face. "Aren't you happy for them?" Jenny asked quietly.

"Indeed. I am deeply happy for them. And for you, too. Did you have a pleasant time last evening?"

"It was really nice. Bobby's sweet."

"I love you, Jenny. Very much." Her eyes held Jenny's for a long moment, then she looked away. "I'll put on the kettle. Those two will be glad of a bite to eat, I expect. I'll fix a tray, welcome him properly."

"Pat?"

"Yes, dear?" She turned, looking back.

"I love you, too, you know."

Pat nodded.

"What happened with Walter? How come you won't see him?"

"It's too complicated to discuss just now. It's all for the best. You run along now and get yourself dressed. Then we'll take them down some lunch."

It isn't for the best at all, Jenny thought, heading through to the bedroom. Something's gone really, really wrong. And I wish I knew what it was.

It seemed as if every day Pat was getting a little older, a little quieter. It scared her, what was happening. It felt all wrong.

"Did you know Gabe and Gillian are living together?" Jane was leaning on the edge of Carl's board.

"I knew." He didn't look up.

"You knew and you didn't *tell* me?"

He shrugged.

"Sometimes," she said, "you're really something else. How could you know and not tell me?"

"It was easy." He looked up at her and smiled.

"Who told you?"

He shrugged again.

"Okay," she said. "I know when to give up. D'you suppose everybody knew when we were living together?"

"Probably."

"God! You know I never even *thought* about it."

"Probably nobody else did either."

"Up yours, buddy."

He looked up. They both laughed.

"I got this very interesting change-of-address card in the mail," Pierce said. "Very interesting. Amy and I agreed it was an intensely interesting piece of mail."

Gillian's face was burning. "Intensely?" she said.

Pierce laughed. "How about 'moderately'?"

"That's better, I should think."

"Are you happy, Miss U? You look happy."

"I am, yes. Are we a topic of conversation?"

"Not with the Downtown Irregulars. That's too much like casting the first stone. You know?"

"That's good. I shouldn't like to think people were talking."

"That'd bother you?"

"I don't know," she said, thinking about it. "I expect not."

"But you still wouldn't like to be the main topic over lunch."

"No particularly."

"Who answers the phone?" he asked.

"The telephone? Whoever's closest. That's a peculiar question."

"No. It so happens that's a very telling question. Ever lived with anybody before?"

"I've lived with people."

"Okay." He smiled. "Ever live with a man?"

"No. Does that make some sort of difference?"

"Nope. I like your judgment. Matter of fact"—his smile widened—"I like *you*. You two want to make it over to dinner next Saturday night?"

"I'd love to. Let me check with Gabe. Though I'm sure it'll be fine with him."

"Let me know."

"I will. Shall I ring Amy this evening?"

"Absolutely."

"You're not laughing at me, are you, Pierce?"

"Miss U," he said carefully, "I find you highly interesting to talk to. A definite ten to look at. But funny? I'd have to be well into senility to find you funny. Still think you're a clown? Is that it?"

"Sometimes now," she said, "I feel as if, if I were small again, I could ride that horse at the circus and come away laughing."

"I take it you didn't."

"I cried and wet myself."

"I'm happy you're happy, Miss U."

"Thank you," she said quietly.

"Are you happy, Gabe?" she asked, an anxious look to her eyes.

"I'm very happy," he answered, watching the anxiety fade away. "Are you happy?"

"Oh, yes. Very. It's odd, you know. But I don't think I've ever really been happy before." Perhaps, she thought, that's why I still feel so frightened at times.

"What do I have to do to get to see you, Pat? Tell me and I'll do it. This is crazy, all this business. Couldn't you just tell me what's so terribly wrong?"

"I can't take very much more," she said. "Won't you please give it up? What is it you want me to say to you?"

"Tell me you don't care for me. Tell me that."

"I . . . I can't."

"Come out. Let me buy you dinner. I won't say a word. I'll just sit and look at you. Not one word. Not one."

"All right," she sighed. "All right."

She'd entirely forgotten writing to her father. And so was very surprised to find a letter bearing an Antiguan stamp in the day's mail. She carried it through to the bedroom, finding it strange to see her father's handwriting after so long. She stared at the writing, not reading, holding the letter in one hand, the enclosed clipping in the other. Then she read the clipping and abruptly sat down on the foot of the bed, steeling herself to read her father's letter.

Coolly removed, as always. Glad to have finally heard from you. Feared all contact had been severed. More along that line. News of his family, goings-on on the island. Hoped she'd come to visit. So forth and so forth. Always welcome here. Deeply grieved at the news of Megan, your mother. Shocked, devastated. His words making her heart start beating wildly, reviving it all, making it too new. She hurried on to the last paragraph: About Brooke.

He'd been attacked by his manservant. With a machete. And had died en route to Holburton Hospital. A year earlier.

You never intended coming to fetch me. *You lied.* Knowing I was there, waiting. With your child. You left me to see it through all alone. Years and years of believing, gradually becoming convinced you'd used me, taken advantage. True. All true. Mother saying, "The man's a bastard, darling. He never had the least intention of coming for you. Put him out of your mind and get on with your life. Forget him."

All the years of anguish, naive optimism. And you never had even the decency or the kindness to respond to my letters. Those dozens of letters. Did you laugh at them? Or throw them away unopened?

Crying until she felt drained, weary. Slowly dropping down, still in her boots and overcoat, turning, eyes closing. Feeling drugged, emptied.

He let himself in, a little surprised to find the apartment dark. Turned on the lights, hung away his coat and hat, removed his boots, and went through to the bedroom. To find her sleeping. He leaned over, stroking her cheek until her eyes flickered open.

"Bad news?" He indicated the letter.

She lifted her hand to look, then remembered, her hand tightening around the handwritten pages.

"What is it, love?"

She pressed the letter into his hand, then rolled over onto her stomach, resting her head on her forearm, eyes closed.

"Someone you knew?" he asked at last, setting the letter down on the drawing board.

"Megan's father."

"D'you want to tell me about it?"

"I don't know that I can."

"Okay, if you'd prefer not to."

235

"There's not a very great deal to tell, actually. I was sixteen. Morbidly shy. He spent a lot of time with me. Claiming he loved me, at the last. I believed him. Idiotic. He induced me to do . . . say . . . a number of things. I did them, said them, thinking it was love. Wanting it to be love, really.

"All these years I refused to believe he'd lied to me, despite all the evidence. Mother told me over and over to forget him. She thought he was a bastard. And she was right, of course. I was a bloody fool. Letting him do the things he did simply because he said he loved me."

"I'm sorry," he said.

"And me," she said. "It all—every bit of it—came to nothing. I suppose I'd best get up, see to dinner." She turned around and sat up.

"Thirteen years?"

"That's right."

"Jesus, Gillian!"

"Stupid, isn't it? Blind, stupid faith. I created all sorts of fabulous alibis, reasons why. But the truth is he *was* a bloody bastard. He knew I'd had his child. He knew. And didn't reply to one of my letters, not one. Not even so much as a Christmas card."

"That's rotten."

"I love you, Gabe. I do love you. I'll never ask anything of you if you'll just be truthful with me."

"I love you."

"Do you?" She looked at him, feeling the words slicing through all the anger.

"I love you."

He put his arms around her, wondering why it had taken him so long. When it hadn't been so very hard to say it after all. Wondering about the rest of the letter, about her mother, Megan. Shocked? Devastated? Why?

"Are you ill, Pat? Is that it?"

"I'm not ill. I'm simply not very hungry."

He once again had possession of her hand. His eyes beseeching her.

"Whatever it is, it couldn't change my feelings for you. Nothing could. I *love* you, Pat. Have you so much of what you want you can just walk away from someone who loves you?"

"Oh, yes," she said bitterly. Thinking, I've done it before. But I was infinitely stronger then. And forty-odd years younger.

"You shock me," he said, his hand easing slightly around hers. "You want me to believe that?"

"It's the truth. Believe what you like."

"Pat, I'm sixty-seven years old. Life gets very lonely. There are women and women. I've known some. But you. You're a once-in-a-lifetime woman. I have a house, money. I still try a case every now and then. I keep active, keep busy. Everything I want I've got. Except for you. And for some reason known only to yourself and God, you're doing everything in your power to drive me off. The part I simply cannot, do not understand is why, when I know absolutely that you love me. I know you do. I knew New Year's Eve. For a few hours you made me a very happy man, Pat. And you were happy, too. Have you committed some crime? Is there still a husband? What is it? What?"

"You promised me you wouldn't do this."

"How can you believe the promises of a desperate man?" He smiled coaxingly.

"Walter, if you make me cry in this restaurant I will never forgive you. You have my most solemn word I will never speak to you again."

"I don't want you to cry. I'm not enjoying this. For this I *am* too old. All right, Pat." He released her hand, looking defeated. "I can't keep on and on."

She lit a cigarette, using every ounce of her self-control not to cry. He'd go away and that would be the end of it, once and for all. The miserable irony of it all, she thought grimly, is I don't want you to go. But to keep you is to begin at the beginning and tell and tell and tell.

"I'll take you home," he said, signing the check before looking up at her.

She stubbed the freshly lit cigarette, nodded, and got up, walking quickly away from the table. Waiting by the door while he got their coats. Holding it in, holding it down. The voice in her head singing, You're a fool a fool a fool. You'll end alone, die alone. And what for? Suffering the incidental touches of his hands as he helped her into her coat, put his hand under her elbow as he held open the door for her. Keeping it tamped down until they were in the back of the taxi and he put his arm around her, drew her close against him, softly saying, "I don't think I can give up on you, Pat. I don't think I can." And his arm around her, his hand on her face, were so gentle, so loving, she began to choke on the accumulation of tears.

"Ah," he whispered. "Don't! You're breaking my heart with all of this. What can I do for you? What do you need? I can't stand having you cry this way. Ah, Pat, Pat. Surely nothing's so bad you can't tell it to someone who loves you." He pulled out his handkerchief and dried her face, pressing kisses on her forehead, her cheeks, her mouth. Gratified to have her arm go around him, to feel her holding him hard, returning his kisses.

Until finally she drew away from him. Saying, "I have to think. A month. A month's time. I'll decide."

"A month," he repeated. "That's a long time at this end of the scale, Pat."

"A few weeks, then. Surely, having waited this long, you can wait a few weeks more?"

"All right, Pat. Take as long as you need."

"When I've decided—yes or no—I will tell you. It's only fair that I do. But I must have some time. To think."

It was getting hard to sleep, hard to move around, hard as hell working on the windows. Trying to crawl around getting the displays put together with her belly in the way. She was slow, slow, slow and knew they were just counting down the days until she'd leave. And sometimes she felt so angry with this baby for wrecking her job. Other times she wanted so badly to get it out of her, have a look at it, see it.

The only really good part of the job now was Bobby. Casually strolling by every so often to waggle his fingers at her or say hi. And working on the finishing touches of his place. Not doing a whole lot else. Because even making out was getting difficult. And he was scared half to death of doing something that might hurt her or the baby. Never mind how many zillion times she told him it was weeks yet before the obstetrician said she'd have to cool it.

Bobby. She'd never known anybody like him. Buying her little things all the time. Trying to talk her into keeping the baby. She was about halfway persuaded already to keep it. And never mind all the hassles there'd be. Because she had this growing feeling maybe she and Bobby might get to be a thing. But scared to want it too much or hope for it, after Sandy. You couldn't make mistakes like that with a baby to look after.

It was weird, too, how emotional she was. Wanting to cry all the time. Or she'd start laughing for no good reason. Getting depressed sitting in the middle of the stupid window looking at the stuff she was supposed to be sticking on the mannequins. Then Bobby would come poking his head inside to smile at her, putting down a paper cup of hot chocolate for her to drink, and she'd be way up there, on this terrific high.

And then there was Pat. It seemed all Pat did lately was make tea. All the time. If there was a gap in the conversation or the telephone rang. Anything. "I'll just go put on the kettle." And off she'd go. And none of the phone calls were from Walter anymore. Just like that, he'd stopped calling. She couldn't help thinking that was probably why Pat was off on such a downer.

But the other thing was that every time Jenny asked her something specific about having babies or anything about babies in general, Pat would go all vague, nine times out of ten changing the subject. Which was kind of weird, considering she'd had five. But she kept thinking about the way Gran used to put the dough to rise and go sit in her rocker to have a smoke while it was rising. And then she'd come back and the dough would just be sitting there, doing nothing. Because she'd forgotten to put in the yeast. Always doing stuff like that. So maybe it wasn't anything more than the fact that old people got a little forgetful sometimes.

Still, Jenny was worried about her. And kept meaning to have a talk with Gabe and Gillian about it. But kept on forgetting. Because she was going out to see a flick with Bobby or going home from the store with him to work on his apartment.

Jenny was spending quite a number of evenings out with Bobby. And for as long as she was out, Pat worried. About Jenny's well-being. About everything.

She'd had a long meeting with Matthew and the paperwork was underway. He was tactful and made no comment—beyond asking specifics having to do with sums of money, legal wording—and she was tremendously grateful. But she was now overtaken by the dread that something might happen to her before all the loose ends were tied.

Too much to think about. Walter's maintaining his promise of telephone silence bothering her almost more than his nightly calls had. She paced the apartment, agonizing over a decision she wished she didn't have to make. But knowing either way that at the very least she owed him an explanation. And couldn't bring herself to think about it, let alone begin putting it into words in her own mind. So her fears took off in other directions.

Time, which had previously dragged, now seemed to be flying away from her. And she longed to be able to slow down the hours, establish some sort of control. But she couldn't. Constantly brooding over how terrible it would be should anything happen to her before Matthew completed the drawing up of those papers.

She did manage to forget herself on those occasions when she and Jenny went downstairs. Or when the two came up to have a meal. And when she had to spend the evenings on her own or when she found herself awake in the early-morning hours, she lay quietly in bed thinking about how Gillian used to ask her down to breakfast at the beginning. Seeing herself and Gillian chatting over good strong cups of tea. The autumn sun streaming in through the windows. She did miss those mornings.

Things always changed so when men entered the picture. Look what had happened to her life.

Oh, Lord! How can I tell him? To have him think me more of a fool than I already am. How could anyone be expected to understand it all? How could they when I scarcely understand it myself? I miss the sound of his voice, his hand holding mine. At the very start I should have been stronger. But it didn't begin with him. It began with me. And must end with me, as well.

She went into the kitchen to make a pot of tea.

14.

The school was coming to completion ahead of schedule. And the site visits were becoming tedious. Keeping track of who was doing what, who was working, who wasn't, checking the logs. Then returning to the office to write up the reports—for the school board, for the chief contractor, for the office. Reports. The files were huge. Half a dozen of them she hefted back and forth between her board and the file room, checking this, that, and everything else. Writing up reports, more reports. Presenting them to the secretary, who'd look at them and groan, then somehow manage to find the time to get them typed up, properly distributed, filed.

She was putting almost half her salary into the savings account she'd started with the balance of her transferred money. Making twice-monthly deposits, each time questioning what it was she was saving for. Watching the balance grow, trying to think of what she might do with this money. Perhaps she and Gabe might vacation together in the summer. Of course they would. Why couldn't she automatically include him in her thoughts without attendant qualifications?

Since receiving the letter from her father, she'd found herself on edge once more. Hesitant in her thoughts, her speech. Unable to understand why—when she should have been feeling finally free—she felt almost more apprehensive and uncertain than before.

And along with this, she was growing very concerned about Pat. Worried that now that Jenny was spending such a lot of time with Bobby, Pat might be feeling somehow abused. Something. Or perhaps it had to do with the departure of Walter Meyers. Something was definitely wrong. Her concern for Jenny, her growing affection for both Pat and Jenny, daily contributing to her nervous state.

Gabe seemed contented. But she was covertly watching him, too. Looking for signs. Of what, she wasn't sure.

She managed to get Jenny on her own one evening when Pat went out saying there was something she had to do she'd forgotten and Gabe was late at the school with parents' night. And tried circuitously to find out from Jenny if there was anything specific Pat was upset about.

"It's got something to do with Walter," Jenny said, sitting tailor fashion on the floor. "But when I ask her—about anything—she just goes off to make another pot of tea."

"I was hoping you'd know," Gillian said.

"I wish I did."

"One other thing," Gillian said. "I'd like to come with you. To the hospital."

"What for?"

"To be with you when the baby comes. Someone's got to be with you, Jenny. You can't go on your own."

"Why would you want to do that?"

"Because I would. Wouldn't you like someone to be with you?"

'You'd really want to?' Jenny asked incredulously.

"Of course I would. I do care about you, Jenny. I'd like to be with you if you'd like to have me there."

"You really mean it."

"I do, yes."

"I'd like that," Jenny said. "Okay."

"Good. That's settled, then. Now, if we could just get to the bottom of what's bothering Pat, *I'd* like that."

The nearer the time came to the baby's due date, the more anxious Pat found herself becoming. Her stomach churning at night when she lay down to sleep, her dreams disturbed, upsetting. She'd sit up in bed and look across at Jenny, sometimes getting out of bed to lean down close to her, making sure she was still breathing. Then, relieved, drawing in a ragged breath, she'd go out to the kitchen to make a pot of tea and sit at the kitchen table, staring out at the night, drinking her way to the bottom of the pot. Something so reassuringly comforting in the familiar habits, rituals.

She was spending far more time than usual at home, reluctant to go out. Except for that one evening when she'd felt she'd suffocate or go completely mad if she didn't escape for a while. So she'd gone to see a film and returned home in a taxi, unable to recall any detail of the film she'd seen. Such a lot of snow. The streets were icy, treacherous. And she'd become unreasonably fearful of taking a fall, breaking bones. Angry with herself for it because she'd never been one of those frail old sorts, the stay-at-home with their tatting, their feet forever on the fender, warming. With chilblains. Rough, reddened hands from doing dishes that didn't need doing but got done because there was so little else to do. Old women peeping out from behind the curtains, watching the comings and goings along the road, reading meanings into the harmless meeting of two neighbors, lending anile interpretations to the most innocent of events. It had always appalled her, this waste of lives. It appalled her now to find herself becoming one of those women. When she'd been so active, so involved in outside goings-on. To see herself as old and useless, a victim of her own fears and fanciful imaginings.

I have many things to do, she told herself. Haven't been to the library in weeks, the books are long overdue. Haven't been down to the shops since the start of the new year. Going only to the local shops to buy the food. Paying far more. This isn't the way to live. I simply must pull myself together and get on with it.

But she couldn't. And sat out the days while Jenny was off at work. Sat rereading old books or dusting, watching films on television. Taking down the good china to give it a washing. Polishing the silver, then putting it away again. Running the vacuum cleaner every day. Avoiding thinking. Standing for long stretches of time staring down at the street, at the snow. Transferring her anxieties to the snow. Viewing the snow and ice as enemies that robbed her of the previous momentum of her life, her incentive. Cold, slick, and dangerous, down there laying in wait to trip her up, send her crashing to the pavement with shattered bones. She was afraid to go out. Chided herself endlessly for staying in. Talking aloud, telling herself, "You're a damned silly old woman. Letting yourself get trapped in here like an invalid. A fool. Bringing all this down on yourself. No one but you."

Wishing the spring would come, put an end to the snow and ice, lighten the air, send the trees to budding. So much easier to think in warm weather. Easier to breathe, function. Thinking, Dear God, it isn't right or just that it should all come to this. All the fine plans and promises, none of them kept. Years and years promising myself the changes. Hanging myself with all the thoughts that should never have been allowed to find access to the air and other ears. I must not allow myself to give way. I must decide. Think. Decide.

But first she'd put on the kettle. And mend that tear in Jenny's shirt.

The last week of February, Gabe announced, "The sixth-graders are giving their concert next Tuesday afternoon. Our music man, Rowell, usually does a great job. I thought you might enjoy it. You've got a site inspection that day, right?"

"It's report day."

"Okay. So why don't you get whoever's chauffeuring you Tuesday to drop you off at the school? We'll see the concert, then go out to dinner. There's a new Greek restaurant downtown I've been hearing about."

Why did he have to talk that way about people "chauffeuring" her around? It hurt in a small way every time he did it.

"Gabe, have you noticed? Something's up with Pat. She's not herself at all. I don't think she's left the house in a week."

"It's cold outside, Gillie. I was her age, I wouldn't feel like going out now either."

"No. It's not just the weather. It's something else."

247

"Well, maybe the two of them are getting on each other's nerves up there."

"I don't think that's it," she said.

"Jenny's getting pretty anxious to have that baby, finally. Which is only natural, I guess. Weren't you?" Realizing what he'd said, he looked over at her to see how she'd taken it.

"I was, actually."

"Okay, then. So Jenny's a little uptight and antsy and it's getting to Pat."

"I've promised to go along to the hospital with her when it's time. She still won't say if she's going to keep the baby."

"It's her decision."

"I know it is. But I do wish ... I ... "

"What? You'd like to volunteer to have the baby if she doesn't want to keep it?"

"I had thought about it," she admitted, everything he was saying striking her wrong. "But it wouldn't be right. As if I was somehow *stealing* Jenny's baby."

"Hypothetically," he said, playing with his knife, setting it to spinning on the table, "I wouldn't mind one bit. I'd love another kid."

"I'd rather not talk of it anymore just now."

"You'd rather not talk about cars or babies. All kinds of things. It's getting a little hard remembering all the things you'd rather not talk about."

She looked as if he'd hit her. "I'm not trying to be difficult," she said almost inaudibly. "I ... uh ... un ... "

"Jesus! I know you're not *trying* to be." His voice going sharp. "It's a little rough, that's all. I wish to hell we could get all the mysteries out of the way. It would help a hell of a lot, Gillian, if I knew *why*. That's all. Maybe you could explain to me."

She sat staring at him, her heart pounding. She couldn't speak. Got up slowly, carefully and walked out of the kitchen, through the living room to the bedroom. Quietly closed the bedroom door. No place to go. How they'd all come clamoring at the doors and windows, wanting to come in, shouting questions through the doors. Somewhere to hide. Somewhere dark. Leaving the lights off, she went around to the far side of the bed, sat down on the floor under the windows, hiding, her fist wedged into her mouth. Uncle Max, please send them away please please. The linens on the shelf above. The airing closet. Mother folding the linens, putting them on the shelf.

He watched her go, thinking, It didn't work. A dumb stunt that didn't work. Going around playing amateur shrink with somebody else's head. Blew up right in your kisser, dope. Go say you're sorry, you were just trying to play with shock tactics, thinking you could stun her into talking about it. It didn't work.

He got up and went through to the bedroom, the light from the living room showing her sitting huddled against the wall, soundlessly sobbing. She put her face down on her knees, turned to the wall as he approached and sat down on his haunches in front of her.

"I was being clever. Trying out a little shock therapy. It was cruel and stupid. Gillie, I'm sorry."

"I . . . I . . . I . . ." He'd taken away her voice and she was suddenly so angry. Furious. Hating herself for being this way, despising him for robbing her of her voice. Her clenched fists vibrating in the air between them. She screamed at him. Screamed until her throat closed and she was pounding at his chest and arms with her fists, hitting him. Hitting and hitting. Seeing his astounded face past the curtain of her outrage. He tried to put his arms around her and she struck at his arms, gulping down the huge sobs.

"I . . . I . . . if I c . . . could t . . . t . . . tell . . ." She screamed again, a rough, rasping sound, the frustration making the blood seem to hurt as it pushed through her veins. "T . . . *tell* y . . . y . . . you." No good. She couldn't. Fell back against the wall, beating the wall with her fist while he sat, thunderstruck, watching. Finally subsiding. The ticking of the clock on the bedside table. The sound of the wind outside. He put his hand on her shoulder. She shrugged it away, turning to glare at him, willing him to read her eyes, read there what she couldn't put into words.

"Want me to clear out for a while?" he asked, ashamed of how badly this little experiment had boomeranged.

She shook her head.

"What, then? I'm not too thrilled with myself. But I didn't mean any of this to happen. In my own half-assed way I was trying to help you."

Her expression cleared slightly, her eyes clouded with such misery he swore to himself he'd leave it alone for good, forever, anything that was so dangerous.

He looked down at his hands. "I know I come on strong," he said in a low, shamed voice. "It's just me, the way I am. Thinking I can force things, make things happen faster or differently. I just thought you might start talking. In self-defense. Something stupid like that. It's something I use on the kids every so often. It works a lot of the time. Those kids. They shout right back at me, a lot of them. They've got such a strong sense of identity, a feeling for their rights. Everyone has 'rights,' even the kids. And they do. I *like* it when they shout back. It means there's a person inside, someone who isn't going to go down, go out without a fight. It didn't work. But you do hit hard." He dared a small smile. "Pack a hell of a wallop."

"I don't like the way I am," she said, her voice hoarse from screaming. "I've *never* liked the way I am, the me I am. I don't claim to be . . . anything. I want to tell you. So many things. *I can't.* Don't you understand that? It doesn't make me happy, living with it all. . . . I can't bear arguments, people shouting. Can't *bear* it. I looked at your face back there, the anger—I thought it was anger—and all I could think was you'd go away. You were finding all the things about me that displease you. You'd go away. I feel so very happy with you. But so often I'm on guard. Waiting for you to say you're leaving. I'm not what you thought I was. Or I'm too this or too that. I love you but you frighten me. When you suddenly become angry again. When I thought that was all done with. Reading the newspaper and something makes you exclaim aloud. And I seize up, waiting for you to turn that anger on me. As you did at the first. It's so frightening. Please, please, don't come at me demanding responses I simply cannot give you. I don't expect you could comprehend how it is to go through one's life finding the world and all its people so alarming. But it's me, the way I've always been. I can't suddenly become bold and confident because you're here. It's taken all these years . . . I can't change all at once, Gabe. I'd give anything to be the bright sort of girl Jenny is. Or the calm, confident sort of woman my mother was. But I'm not, never will be. I can't speak about wh . . . what happened. Please understand. I'm sorry I screamed, hit you. I'm very ashamed, behaving that way."

"I'm not going to leave," he said. "Unless you throw me out. And I guess we're both ashamed. I'll leave it alone, respect it. If you can't talk about it, maybe it's better if you don't."

"I've hurt my hand," she said, holding it out to him. The side of her hand was turning purple.

"I love you," he said, taking her into his arms. "It was a dumb stunt and I just this minute gave all that up."

The telephone rang.

"You answer it," she said, enervated.

He got up and went to pick up the phone.

"Hi," Jenny said. "Everything okay down there?"

"Oh, Jenny. I'm sorry if we made a lot of noise, disturbed you." He felt like an idiot, realizing it must've sounded as if he'd been murdering Gillian.

"I was just worried. Pat, too. Gillian's all right?"

"She's fine. I was just playing smartass and got her upset."

"Gabe, don't push her too hard, okay? Everybody around here's been so nervous lately. Maybe it's the season or something. But everybody I know's feeling it, acting strung out. I didn't think it was any big number, but Pat nearly freaked. She was sleeping and now she's out in the kitchen making tea again. You know?"

"I know. I'm sorry. Tell Pat I apologize. To you, too."

"It's okay, Gabe. Just a very heavy eggshell feeling coming down all over the place. Night."

He hung up feeling even worse than he had before and returned to the bedroom. Gillian was sitting on the side of the bed—the light on now—examining her hand.

"Let's leave the dishes and go to bed," he said. "I'll load the dishwasher in the morning before I leave."

"Yes," she said distantly. "In the morning."

"Pat, why don't you go back to bed? It was nothing. Gabe said to tell you he's sorry."

252

"I'll be along in a few minutes, dear," she said, spooning tea leaves into the pot. "You go on to bed, now. I'll have a cup of tea, a cigarette, then I'll be in."

I wish you'd tell me, Jenny thought, going over to kiss Pat good night.

"Don't stay in here too long," Jenny said. "You need your sleep."

Pat put her hand on Jenny's cheek. "Whatever happens," she said mysteriously, "you'll be looked after, Jenny. Go along to bed, now."

Puzzled, Jenny went. There was no point to asking questions. Pat had stopped answering them.

"What are you going to do, Dad?" Matthew asked, sitting down on the corner of his father's desk.

"What is there to do? If I call her up, it'll be breaking a promise and I can't do that. If I allude to knowing, she'll lose all faith in you and that'll be the end of both of us. So what can I do? Sit and wait and hope she's going to see there's no sin to telling the truth."

"She made me swear not to tell you," Matthew said, inspecting his fingernails. "The two of you pulling in different directions."

"You did the right thing, Matthew. Absolutely the right thing."

Monday morning, after Jenny left for work, the flowers came. Without a card. But one wasn't needed. Pat opened the box on the kitchen table and looked at the mass of red roses. Lit a cigarette and began pacing back and forth, every so often glancing over at the box of flowers. Knowing time was running out. The roses somehow giving her strength. So that for the first time in more than two weeks she didn't feel tired. Or so

253

Charlotte Vale Allen

hopelessly, helplessly frightened. He loves me. And twice in one lifetime is one time too many to say no shut the door go away fare thee well. Not twice. She put the roses in water finally, then sat down to think. Putting the words in order one by one. Framing her thoughts, the sequence. Another day, two days.

Tuesday morning there was a freezing rain. Pierce refused to leave the car, staying inside, reading the morning paper. The car heater on high.

"I'll be right here when you're done, Miss U. No way I can hack the elements this A.M. I'll just have a look through the paper, then get a little work done. Take your time."

She toured the site, feeling chilled right through to her marrow, anxious to get done and be on her way. Anxious to get back and talk to Pierce. By the time she got back to the car her hands were numb. She was shivering, teeth chattering. The car interior warm, smoky. She climbed in and sat hunched over her briefcase for several minutes, feeling the sting in her hands as they started to thaw.

"Let's go grab something to eat before I drop you off," he said. "You look as if you don't get something hot inside you, you'll gel."

"I think I may have done already. I can feel the blood sliding through my veins in chunks."

He laughed and gingerly reversed his way out of the lot.

"Some mess," he said once they were on the road. "A little more of a drop in the temperature and we'll all come skating to the office in the morning."

"I simply will not come. I'll stay at home. I've had quite enough."

"How's it going?" he asked, sensing she wanted to talk. "Everything copacetic with you and Gabe?"

"Will you tell me something, Pierce?"

"Sure."

"Do you feel worthy? What I mean to say . . . What do I mean? Do you sometimes wonder why the people who love you love you? Do you wonder if there's enough . . . *in* you worth loving?"

"You're lovable, Miss U. Don't you think so?"

"I don't know."

"Thinking about the clowns again?"

"Not quite. Pierce, I'm not great fun or a marvelous mixer. Stupid things make me cry. Stupid things terrify me. There are . . . other things I want so much to talk about, but can't. I know it bothers him. We talk about love and sometimes I seem to feel it. But I'm not sure I know what it is, love. And it seems I'm too old not to know. So many things . . . Great segments that are unsafe, not spoken of. He tried to . . . shock me into telling. And I beat at him . . . because I'm not . . . *able*. I hated him for trying to force me to talk about it." She cleared her throat, then rummaged in her bag for a cigarette. "There's no reason really, but I feel . . . apprehensive. Frightened. Something will happen."

"What sort of something d'you have in mind?"

"He'll force me to tell. And his forcing me will destroy us."

"Are you sure that's what'd happen?"

"I'm not. It's what I fear."

"Gabe's not stupid, you know, Gillian." He pulled into a parking slot, turned off the motor, and swiveled around to look at her. "And I get the feeling it's not so much his forcing you to do all this telling as you, inside there, wanting to get it out, get rid of whatever's eating at you. As to feeling worthy. Well. There are times when I feel all kinds of worthy. And other times when I don't know how anybody in the world can *stand* me. It's the human condition, Miss U." He reached across and took hold of her hand. "I know you," he said. "And that something that's eating at you. We've all got those 'somethings.' So you'll do what needs doing. Because you're someone who does. Maybe even in spite of yourself. Cause you're stronger than you think you are. I was a woman, Miss U, I'd be you. I'd *choose* to be you. 'Cause looking at it from all sides, I think it's better being able to cry when it hurts. Never mind how stupid it is or isn't. Better to cry. It gives other people a chance for their own crying time. You know? You're worthy. And as for love. Well"—he smiled—"I think you know. You just don't know yet you know. That's all. If something's going to happen, maybe it's going to be for the good. Maybe it's going to be better than good. It's time, wouldn't you say?"

"Yes."

"And let me tell you something about Gabe. He put in about four years with a woman I used to call Numb. When she'd come to my mind, when I saw her, I'd think, Hey, there's Numb. 'Cause she was. If anybody knows about wanting to strike back, it's Gabe. We all just have our different ways of handling things. So okay." He grinned, patting the back of her hand. "Let's go eat."

He dropped her off after lunch in front of the school.

"Let it happen," he said, leaning across the seat to kiss her cheek. "Just let it all happen. Take it easy walking. It's icing over fast. Probably start to snow anytime now."

She thanked him and made her way carefully to the nearest door. Still thinking about everything Pierce had said. The doors were heavy. So heavy she could scarcely manage to open the nearest one. And wondered how the original architect could have installed such massive doors in a school for small children. Something about the doors triggering a signal in her brain. But she was later than she'd intended to be and hadn't time to stop and think about it.

"I've been waiting for you," he said. "Like a kid. Anxious for you to get here."

"You look very dignified behind your desk."

"The program's just starting," he said. "I ducked out to wait for you. Want to leave your coat here?"

"I think I'll just keep it on for now. I still feel chilled from my visit to the site." More than chilled. Jumpy inside. Bursts of adrenaline making her heartbeat rapid.

At the foot of the stairs to the mezzanine he held her back—quickly looking around to make sure they were unobserved—to kiss her. Then, smiling, he took her hand and they continued on up the stairs. He was about to push in through the glass doors when he became aware of her hand gripping his arm and turned to see her frozen, rooted. An expression of absolute terror on her face. Bewildered, he looked back to see a small girl of eight or nine on the far side of the door, pulling against the inside handle, trying to get out.

"What?" he asked Gillian.

Her heart was exploding. The silence. Where was the light? A blinding flash of light. She whirled around to look at him, her mouth opening and closing, no sound emerging. She could see his mouth moving but couldn't hear what he was saying. Screams, echoing, echoing. Screaming. She had to get away. Turned and ran. Megan! The doors. Her heart trying to force its way right out of her. Mother! *Run!*

He held the door open for the child, then took off down the stairs after Gillian, arriving at the foot of the stairs in time to see her run straight out of the building. Her arm flying out as she tried to maintain her balance, running down the icy walk. He flew into his office, grabbed up his coat, called to his secretary that there was an emergency, he had to leave, and raced out of the building. Squinting through the driving rain, seeing her several hundred yards ahead of him, tearing along the sidewalk. What the hell was happening? He started after her, almost falling—forgot his damned boots—chasing after her, the rain leaking in down the back of his neck. He wrenched up his collar, sending a stream of gelid water down his neck and back.

The voice in her head shouting, *Get away! Run! Run!*

When he saw her go down, he sucked in his breath, wincing. She went down so hard. A moment of awful silence. Then he hurried on, his feet seeking purchase on the treacherous sidewalk. She was picking herself up, sitting on the ice, her mouth still opening and closing. Her eyes round, unblinking. He helped her up, asking, "What's wrong? What happened? Gillian!"

She could hear. How was it she could suddenly hear? His voice slashing through her head, hurting, echoing inside. So loud. All wet and she'd hurt herself. Hurt. Her heart out of control, rapping against her ribs. Hurting, too.

"The doors," she whispered, grimacing as his hand closed around her arm. Hurting there, as well.

"What about the doors? What? Why did you run that way?"

She couldn't breathe. Her lungs working, fighting. So little air.

"She was there. Behind the door." Searching his face

for an understanding. Why didn't he know? Hadn't he seen?

"You're soaked, love. Let's go back to the car, get out of this rain."

"Didn't you *see?*"

"You mean the kid, the girl? Who?"

"She couldn't get *in*. I couldn't g . . . g . . . g . . ." Her teeth chattering so hard, the sounds—all the sounds—locked inside her mouth, caught in her throat.

He steered her along back to the school parking lot. Scared. The lock on the passenger door frozen. He nearly tripped, almost fell running around the front of the car to unlock the door on the driver's side, jammed the key into the lock, got the door open, then reached across the seat to unlock the other door. She wasn't moving. Just standing there staring, the rain running down her face, into her hair. Her eyes fixed. He ran back, pushed her in, slammed the door. Finally he got the car started and turned to look at her. Her hair saturated, dripping. Her teeth clacking together audibly. He opened the glove compartment, took out an old towel he kept there for cleaning the interior of the windows, and made a rough attempt to dry her hair, asking, "What *is* it? Gillian, for God's sake, what's wrong?"

She simply stared at him.

"There's no point to sitting here," he said. "We'll go home."

Tell him tell him. Get it out all of it out finally tell him if you do some of it please perhaps some of it will go away go and not keep coming back and back and back tell him.

She sat the entire way staring at him, her head moving back and forth as if she couldn't stop. Shuddering. He had to half carry her out of the car. And once

259

inside the apartment, forced her down into a chair after removing her coat. She immediately jumped up. Then stopped, turning slowly, looking around the room as if she hadn't any idea where she was.

He hung their dripping coats over the shower in the bathroom and came back, towel in hand, to dry her hair more properly. Sitting her down on the sofa. She clutched at his arm. The way she had outside the auditorium.

"I . . . I . . . wh . . . what . . . I . . ."

"Go easy," he said, dropping down beside her. Her hands gripping his arms. Her eyes raking his, frantically searching. "Start at the beginning and take it nice and slow. Take your time. You can talk about it."

"We . . . we . . . w . . . w . . . w . . ." She took a deep breath, her fingers digging into his arms. Closing her eyes for a moment. Thinking perhaps deep breaths, several of them, would dislodge the stones in her throat. Opening her eyes. "We went to the West End," she said. "Shopping. For a treat. Mother. And Megan. And me. To the West End. On the bus. The number seventy-three bus. Oh, *God*. Oh!"

"It's all right. Go on. Slowly."

She nodded her head. "The bus. Megan. Hated my smoking. So. So we sat below. But there weren't. Three seats together. I had a seat. Near the front. Mother, Megan, found seats at the rear. Oh! *Help me!*"

"Go on," he urged. "Keep going."

"We . . . we . . . planning a super lunch after . . . after . . ." Her chest heaving, eyes filling. "The bus." Her eyes slid past him, connecting with something only she could see. "The bus . . . stops. Not at the proper stop. Curious. A bit before the stop. Because there's a . . . car. A car. The *car*. I get off. Turn. See Mother, Megan, coming off the bus. They're right behind me. Coming along. I turn again. Something inside the window. A jumper. Perfect for Megan. Yellow. The color of sunshine. It will go so well with her hair. Here, they're coming. I pull open the door. My God. So heavy. I can barely get it open, get inside before it's closing, almost catching me. I don't want the door to close that way on Megan, she might be hurt. Mother. I'll hold the door for them. Turn back to pull open the door. Here they come Megan's laughing I can see Mother's telling her something they're holding hands. Oh, my God. God oh my God the car it's a bomb! I can't get out. *I can't get out!"* She started to scream, pushing with all her might against his chest, shoving against him.

He tightened his hold on her arms, deafened, stunned by her screaming.

Pat's teacup went smashing to the floor. She jumped to her feet and went hurrying through the apartment, down the stairs, to knock at the door.

Gabe called out, "Come in!" and Pat opened the door, stopped.

"What's happened?" she asked Gabe, taking several steps into the room.

"Help me with her," he said, afraid she'd never stop screaming.

Pat came quickly across the room, pried Gillian's fingers off Gabe's arms, pulled Gillian into her arms, stroking her, whispering into her ear. "Come, now. It's all right. Hush, hush."

Sudden softness, sweet scent. The scream died in her mouth. Hunched inside Pat's arms, torn by sobs. Returned in some measure to the present. Pat's arms strong about her, the cushion of her breasts. She closed her eyes tightly, wanting the last of it out, done. "It . . . tore

261

them to p . . . *pieces*," she cried. "The glass . . . in the
door . . . blew out, shattered. The explosion. Deafened
me. I couldn't *hear*. No sounds. I didn't know. All the
blood. Everywhere. And I couldn't get to them.
Trapped. People . . . rushing up . . . like the ocean behind me. Out there. And p . . . p . . . *piece*s of M . . .
M . . *Megan, Mother* . . . all over the street. Arms . . .
legs . . . Oh, God. Please. I want them back I want
them back.". . . .

Pat's and Gabe's eyes connected. He'd completely lost
all his color.

"Fetch some warm clothes for her," Pat said calmly.
"And a bit of whiskey. Go along, now." She seemed very
much in control, he thought as he went to the bedroom
for Gillian's robe, her slippers.

Pat held Gillian's face between her hands, forcing her
head up. "It's ended," she said firmly. "Done. Are you
hearing me, Gillian?"

Gillian lowered her eyelids, then lifted them.

"I *know,*" Pat said. "You understand me? I know all
about the bombs, the deaths. I've seen. Let it go away
from you, dear. Let it all go, now. Take yourself past it."

"Why didn't I die? I wanted to."

"Not now," Pat said. "That was then."

"They had to bury Mother, Megan, in plastic bags. Inside the coffins. *Plastic bags.*"

"Yes, I know about all of that."

Gabe, returning, heard and stopped. Feeling sick.

"I screamed and screamed. I didn't know, you see. I
couldn't hear, couldn't get out."

"Go on," Pat encouraged her. "Get to the finish. Let it
end."

Pat's eyes so clear. How clear your eyes are. Green
like the sea. "Cut my hands on all the glass. People

screaming but I didn't hear. Seeing their mouths open. A woman sitting on the pavement all . . . blood. Sitting, weeping. People strewn all over the street. But only Megan and Mother dead. They'd been directly in front of the car. The doors flew off. Hitting them . . . bits of metal . . . " She stopped and wet her lips, blinked. "My mother, my daughter."

Pat's hand was moving, pushing the wet hair off her face, her lips forming sounds. Gillian shook her head to clear it. "I'm cold," she said. Pat's words sliding past her.

"Come get her out of these wet clothes," Pat told Gabe. "I'll see to the whiskey."

Pat got up, went away. Gabe came, took her place. She looked at the robe bunched on his lap, then at his face. His hands beginning to unbutton her cardigan, removing it. Then the buttons on her shirt. She sat shuddering, watching him closely. He was crying. She put her hand on his face. He put the wet clothes down on the floor, gathered her into his arms.

Pat returned from the kitchen—three glasses on a small tray she'd found in the cupboard—halted by the sight of Gillian's naked back, the two in each other's arms. The intimacy, a truth that stabbed into her. They separated and Gabe was putting Gillian into the robe. Pat moved forward again. "Drink that down, now, dear," she told Gillian, putting a glass of whiskey into her hand. "It'll ease you." Then she beckoned Gabe to come with her and the two of them went into the bedroom.

"See she has a good hot bath, something to eat, and then straight to bed. She'll be all right now."

"I didn't know what to do," he said. "I'm grateful you were here."

"One thing," she said, preparing to go. "Don't expect the nightmares will stop now. It seems they never do."

"It happened to you?"

"Indirectly. And I've seen enough, heard enough to know. Drink this now and see to Gillian. I must get dinner. Jenny will be coming in soon."

"Pat, thank you." He pressed a kiss on her cheek. "Thank you."

"Not at all," she said. "I'll be upstairs should you need me."

"Pat? How did you know about the nightmares?"

"I've heard her in the night. I guessed." She continued on her way, pausing in the living room with Gillian, who said, "I'm all right now," and smiled thinly.

"You'll feel just fine comes the morning. I'll be going along now."

She lowered herself into the water, at once feeling the heat penetrating the cold. Her chest felt curiously light, emptied. She sank all the way down until only her face was above the water, then sat up a little, resting her head on the back of the tub.

Gabe set a mug of steaming coffee down on the side of the tub, then sat down on the floor, his hands closed around his own mug of coffee.

"Can we talk?" he asked hesitantly.

"I think so. I feel quite peculiar. Very emptied."

"Better?"

"Somewhat."

"What happened after?" he asked.

"Newspaper people, that sort of thing. Hounding me, driving me mad. I finally hid in a closet and Mother's brother, Uncle Max, took charge. Made all the arrangements, kept everyone away. Telling me I must keep going, return to work. And I did. Return to work. But having to come home every night to the house. Seeing Mother's dresses hanging in the closet. Her shoes. I'd open the closet door and her scent clinging to the clothes . . . Megan's toys, books. I simply couldn't live there. I took a few things I wanted, moved into a flat in South Kensington, and listed the house with an estate agent. Lady Nora used her influence to help me get a visa. I came here, bought this house. That's all, really."

"Did they find out who was responsible?"

"Some terrorist group. The IRA or the PLO, one of those. I don't know. It didn't matter. What mattered was Megan, my mother. How they died." She looked down at the water, the tears starting up again. "I could have accepted their dying. But not that way. Seeing it all. The tremendous flash of light, the fire. And their eyes. Oh, God. Gabe, *their eyes*. Five seconds and everything was ended." She sniffed and looked at him. "You're the only person, outside Mother and Megan, who's ever made me feel of any importance, value. Brooke did. I thought. But that was only eight weeks when I was barely sixteen and believed it was love because I knew no better." She took a sip of coffee. "My mother was so beautiful, Gabe. *So* beautiful. Warm and soft and so wonderfully alive. And Megan. She was my *life*. Nine years old. No chance at all for her. They were all murdered. Mother and Megan. Even Brooke. By mad people. *Mad*. For no reason. None at all.

"After I returned to work, I began frequenting the pubs again. I was searching for a madman to put an end to me as well. I would have prayed for it had there been anything left I believed in. And there was one night when I thought I'd succeeded. A very violent man. Wanting . . . performances. He used me so badly. All

265

the while it was happening I kept thinking, He'll kill me once he's done. He'll take my life and it will all be over. And suddenly I didn't want to die. I had no feelings for life. I simply didn't want to die. There's something more I want to tell you. But you must give me your promise you won't speak of it."

"You know I won't."

"It has to do with Jenny."

"Go on."

"She took the apartment with a young man. Sandy."

"I've heard you all talk about him."

"Yes. Well, one evening he came down to bring the rent check. And tried to rape me. Hit me, tore most of my clothes off. He . . . I was able to fight him off. And that's why he left, moved out, leaving Jenny on her own."

"And you never told her."

"Gabe, how could I tell her that? It would have hurt her terribly. I couldn't. But I wanted you to know. There's nothing else. Nothing at all."

"Jesus!" He looked at the bruised areas on her arm and leg. Livid bruises. "That was one hell of a spill you took. You're bruised all to hell."

She looked at herself, touching her arm and leg almost disinterestedly before taking another swallow of coffee.

"Hurt?"

"Mmm. I feel so tired."

"Finish up and we'll get you to bed."

"I'm sorry if I embarrassed you at your school."

"You couldn't help it," he said. "Any more than I can help shouting sometimes to make my points."

"Pierce was right," she said. "I do know. I didn't think I did, but I do."

Mystified, he said, "What?"

"What love is. I do know. It's what we have."

"Damned right." He smiled. "And don't forget to dry your hair."

15.

"When's your last day?" Bobby asked her.

"Friday."

"You want to go out and celebrate Friday night?"

"Sure. What should we do?"

"I'll think of something. Take it easy going home, eh? It's getting really bad out now."

"Don't worry. I will."

"See you tomorrow?"

"Unless there's a blizzard or I get hit by a truck or something."

"That's not funny," he said.

"Come on, Bobby. It's just a joke."

"It's still not funny."

"You're so sweet. You're really sweet. You take it easy going home. And I'll see you tomorrow. Okay?"

"Okay."

"Dad, the forecast's bad. Let's cancel tonight. You stay put out there and we'll get together another night."

Gifts of Love

"You're probably right," Walter said, looking out the window. "It's already coming down pretty thick."

"She didn't call?"

"Not yet. But she will."

"I hope for your sake she does. I really mean that. You both deserve some happiness. No disrespect to Mother. But I know how it was. I was never fooled. I hope it all works out."

"Matthew, you never fail to amaze and delight me. Now, do me a favor and get off the line. Someone might be trying to reach me."

They ate in front of the fire. She seemed considerably calmer. And ate with appetite, drinking a second glass of wine before lighting a cigarette, leaning back against the sofa with a sigh, looking into the fire.

"It's easier to breathe now," she said. "It seems years since I've been able to draw a deep breath."

"Snow's really starting to come down," he said, watching it drift past the window. "Looks like the forecasts were right."

"If it keeps on, how will you get to school in the morning?"

"Hell, I won't. Nobody will. The school won't open. We close with two inches of snow. With this kind of weather there probably won't be any classes for days."

"I adored staying home from school. Mother would tuck me up in her bed, give me a bowl of fruit and biscuits, and I'd stay the day, listening to the BBC Light, drawing, napping. She'd come sit with me and we'd draw together. I'd try to put how she looked and felt to me down on paper. I never could. But she was wonderful, could quite easily have sold her paintings."

"Why didn't she?"

"She'd say they weren't good enough. After the . . . after, I gave them all to Hugh. He took me to Claridge's one afternoon for tea. Held my hand and cried. It was so unbearably sad. He said he hoped I'd understand and not feel he was abandoning me but he was going to move permanently to his country house. Retiring. Closing down the business, selling out. Said he hoped I'd come visit him in the country. In any case, I gave him the paintings. He sent the car the next afternoon and they were gone.

"Such fine times we had together, the three of us and Hugh. Going to Kew Gardens, Festival Hall, the Royal Albert. My mother was only forty-six, Gabe. Megan just nine. So many plans we had, things we'd do, holidays. I miss them so."

He put the plates aside and leaned back beside her, listening.

"When I first came over here," she said, "it didn't feel real to me. Everything so unfamiliar, different. None of it began being real until that night at the party. I was so desperately afraid I'd hate you the next morning. And it didn't happen. You didn't allow it to happen."

"At that Mexican restaurant I felt like such an ass," he said. "After you left, I went back to the table and sat there convinced I'd driven you away."

"It doesn't matter. Truly, it doesn't." She yawned. "The fire's making me very sleepy," she said, putting out her cigarette. "It's always been my understanding that school principals—headmasters, you know—were older gentlemen. White-haired, of stern moral fiber, ethically impeccable."

"You obviously never read *Peyton Place*." He laughed. "Good old Grace Metalius did wonders for enhancing our image. Mind you, he was high school and I'm only primary."

"I'll have to read it."

She yawned again, closed her eyes, and within moments was asleep. He grabbed a pillow from the sofa, eased her down. Then got up, carried the dishes out to the kitchen, and began cleaning up. When he'd finished, he brought in some more firewood from the back porch. Gillian was sleeping soundly. He sat down with a cigarette, listening to the silence, the crackle of the fire, looking every so often at the window, the snow falling steadily. Thickly. Whirling, the patterns of its fall changing as the wind climbed. Drifting. The cars parked outside already half buried. Nothing moving. The silence heavy, weighted. Quiet movements upstairs.

Jenny came in complaining, "I'm frozen. Boy! You can hardly walk out there it's so icy. If it's like this in the morning, I'm staying home. Does something ever smell good! I'm so glad to be home."

Pat smiled over at her, finishing laying the table. "They say on the radio there's to be six to ten inches. I think you'd be wise to plan on staying indoors tomorrow."

"What're you cooking? It smells so *good*."

"Curry. Do you like curry, dear?"

"I've never had it."

"I'm sure you'll like it. I've kept it mild. Shall we have some wine?"

"Sure. You know something?"

"What might that be?"

"I was really glad to be coming home today, knowing you'd be here."

"That's very nice to hear."

"I mean it," Jenny said, moving closer. "You've been so good to me. You're like my gran was. Only better. I love you a lot."

Pat stood there, the cutlery in her hand, looking as if she'd start crying. Jenny hugged her, then said, "I'll go wash my hands, see if I can get them thawed out."

Pat exhaled slowly, then finished setting down the knives and forks. She felt tired. Such an emotional afternoon. That moment coming through the kitchen door to see them embracing. She could close her eyes and see it again. And feel it all cutting into her deeper and deeper. The vision of so much missed emotion, all she was willing to reject.

Get on with the dinner, she told herself. But still. That moment when he'd held the robe out. A glimpse of rounded breasts, silvery skin. A glimpse that had once been a mirror image. And a view of something that was not yet lost to her. All it required was picking up the telephone. Her back aching, she moved over to the stove.

It crept through her sleep so that she lifted closer, then closer to waking. Turning from one side to the other, her dreaming self thinking to ease it that way, slipping down again.

Pat sat reading, looking across from time to time, noticing how Jenny's sleep was changing, becoming disturbed, restless. Poor child, finding it so hard to rest properly with the baby kicking away inside.

She couldn't concentrate on the book. That irrational agitation once more overtaking her. Making her skin feel taut, tight. Watching Jenny sleeping. A sensation of impending disaster. So that her heart double- and triple-beat and she kept swallowing in an effort to moisten her

272

throat. It felt so dry. Faintly nauseated from lack of sleep. Waking so often—most nights—with her heartbeat rapid, to look across and ascertain nothing was amiss. Jenny was there, breathing evenly, regularly.

If only she could face it all. Get it done, get it said. Accept the consequences, knowing she'd at least made a decent effort to remedy past errors. The necessity of providing Walter with an answer putting her in a state of malaise. With skittering fears that danced about in the corners of her brain, peeping out at her from the shadows, waggling their fingers mockingly before darting away. Like those tots towing about sacks of lumpy clothing on Guy Fawke's Day, crying, "A penny for the Guy!" Insistent, demanding. She'd seen them that visit to London. Their voices so high, abrasive.

So weary. The reading glasses pinching at the bridge of her nose. Removing them, holding them, thinking with a twinge of anger at the steadily erosive damage of time's passage. Drawing her thumb and forefinger back and forth to ease the pinched place, closing her eyes a moment to rest them. Knowing they'd condemn her as a witless old fool, consign her to the backstairs regions of their interest and attention. The book slipping away down the blankets. The glasses dropping noiselessly to the rug.

"Let's get you to bed," he said. "Here we go." Got her to her feet and propelled her into the bedroom, untied her robe, urging her down, under the blankets. She scarcely woke up. Just opened her eyes, then closed them and was deeply asleep once more. He returned to the living room to put up the fire screen, set the pillow back on the sofa. Tidying up some before going around, making a last-minute check. Sure all the burners were off, the lights, thermostat turned down for the night. Stopping to stand at the kitchen window, watching the snow fall. Nothing was going to get through that. They'd spend a relaxed day at home tomorrow. He yawned, then stretched so that his bones seemed to crack.

It had finally happened. She'd managed to get it all out. He was so overwhelmed by the afternoon's revelations he hadn't had a chance to stop and think, react.

While he was showering he tried to imagine himself trapped behind a heavy door seeing a woman and a small child blown literally to pieces. Turned it into Aunt Dora and Craig and not only saw it but felt it. Too clearly, too strongly. Jesus! What she had to have been through. Going ahead with her life with all that behind her eyes. He dried off, hung the towel over the rack to dry. Picked up the talc, shook some out, applied it without thought. Sleepy.

Her body was wonderfully warm as he curved himself against her, ready for sleep. Letting his hand trail over the hard rise of her hip, down into the deep curve of her waist, settling over her breast. Kissing her shoulder before sinking back, finally closing his eyes. Sighing deeply.

It woke Jenny up. Pat was sleeping. The light still on. She pushed the pillow up against the headboard and sat with her hands on her belly. Waiting, thinking she had to be mistaken. But no. There it was again. A dull, circular pain. Lasting only a few seconds. It can't be, she thought. It's too soon. Five weeks too soon. A mistake. So many weird things happening inside her with this baby. Going to the john almost every ten seconds. Indigestion. Heartburn. Nutty, old-people stuff. But that's what happened, being pregnant. The doctor said so.

Telling his dumb jokes, distracting the hell out of her so that half the time she couldn't remember the serious stuff he told her.

She got up and went into the bathroom to lift her nightgown and stare down at her belly, feeling around it with her hands. Caught again by another pain. Slightly stronger, lasting a little longer. Suddenly afraid. Because it was too soon but it seemed to be happening. She'd have to start timing the contractions. Standing there thinking about timing them when she realized there was water running down her legs, getting all over the floor.

She cleaned herself, then mopped up the floor with the sponge and returned to the bedroom to sit on the side of her bed, holding her wristwatch, staring at the face as the second hand ticked its way around. Nine minutes and there was another one. Lighter than the last one. Eleven minutes later, another one. Then eight minutes. Then fourteen. This wasn't the way it was supposed to be. They were supposed to come regularly. Ten minutes apart, then eight, six. Not this way.

She continued to sit, timing the irregular contractions.

Walter couldn't get to sleep at all. He got up, put on his robe and slippers, and went through the darkened house to the kitchen. Something to drink. Not coffee. That would guarantee his being up all night. Tea was just as bad. He closed one cupboard door, opened another. Hot chocolate. Now, that was a good idea. He'd always had a sweet tooth. Hot chocolate.

While he was waiting for the water to boil he walked over to the sliding glass door at the side of the kitchen, switched on the outside lights. Watching the snow fall. Wonderful. Snow was one of God's more opulent gifts, he thought. And opened the door, allowing flakes to fall on the sleeve of his robe. Studying their exquisite design before they melted away. Closed the door and blotted the water from his sleeve with a paper towel. Stirred up his cup of hot chocolate, chuckling to himself, recalling how Matthew as a child had one time asked for "a chock of hot cupolate."

Putting off the lights, he made his way back to the bedroom. Sitting down in the armchair, looking at the bed. Remembering New Year's Eve. How they'd danced. The champagne. The superb dinner. Dancing and dancing. Then returning here. To this room. To that bed. To make love with a passion, a swelling passion the likes of which he hadn't experienced in so many years. Something that dated back to the start of the marriage when, all unknowing, he'd made love for the first time to Catherine. And, all too soon, discovered she suffered through it all. Deriving no pleasure whatsoever from any of it. But persevered. Attempting variations. Anything, everything. Slowly realizing nothing on earth was ever going to make Catherine respond to him.

And took his first lover—outside the marriage—the year Matthew was twelve. Staying faithful to her for seventeen years. Both of them dying that same year. Catherine first. And then Lillian. Gone.

From then till now there'd been half a dozen others. None of them holding his affections or attention for any appreciable length of time. Until Pat. And, oh, the irony of it all. To find the one woman who, in every way, stimulated and sparked him. And would accept nothing he sought to offer. Trying her hardest to deflect his interest, turn it away.

The look of her, the feel of her. Someone still so young in so many vital ways. If you don't call tomorrow,

Pat, I'll begin again calling you. Because I want you here, need you here. And nothing else matters.

Gillian woke up. From a dream she was making love with Gabe. In Trafalgar Square, directly in front of the fountain. Waking to find herself on her back with her hand between her thighs. Stealthily turning her head to find him smiling at her in the reflected snow light.

"You were shaking the bed," he said. "That must've been one hell of a good dream."

She felt her face turning to fire. Then laughed. "We were making love on the pavement in Trafalgar Square. It was very real."

"I'll say." He laughed. "I was right there with you."

She laughed again and rolled over against him. "It seems the more I have," she whispered, "the more I want." His hand gliding down over her buttocks, urging her closer.

"Ditto," he said, moving between her thighs. "Jesus!"

Her hand guiding him in. She shuddered, then whispered, "Oh, it's good," swinging over on top of him, lying full length upon him. A pulsing receptivity and a compelling need to move. Joining her mouth to his, her knees tight against his hips. Whispering, "Hard, hard!" into his mouth. "More." A frantic dance, slippery, sliding. Feeling her go suddenly tense, then go twitching, jolting inside his arms. He couldn't stop. Continuing on. A pulsing, caresslike rhythm inside her. She began to move again. Only seconds and she was once more convulsed, then again. Long minutes while her tongue explored the interior of his mouth and her body shook, spasms that ended only to begin again until she was at last still on his chest and he lifted once, twice, and it was ending. Holding her secured to him. Hard. Soft inside. She kissed him deeper, harder, knowing, remaining utterly open, receiving. Then lowered her face into the soft curve of his neck. Turning her head finally to whisper, "I didn't take a pill."

It took a moment or two to register. He tightened his hold on her, speechless with hope. Cooling now, her head became suddenly heavier. Her body untensing even more, more. She slept. He lay caressing her until his hand came to a stop mid-motion, at rest in the small of her back.

Six A.M. The sky was starting to get light. And the pains were still all over the place. She dozed. Then came awake to see Pat setting a cup of tea down on the bedside table. "You've been making noises, moaning. What is it, dear?"

"I think it's coming," she said. "But it's too soon."

Pat paled, her hand flying to her mouth. Of all the things she'd been fearing, it had never occurred to her that something like this might happen. And in the face of this reality, all her prior resolutions fled, leaving her weak with fear.

"My God," she said, aghast. "What shall we do?"

That's funny, Jenny thought. You're supposed to know what to do. You've done this five times. Do people forget when they get old?

"I guess we just wait. I'm having contractions, all right, but they're not regular. My water broke, though. Hours ago."

"I think we'd best ring your doctor, Jenny."

"I'd feel really stupid calling him and having him tell me I was wrong. I'd rather wait a little while longer, see if they go away or get worse or whatever. I might as well get up now anyway. I'm starving."

"Should you eat?" Pat asked.

"Sure. Why not? I mean, if I was having them every two minutes or like that, I wouldn't. But the way things are right now, it could be days."

"All right, then," Pat said, her hands tightly clasped in front of her. "I'll make breakfast. Yes. I'll start straightaway." And she hurried off to the kitchen.

Jenny got up, went again to the toilet, pulled on her robe, and wandered out to the kitchen to finish her tea, watching Pat rush back and forth. Disorganized. She was usually so effortlessly orderly in the kitchen. Now she was doing six things at once, looking plain scared.

"You're not worried about me or anything, are you, Pat?"

"No, no. Not at all. Will you have one egg or two?"

"Just one. Are there any sausages left? I could do them."

"They're on the broil," Pat said. Then looked doubtful and opened the oven door to have a look. As if to make sure she'd actually put them in there.

"Anything I can do to help?"

"No, nothing, dear. Nothing."

"I sure wouldn't mind being in Florida right now," Jenny said, thinking of the Bradleys. Down there with all those beaches, the sun. She went over to look out the window. Still snowing away. "Boy, oh boy! Look at it. There must be six feet of snow at least. You can't even see the cars." She laughed, delighted. "It's like wonderland. Come look, Pat! It's beautiful."

"I've seen," Pat said shortly, anxiously watching the eggs in the pan. She'd gone ahead and put in two when Jenny had said one. I can't think, have no idea what I'm doing. What will I do? "I can't imagine how they'll manage the snowplows."

"Boy, I wish I wasn't pregnant. I'd love to go down there, jump in the snow, make angels. We used to do that. D'you ever make angels? Lie in the snow and move our arms up and down, making an—" She stopped. Pat looked over to see her face had gone very tight, her eyes staring.

"What is it?" Pat asked as Jenny let out her breath and wiped her upper lip on the sleeve of her robe.

"Another one," Jenny said casually, once more looking out at the snow. "That one was eleven minutes. They're really all messed up." She doesn't know what's happening. Can that be? She's supposed to know about contractions, all of it.

The toast popped up. Pat visibly started. Shakily buttering the toast. Keeping busy, staying on the move. Too afraid to stop and find herself faced with this overwhelming reality.

"There you go, dear," she said, her voice as brittle and falsely bright as cheap glass. "Eat now before it goes cold."

Jenny said, "Oh, good," and sat down at the table, looking at the two eggs. Oh, well. Might as well eat them. She picked up her fork while Pat stood watching. Fear whispering to her. She smiled whenever Jenny looked up, praying none of it showed on her face.

Seven-thirty, the alarm went off. Gillian's hand shot out to turn it off. Gabe sleeping right through it. She slipped out of bed, taking care not to disturb him, and went to look out the window. Smiling, an expanding sensation inside, at the sight of the back garden completely lost beneath the still-falling snow. The trees. Branches heavily spread with snow. All of it blinding, brilliant. They'd have the day at home. She went into the bathroom, pushed her hair up under the shower cap, and took a long, long shower. Feeling marvelous. Exhilarated.

Not bothering with a bra, she pulled on her pants. A shirt, jeans, one of Gabe's sweaters on top. A pair of his woolen socks. And went shoeless through to the kitchen to start breakfast. They'd have it in the bedroom. On trays. Omelets, she decided. With bacon and mushrooms. Humming softly, she took down the omelet pan and set it to warm on the stove, turned the radio on low to get the weather report, the news. And smiled again at hearing everything was at a standstill, the city completely immobilized by the snow. With another four to six inches expected. "Lovely," she said to the radio. "We'll stay indoors for days. Days and days and days." Humming as she opened the refrigerator to get the eggs, the butter and bacon, the mushrooms. Pausing to stand motionless, breathing in the first truly contented lungfuls of air in her life. Then sang, "Food, glorious food," forgetting the lyrics, making them up as she cracked the eggs on the side of the bowl.

"Aren't you going to eat?" Jenny asked her.

"I'm not hungry, dear."

"You're not coming down with something or something, are you?"

"I shouldn't think so. I'll have a piece of toast a bit later on."

"Oh, boy. Here's another one." She gazed at the far wall throughout, then looked at her wristwatch. "Eight minutes. I wish I could be sure this is really it. Did it ever happen to you this way?"

"I'll just go have a wash," Pat said. "Have another cup of tea, dear."

She locked the bathroom door and stood grinding her hands together. Cursing herself. Thinking, You've done it good and proper now, you silly old fool. This is something you can't talk your way out of. You'll have to cope, handle this.

Gillian's eyes went to the ceiling, hearing them moving about upstairs. Considered inviting them down to breakfast. But no. Gabe was sleeping. Let him sleep for a change. He was always up so early in the morning. They could come down another morning. But not this morning. Not when he had so few chances to sleep late. Such a lovely, lovely morning. Glorious. All that whiteness, blinding. And more coming.

The pan was good and hot. The bacon draining on a paper towel, the mushrooms turning golden in the other pan. She started the first omelet.

"Up you get. I've brought you breakfast."

He sat up, rubbing his eyes as she set the tray down on his lap.

"Hey! This is fantastic, Gillie. What kind of omelets?"

"Bacon and mushroom."

"Fantastic." He unfolded his napkin. "Remind me to order snow again next week."

She sat down on the floor with her tray on the side of the bed. "They say on the wireless we're in a state of emergency. Everything's completely shut down. You must see outside. It's quite, quite beautiful. Your car has vanished. There's a long row of rounded objects up and down the street." She laughed happily.

"Wireless?" He bit into a piece of toast. "*Radio.* I'll go out later, start up the car just so the battery doesn't go dead. Say? Are you interested in hearing one of my better fantasies?"

"Yes, absolutely."

"You might not like it," he warned her.

"Perhaps I will."

"Well, okay. It has to do with cars, though."

"Carry on. I'm listening."

"A beautiful woman alone, driving a Mercedes four-fifty SEL."

She looked at him blankly. "Is that it?"

"Christ! Are you *kidding?* That's my top romantic/sexual fantasy."

"Seriously, Gabe?"

"Okay. I'll make it a two-thirty. It can be a two-thirty or a two-eighty. That doesn't matter. It's you in a Mercedes. Maybe wearing a mink."

"And not a stitch on underneath." She laughed.

"Hey! That's even better. Maybe I'll trade in the old tank, scout around for a good used two-thirty. So *you* can drive it. And I can get all turned on watching you climb out."

"I have a driving license, you know. A British one."

"You mean you *can* drive, after all?"

"I never said I couldn't drive. I simply said I didn't have any wish to."

"Well, anyway. What'll we do today?"

"Bloody nothing," she said. "You don't actually want to *do* anything, do you?"

"Jesus, no." He reached across and took a piece of her toast.

"Don't eat mine. Eat your own bloody toast."

"Yours tastes better. You probably put saltpeter on mine."

"I know what that is. Why on earth would I do a thing like that?"

"Never know."

Charlotte Vale Allen

"Daft bugger. Eat your own."

"You *did* put something on mine. I can tell by the way you're smirking."

"An aphrodisiac." She laughed. "It's in the butter."

"Jesus, you're beautiful."

"You're positively demented."

The contractions were starting to come closer together. Seven minutes, then nine. Five, then eight. Maybe, she thought, it'd be a good idea to go down, talk to Gillian. Pat was in the bedroom. Maybe she'd gone back to bed. Jenny put the door on the latch and went downstairs.

"Someone's at the door," Gabe said.

"I didn't hear anything."

"Want me to go?"

"You go and take your shower. I'll go."

She put the trays down on the coffee table and went to the door.

Jenny said, "Hi. Okay if I come in?"

"Of course. Is anything the matter?"

"I think so. That's why I thought I'd come down."

"Where's Pat?"

"In the bedroom."

"Come, keep me company in the kitchen while I clear these trays. Have you had breakfast?"

"I ate ages ago. The thing is, I'm having contractions."

"For how long?" Gillian put down the trays.

"Oh, hours. A long time."

"Close together?"

"Five or six minutes apart."

"Jenny, ring your obstetrician."

"I'm having it, aren't I?"

284

"From the sound of it, I would say you are. Use my telephone."

"Okay."

"I'll just be a moment. I want a word with Gabe. You go ahead, ring up."

She went through to the bathroom, knocked on the door. He opened it.

"What's up?"

"Jenny's having the baby."

"What? Right now?"

"Soon, I think. Her contractions are coming five or six minutes apart. She's got to go to the hospital."

"Gillian, everything's shut down. How in hell can we get her to the hospital?"

"An ambulance?"

"About the only thing that could get through that would be a tank. What do we do?"

"We'll have to do something. Let me go find out what her doctor has to say."

Jenny was standing, holding out the receiver. "Will you talk to him? He says he'd like to talk to you."

Gillian took the phone.

"This is Dr. MacCauley. I'm sure you know by now nothing's moving outdoors. We've got a little problem."

"I do realize that," she said, smiling reassuringly at Jenny.

"I understand you've had a child. Were you sedated?"

"No. It was a LeBoyer birth."

"Well that's a break. Think you can deliver a baby?"

She'd known he'd say that. Her hands were suddenly wet, her mouth dry. "I'm going to have to. Isn't that correct?"

"Afraid so. Anyone else there to help?"

"Yes, two more."

"Okay. First off, I'm going to give you my private number. And a list of things you'll need. You'd better write all this down."

"Yes. Hold the line a moment, would you?" To Jenny she said, "Get me a piece of paper, a pencil from the drawing board in the bedroom. There's a good girl."

As soon as Jenny left the room, she asked, "There won't be any complications, will there?"

"Shouldn't be. Everything's so far been absolutely normal. D'you have any idea at all how to tell if she's dilated?"

"My God. I haven't!"

"Okay. Just listen. Stay calm and I'll tell you exactly. Step by step. Okay?"

Jenny came back, holding out the pencil and paper.

"Yes, all right. I'm listening." Perspiration was trickling down her sides. She looked over at Jenny, who was sitting on the edge of the sofa, following Gillian's half of the conversation. Gillian smiled at her, then turned her attention to what the doctor was saying.

16.

She put down the telephone at last and looked again at Jenny. It didn't seem possible this was happening. But it was. The snow still floating past the windows. Jenny sitting, waiting to hear what the doctor had said.

"We're going to have to deliver the baby here," she said.

"Here? Boy! I had a feeling this was coming."

"Look, Jenny." Gillian sat down beside her on the sofa. "I had my baby at home. I wanted it that way. And think about it. Wouldn't you prefer to be having the baby here, with people who care about you, rather than at the hospital, where no one but your doctor knows you? Bearing a child isn't a surgical procedure. It's something perfectly natural. And we'd like to share it with you."

"I don't have too much choice," she said. Then was caught by another contraction and rode it out, holding on to the hand Gillian offered.

Charlotte Vale Allen

"They seem to be coming closer. You've been timing them?"

Jenny nodded.

"Pat's sleeping, you say?"

"I don't think so. She's just in the bedroom. I wish I could figure out what's been bringing her down so hard all this time. She just clams up every time I try to ask her what's wrong."

"There isn't time now to sit discussing it. We've got to start making preparations. Are you all right?"

"A little scared."

"There's not a thing to be scared about." She put her arm around Jenny's shoulders. "I'll tell you exactly what's happening. Each stage. It's really very exciting. Now you rest here. I've got to start collecting things. Gabe will be out in a minute or two and he'll stay with you while I get everything organized. You'll be all right here for a few minutes on your own?"

"Oh, sure. Is it going to hurt a lot?"

"Some. But you'll find you won't mind. Just think. You're finally going to get to see your baby."

Gabe was shaving. She closed the door and sat down on the lid of the toilet. "We're going to have to deliver the baby." She looked at her hands. They felt strange, looked huge. Surely not the sort of hands that could, with any effectiveness, bring a baby out of a woman. She'd have to cut her fingernails.

He turned to look at her. "We?"

"We've no choice. We can't get her out and the doctor can't get in. Could you pass me the nail scissors, please? Thank you. He's told me what to do, given me a list of things we'll need. I'll go in just a moment and start collecting up the various bits and pieces. I'm not at all sure I'll find all we have to have. We may have to do a

288

bit of improvising." She paused. "You will help, won't you? I really will need you."

"I guess I'm going to have to. What're you doing?"

"Trimming down my nails."

"Why?"

She passed back the scissors. "The emery board there? Thank you. I have to cut them," she said. "I've got to examine Jenny, see if she's dilated." How on earth, she thought, can I do all this?

"Internally?"

"It's the only way of knowing what stage she's at."

"Jesus!" he said, staring at her. The whole thing was suddenly assuming very scary proportions. "Doesn't the idea of it make you feel a little . . . peculiar? I mean, performing an internal . . . whatever . . . on another woman?"

"It makes me feel quite, quite indescribable. I daren't stop to think about it." She was quickly smoothing down her nails. "When you finish up in here, would you go out, sit with Jenny, time the contractions? You might even help her with the breathing. It's very simple. I'll do it for you now, show you how. Just remember to count, do it properly. We can't have you hyperventilating."

"Jesus!" he said again. "Okay. But what do we do if something goes wrong?"

"Her doctor assures me there's nothing will go wrong. But he did say that if it appears there's a problem, I'm to call him at once. He's ringing the police to put them on standby. He said he thought they might be able to get him through or bring Jenny out with a snowplow and is seeing about that. In the meanwhile he was quite sure we'd be able to handle it."

"Aren't you scared?"

"I'm bloody terrified. But rather excited, too. Mother

289

and I did the childbearing course together. Megan was a LeBoyer baby. Are you familiar with his methods? I'm going to try to do it that way. No bright lights or loud noises to frighten the baby. And it's wonderful seeing the baby come, Gabe. Didn't you see Craig born?"

"You've got to be kidding. Penny wanted out. *Out.* 'Give me a shot and get it over with.' She didn't even want me in the hospital, never mind the delivery room."

"Did you want to be there?"

"I . . . Sure I did!"

"Well, then, here's your chance."

"It's hardly the same thing."

"It doesn't really matter whose baby it is, Gabe. It's wonderful. And Jenny's not just anyone. She's a friend. More than a friend. I'd planned to go along with her to the hospital, told her I would. I'd have been with her in any case."

"You've got balls," he said. "You know that? You really do."

She ducked around him to return the emery board to the medicine cabinet. "One does what needs doing," she said. "I'm going up now to have a word with Pat. You'll hurry, won't you? I shouldn't like to leave Jenny on her own too long."

"Two minutes," he said, turning back to the mirror.

She went out. Nervous, trying to work too quickly, he nicked his chin. Balled up a piece of tissue and stuck it onto the cut. Rinsed his face, and hurriedly dressed. His movements so frenzied he nearly broke his leg trying to get his jeans on, pull them up.

Gillian knocked at the door. Getting no response, she tried the knob, opened the door, and went inside. After looking into the kitchen she went through to the bedroom, tapped at the door, and went in. Pat was sitting on the side of the bed. Looking very, very old and not at all herself.

"Are you ill?" Gillian asked.

Pat shook her head. "Weary," she said. "Old and weary."

"You're not old, Pat. Some women your age are. But you've never been. I wish you'd tell us what it is that's been bothering you so. We'd like to help."

Pat said nothing.

"Jenny's started. We're going to have to deliver the baby."

"You *can't*!" Pat looked at her questioningly. "Can you?"

"Of course we can," Gillian said calmly, sitting down beside her. "Babies are born at home every day. Jenny's perfectly healthy. The baby's a bit early. But aside from that, there's not a reason on earth why the three of us can't make the delivery."

"I couldn't. Not possibly."

"But surely you could, having had five of your own. And we really could use your help, Pat. I thought Gabe would help her through her contractions, do the breathing with her, and you'd assist me with the actual delivery."

"I'd be no use to you," Pat said. "None at all."

"I don't understand. Were you anesthetized for your births? Or were they cesareans?"

Pat turned her head away. "I've had no children," she confessed. "Not one. And I've never been *Mrs*. O'Brian. It's *Miss*. Miss O'Brian."

Gillian took hold of her hand. "Tell me about it, Pat," she said softly.

"It's a dreary story," Pat said, keeping her eyes averted. "Told far too often, heard too often. I was the one who stayed. To tend to the younger ones. And, at the last, to a tyrannical old man whose voice terrified me as a child, whose ludicrous Protestantism made me send away a man I dearly loved. But I stayed nevertheless. Duty-bound and intimidated for far too long, until it was much too late."

"He was a Catholic?" Gillian asked.

"Dr. Peter Flannigan. Loved only me, he claimed. Went off to become a medical missionary. And died in China at the age of thirty-seven. I read the obituary. A small piece in the newspaper. I had no courage. None at all. A small measure of defiance. Sweetening an hour here and there for grateful young soldiers during the war. In the sitting room. Directly below his bedroom. Retaliating by hurting myself. But I stayed. And then it was too late and I was too old to do more than sell up and come away to a new country.

"It was never my intention to create problems. The children just came to my mind, one by one. So clear to me. Their ways. But there's not a particle of truth to any of it."

"And that's why you've stopped seeing Walter," Gillian guessed. "Because you didn't want to tell him."

"I was gearing myself up to tell him, show myself for the fool I am."

"Oh, Pat," Gillian sighed. "How unhappy you must have been. I am sorry. Don't turn away, Pat." Gillian put her arm around her. "None of us would pass judgment on you. Not one of us would dare to. We've got too many tales of our own to tell. I've done some truly shocking things over the years. And told myself any number of stories to justify it all."

"But you had *reason*," Pat argued.

"No, Pat. I hadn't any reason. Self-pity. Because I was this way or that way. Because this happened or that. Because I was afraid and a drink or two was liquid courage and I could safely escape afterward. How could we condemn you for creating a family for yourself? I can't conceive of Jenny or Gabe or Walter—although I don't know him, but he appears to care very much for you—condemning you for something so human, so forgivable. None of that *matters*. What matters is right now. I care very much about you. And your having or not having five children doesn't in any way affect how I feel about you. I care because of you, the way you are, the way you've been. The rest of it simply does not matter. Right now we need you. Wouldn't you like to be there, see Jenny's baby born?"

"I would," she admitted. "I would."

"All right, then." Gillian smiled. "You get yourself dressed. And perhaps you'd have a look see if you've any of these things." She handed Pat the list.

"I've a tub," Pat said. "I've been putting things by for the baby, hoping Jenny would decide to keep it."

"Super. Gather up whatever you can find that's on the list, get dressed, and come down."

"You'll all think I'm a fool," Pat said warily.

"No." Gillian shook her head. "I promise you no. And why not think of this, Pat? You've got Jenny and Gabe and me. And another on the way. That's four. Someday Gabe and I will have a child and that'll make up your five. And there's Walter." She stood up. "I must hurry. Come along down as soon as you're ready. You don't happen to have the gloves, do you?"

"I believe I do."

"Good. Pat, none of that other matters. Believe me, it doesn't. What matters is how much you've done for

Jenny. And for me. Gabe, too. You've been generous, tolerant, so understanding. That's what matters. Your kindness. Your being there yesterday meant such a lot to me. You allowed me to hold on. You mothered me. And I've been needing that so. I've thought for such a long time that it was a question of getting through on one's own. Something having to do with self-reliance, independence. I'm not quite sure. But you and Jenny and Gabe have shown me closeness. All families aren't born together, Pat. I've learned these past months they're sometimes created. You'll hurry now, won't you?"

Gabe held Jenny's hand, his eyes following the second hand of his watch until Jenny exhaled noisily, saying, "That's it. Boy! That was a tough one."

He mopped her face with his handkerchief, smiling. "You're doing fine, Jen." Wondering, What in the hell am I doing? What are we all doing? It's all fine and well for some guy miles across town to say there'd be no problems but what were they supposed to do if some started happening? By the time that doctor arrived via snowplow Jenny could be dead. Or the baby. Jesus! He wanted Gillian to hurry up and come back. She seemed to have been gone for far too long.

She came through the door, asking, "How is it?" and at once he felt better.

Jenny smiled tiredly. "Okay. Is Pat all right?"

"She's just fine. She'll be down shortly."

"Did she tell you finally what's been bothering her?"

"It isn't anything serious. How often are they coming now?"

"About every four minutes," Gabe answered.

"Good. I'm going to ready the bed, then I'll be back. Don't forget to breathe with her, Gabe."

As she stripped the bed, she thought of Mother. Before the midwife came. Her hand on my breast, saying, "Are you awfully sore? You're so swollen. But once the baby's come and you've started nursing, you'll feel much better. Another one, darling? Hold my hand. Hold my hand."

All the things you did for me. With such caring, such a lack of pretense. Sitting beside me on the bed, watching me nurse Megan for the first time. Laughing softly, your hand stroking my arm. I loved you so much. Loved you both. And I must try now to think of how we lived, not how you died. I must think of that. Perhaps I will give Pat the diamond earrings. I think you'd have liked the idea of that. You'd have liked Pat. And Jenny, too. Gabe. Megan. You'd have liked seeing this new baby born. You'd have asked your hundreds of questions and watched every bit of it.

She closed her eyes tightly for a moment. Then opened them and kept going. Setting some newspapers and a clean sheet at the ready, in the hope that Jenny could be induced to get down off the bed. In the bathroom she located the small, sharp scissors. A belt and pad she'd put away in case she sometime ran out of tampons. She crossed items off the list one by one. Then went to the kitchen, cleared the counter and stove top, set a large pot of water on each of the front burners.

"Still okay?" she asked Jenny, returning to the living room. Seeing that Gabe had lost his look of nervousness.

"I'm getting tired," Jenny said. "This has been going on for ages."

"When did it start?" Gillian dropped down in front of her, taking hold of her hands. Small, soft hands.

"I don't know for sure. Maybe one or two o'clock. At

first I didn't think it was anything. But then, later on, my water broke. It's going to be all right, isn't it?"

"Fine, just fine. You're going to have to think about the baby and not about yourself, Jenny. If you're embarrassed, it's going to be just that much more difficult for all of us. Tell yourself it's natural, it's proper, and allow yourself to enjoy what's happening. You're young and strong, healthy. Your doctor says you should be able to do this easily."

"And you know how to do it all?"

"I think we'll manage."

Jenny's hands went tight around hers. Gillian told Gabe to time it.

"Don't fight it, Jenny. Relax, breathe, breathe. Nice and steady, now. Good girl."

"Whooo!" Jenny laughed, easing her grip on Gillian's hands. "They're getting bigger, closer."

Gabe said, "That was three minutes since the last one."

"Let's get you ready, now. Give you a wash, then you'll lie down."

"You're going to *wash* me?" Jenny's face turned bright red.

"Come along." Gillian laughed, getting to her feet. "Pretend I'm your mum."

"Oh, sure. Who does that make *him*, then?"

"Call me Dad." Gabe laughed. "Whatever turns you on."

"Boy, this is really weird. Why don't you just leave me in here for a couple of minutes? I can wash myself. I'd rather."

"Fair enough. But don't lock the door. In case you need help. I'll wait right here."

Boy oh boy oh boy. Jenny soaped the cloth, washed

between her legs, She giggled, rinsing out the cloth, starting to find the whole thing pretty funny. In the john with her nightgown up around her neck. Looking like one of those bad cartoon calendars. She dried herself, then had to wait out another contraction before opening the door.

"Come lie down, now." Gillian took her hand. "Find yourself a position that's comfortable. It shouldn't be too terribly long, now. Gabe's going to stay with you while Pat and I tend to a few things in the kitchen."

"Okay."

Gabe was sitting on the far side of the bed, plumping up the cushions.

"How do you feel?" he asked, looking as if he really cared. It made her want to cry. Going up and down like a seesaw. Finding everything funny one minute, ready to cry the next.

"Pretty good, I guess," she said, turning on her side. Facing him. It didn't feel too bad that way.

He had a damp cloth and wiped her face with it.

"That feels good, really good."

Another contraction and he held her hand, reminding her to "Breathe! Don't forget to breathe. That's right. Good, good." Then he stopped talking and breathed along with her, exhaling when she did.

"You having them, too?" she asked with a laugh as he sponged her face again.

"Feels like it." He smiled. Looking at her, thinking, You're so young. Just a kid. Thinking of New Year's Eve. How gay she'd been. How alive and open to everything. Enthusiastic, excited. He kissed her on the forehead. "It's going to be fine," he said. "I think you're terrific, kid."

"You do? Why?"

"Just because you are."

"Well, I think you are, too."

He squeezed her hand.

Everything that could be sterilized went into the pot. She turned on the burner, telling Pat, "Use the tongs when you take things out. Don't touch anything in there with your hands. We won't be needing any of it for a while yet. You're all right?"

"A bit jittery, but I'll do." She offered Gillian a quivery smile.

"You'll do indeed," Gillian said. Pat seemed to be shedding years now rapidly. Looking, sounding, and acting more like the Pat who'd come down those autumn mornings for breakfast. Erect and bright-eyed.

She went along with Gillian into the bedroom in time to see Jenny emerging from another contraction. Smiling, saying, "Are you okay now, Pat?"

"Perfectly fine. How are you, dear?"

"Pooped."

"Massage her belly, Gabe," Gillian said. "It helps. I'm going to see how far you've dilated, Jenny." This is it! Her stomach tumbling, then going hard.

Pat stood watching, having utterly no idea what to do.

Seeing, Gillian said, "Pat, why don't you come take over for Gabe while he readies the bath? I've already explained to Gabe, but I wanted to tell you and Jenny how it's to be. When it comes time, we're going to turn the lights down. And we'll all whisper. In order not to frighten the baby. It will be very dim in here, quiet. We'll speak very, very softly. After Jenny's had a look at the baby, a quick cuddle, baby will go into the tub. You'll see the most remarkable expression come over the baby's face. Megan actually smiled. It was quite, quite beautiful."

Both Pat and Jenny nodded earnestly, paying close attention to every word she said.

"All right now, Jenny." Wondering how all this could be happening, how she could be doing the things she was doing. "Lie back, bend your knees. And try not to be tense. I'll be very, very careful not to hurt you."

Jenny did as she'd been told, her eyes glued to Gillian's face as Gillian raised Jenny's nightgown.

Oh, God. She felt as if she was disintegrating inside as she pulled on the gloves, lubricated one, parted Jenny's knees. I can't do this. I must do this. Putting my hand inside another woman's body. I mustn't think of it that way. "Relax now," she said. "I don't want to hurt you."

Pat picked up the cloth and began bathing Jenny's face.

Gillian looked down. And suddenly it wasn't dreadful. We're the same, she thought. Exactly the same. There are no differences.

Jenny closed her eyes, telling herself to relax, feeling Gillian's fingers moving up into her. "It hurts," she said, instantly tensing her muscles.

"Steady now," Gillian said, placing her free hand firmly on Jenny's belly. "Ease up, relax."

Gillian waited until she felt Jenny's muscles relaxing. "It'll only take a moment," she said, trying to see with her fingers. Feeling. Finding. Minute movements of her fingertips, feeling the definition of the cervix. "You've started," she said, carefully withdrawing, patting Jenny on the knee. "You can put your legs down."

"How much?"

"I'd say three or four centimeters," Gillian guessed. "More than I'd expected. It won't be very much longer now. Massage her here, Pat." She directed Pat's hand down on Jenny's abdomen. "And when she has another contraction, remind her to breathe. Jenny, remember to keep it nice and steady. Gabe and I will be right back."

She went out to the kitchen, stripping off the gloves, hastily cleaning them. Gabe was filling the bath.

"Make it a little hotter than necessary. By the time the baby's come it should have cooled down to the right temperature. But we'll keep a pot of water at the boil in case I'm mistaken about the time."

"I'm impressed," he said. "The way you've taken over's just fantastic. As if you'd done this dozens of times before."

"I'm petrified," she said, resting against him for a moment. "But, Gabe, I'm the only one here who's had a child. The only one with any idea at all of what's to be expected."

"But what about Pat? Surely she knows."

"It's so sad." She lowered her voice. "It's why she's been acting so strangely, been so upset. She's never been married, never had any children. It was all an elaborate fantasy. And she's terribly ashamed."

"Oh, Jesus! That's really *sad*."

"Don't let on you know, will you? If she chooses to tell you, she will. I think she will. But she was upstairs sitting on the bed, so ashamed and frightened. It's why she sent Walter away."

"All those stories. The kids and the cute things they did. I thought it was kind of all too good to be true all five kids turned out doctors, engineers, what have you."

"You will be kind, won't you? She's been so good to us."

"What am I, Jack the Ripper? Haven't I always been
300

kind to little kids and ladies on the gentle side of forty?"
He ruffled her hair.

"You're kind to everyone. But she's so nervous. And I
don't want her to alarm Jenny. So would you go on back
now and keep the both of them happy?"

"Yes, chief. Okay, chief. Anything you say, chief."

"Oh, don't." She laughed. "I've got to find a clean
apron. And you've got to give your hands a good scrub-
bing. Get Pat to, as well. And no smoking. Have one out
here if you like. But we'll not be smoking now until it's
over."

"Anything else?"

"A kiss, please. To keep *me* happy."

"Yes, sir, chief." He kissed her, drawing her close.

"I love you." She wound her arms around him, taking
care not to let her hands touch him. "You're so good and
I love you so much."

"If it was you in there and not Jenny, I'd be very
damned excited right now," he said.

"I imagine you would."

"Are you planning to catch up on the pills?"

"I don't know. I need a little more time to think. And
I can't think at all just now."

"I know." He kissed the tip of her nose and released
her. "Where d'you want this tub?"

"I think the best place would be my board. Why don't
you clear everything off it, put down a towel, and set
the tub on that?"

"Okay, chief." He lifted the tub. "By the way," he
said, stopping in the doorway, water sloshing over the
side of the tub and down the front of his jeans. "I love
you, too. Can't say I'm too crazy about the bath I'm getting here. But the rest of it's just fantastic."

She found aprons for Gabe and Pat. Tied a handkerchief around Gabe's head. And a spare shower cap for Pat. Jenny, between contractions, looked at the three of them and began laughing.

"You look like bakery workers or something. It gives me the feeling I'm about to deliver a ten-pound sponge cake here."

Even Pat laughed.

The contractions were coming about a minute apart. Gillian did a quick last-minute check to make sure everything was ready, then came back, saying, "I want to have another look, Jenny. If you're starting a contraction, tell me and I'll wait."

"I'm starting," Jenny groaned, bearing down heavily on Gabe's hand. He mopped her forehead, crooning, "Okay, okay."

Pat, feeling useful, massaged Jenny's abdomen.

Gillian looked at the window, trying to concentrate on what she could feel inside Jenny. "I think you're fully dilated," she said, withdrawing her hand. "Things are going to happen rather quickly now, Jenny. I'll get you swabbed down."

Using a wad of cotton—all as the the doctor had instructed—she coated Jenny's upper thighs and lower belly with the iodine. For what purpose she couldn't be sure. Something vaguely to do with antisepsis. But he'd said to do it, so she did.

"Are you comfortable, Jenny?" she asked, disposing of the cotton.

Jenny shot her a look that said, You must be kidding! then went off in another contraction.

"What should I do?" Pat asked.

"You come around down here by me. I'll let you know as we go on."

Gabe took over the massaging. Amazed at how hard and taut Jenny's belly was. The contractions making it even harder. He could feel the mound shifting down under his hand when she underwent a contraction. And was getting caught up in an accelerating excitement. Feeling so involved, so much a part of Jenny. A part of them all.

Gillian came around to sit on the near side of the bed, stroking Jenny's cheek.

"We're going to get down to the final stage in a moment and there's something I'd like you to try. You needn't do it. But when I delivered Megan, the midwife had me squat on the floor. It was easier that way. At least, I found it so. I think you'd find it easier, too. Would you be willing to try, Jenny?"

"What? You mean on my hands and knees?" She wanted to say more but had to get through another contraction first. Gabe wiping her face with the cloth.

"Not quite," Gillian said, smiling. "It isn't a terribly dignified position. But infinitely more practical and less painful. Gravity lends a hand. Will you try? You don't have to."

"Oh, I don't *care*," she moaned. "I feel like I want to push."

"Try to hold off for just a few more moments. Let's get this nightgown off, then we'll help you down."

Gabe supported Jenny and Gillian removed the nightgown. Pat stood at the foot of the bed, watching. Extraordinarily elated, rejuvenated.

"Here comes another one!" Jenny cried, throwing her hand out to Gabe.

She strained back against him and he had to remind her to breathe, doing it with her, feeling her hand loosen as the contraction passed. Then he and Gillian helped her down onto the floor.

"If you lean back against the foot of the bed, you'll be able to brace yourself. Hold on to Gabe for support. That's right. Now, we all have to remember we're going to be very, very quiet once the baby starts to come. After you've delivered the placenta, you'll be able to lie down again. Only a few more minutes and it will be all done. The baby's crowning," she explained as the next contraction pushed the top of the baby's head into view. "Once the head begins coming through, the rest'll happen very, very quickly. You'll have a look at the baby, then another contraction or two, the placenta will come. Then you'll get to rest and watch the baby have its bath."

"I've got to *push!*" Jenny cried. "Have to!" The most enormous need to exert every last ounce of her strength.

"Go ahead. Push!" Gillian told her.

Her face crimson, she held her breath, pushing. Gillian, crouched on the floor before her, holding Jenny's thighs open with both hands. "Next time," she said, keeping one hand on the inside of Jenny's thigh. "Another good push or two and we've got it. You're doing beautifully. Don't forget to breathe this time. Here we go again. *Breathe.* Nice and light. High in the chest. Huh-huh-huh. Keep going. Push! Come on, a nice big push, now."

"*It's not a sponge cake,*" Jenny cried in a strangled voice, her face contorted. "*It's a bowling ball.*"

"Here we come." Gillian's hand cradling the emerging crown. "Keep it coming. Push, push!" She had the baby's head in the palm of her hand now. Pat was down on her knees, open-mouthed. "Give a great big one now," Gillian said excitedly as the baby's shoulders squeezed through. "A little bit more. Here we go. Here we *go!*" Jenny heaved. Astonished, Pat saw Jenny's belly collapse as, in a rush of blood and fluid, the baby came slithering into Gillian's hands. Pat laughed softly, tears springing from her eyes. "It's a girl." Gillian laughed quietly behind her handkerchief. "A beautiful little girl."

She cleaned the interior of the baby's mouth, then held her up for all of them to see, whispering, "Pat, we need the towel now." Pat spread the towel across her lap, ready to receive the baby. Gillian laid the baby down on Pat's lap, whispering, "Hold her still now, Pat, while I see to Jenny." Gabe and Jenny laughing, covering their mouths with their hands. Their eyes glittering.

All just the way the doctor had said it would be. Two more contractions and the placenta was delivered. Then, as Pat moved along with the baby, Gabe got Jenny back on the bed on top of several towels while Pat placed the baby on Jenny's middle.

"Right," Gillian whispered. "The scissors now, Pat. Don't forget to use the tongs. And the thread." She got to her feet, her thigh muscles aching from remaining for so long in one position. Walking around the side of the bed. "Isn't she beautiful?" she whispered to Jenny, who was beaming, gingerly touching the baby's face. Gabe, helping to hold the baby steady, looked ecstatic. "It's fantastic," he said softly. "Absolutely fantastic."

Pat returned with the scissors and handed them to Gillian, who said, "I'm going to milk the cord back. Like that. I know you don't like it, baby, but it won't be another minute. Tie it off down here with the thread. There we go. Cut the cord. And that's it. All ready for the bath."

She disposed of the cord, then whispered, "Bring the baby, Pat."

Three sets of hands cautiously lowering the now-squealing baby into the warm water.

"Watch her face," Gillian told them. "Watch!" Removing her gloves, waving the water gently over the baby, cleaning her, witnessing the look of blissful serenity that overtook the baby's face, the crying stopping at once. "Isn't it lovely, baby? We'll get you all cleaned up and then you'll have a visit with your mother. Here," she said, relinquishing her position to Gabe. "Very gently, very slowly, bathe her. I'll see to Jenny."

Still caught up in the technicalities, she cleaned Jenny, put on the belt and pad, got her back into the nightgown, then straightened. Jenny leaning on her elbows, watching Gabe and Pat bathing the baby. All Gillian's control simply evaporating, she got down on her knees beside the bed, putting her arms around Jenny. Holding her, loving her.

"I've got a little girl." Jenny laughed, hugging her. "I can't believe it. Mine! A baby girl. I can't wait to tell Bobby. He'll go bananas."

"What will you call her?" Gillian asked, studying her radiant face.

"Anne. I like that name. Don't you?"

"It's a lovely name. *You're* lovely, Jenny. You were wonderful. It wasn't too terrible, was it?"

"It wasn't terrible at all," she said, keeping her voice down. "I'm really glad now it happened this way. With everybody here."

"And me. Lie back now and rest for a few minutes. Then we'll bring Anne to you."

Pat was happily humming, rinsing the baby's sparse growth of black hair, looking as if she'd gladly keep on for days. Clean now, the baby lay placidly in the crook of Gabe's arm, half asleep.

"Hate to do it," Gillian whispered, "but you're to come out now." Pat lifted the baby out into the towel Gillian had waiting. And for just a moment, holding the baby, she experienced the same profound feeling of joy she'd known holding Megan for the first time. It rippled all through her, so intense, total. And she thought, I do want a baby. I do. Want it all again.

Clad in a vest and disposable diaper, loosely wrapped in one of the receiving blankets Pat had provided from her cache of surprises, Gabe presented Anne to Jenny, who eagerly held out her arms, laughing again. Gillian stood by, ready to help, but Jenny didn't need any help.

"Look," Jenny whispered. "She knows just what to do. And she's really hungry."

Gabe put his hand on Pat's shoulder. "How are you doing, Pat?" he asked.

"Isn't it marvelous," she said, awed. "Simply marvelous."

Gillian picked up the newspaper and its contents, the soiled towels. Carried the newspaper out to the trash. Skipped downstairs to the cellar to put the towels into the sink, sprinkle some prewash over them, then fill the sink with cold water. Feeling exhausted now, desperately in need of a rest, her arms and legs trembling with loss of tension as she climbed the stairs, went inside to the kitchen to take off her delivery paraphernalia. She leaned against the counter, lighting a cigarette.

Pat came in briskly, back to her old self again, saying, "I'll go up and make some sandwiches. I expect everyone's good and hungry. I'll be down directly."

"You did beautifully, Pat. Thank you for being here to help."

"It was a rare privilege. I feel as if I just might sleep tonight. I'll not be long." She smiled and went off. Thinking, I must tell Walter.

Gabe came in and leaned against the counter beside her, tucking her hair back behind her ears, then taking a puff of her cigarette. "They're both asleep," he said. "Looking so nice, the two of them. Jesus! It was fantastic."

"She's named her, nursed her. Now they're asleep together. She'll keep the baby."

"Looks that way." He smiled, returning the cigarette.

"I'm so glad," she said, starting to cry.

"Why're you crying, love?"

"I'm just so tired."

"That was hard work for everybody," he said, putting out her cigarette, then drawing her head down on his shoulder. "Don't you ever let me hear you apologizing for yourself. Not ever again. You're beautiful and . . . beautiful."

"So're you," she sniffed. "I think I'm going to have to lie down. I feel a bit queasy now."

"That presents a little problem," he said. "We can't move Jenny and the baby. And both of us can't sleep in one of Pat's twin beds. Nor can we politely ask her to give up her bedroom. Which leaves us the floor in the living room."

"Fine. I'm quite happy to take the floor."

"Okay," he said. "Let's go lie down. I could use a nap myself."

"But Pat's gone up to make some lunch."

"So when she brings it, we'll eat," he said, grabbing two of the pillows from the sofa. "Everybody down!"

"Oh, Gabe," she sighed, settling herself against him. "It *was* lovely, wasn't it?"

"It certainly was." He tucked his free arm under his head, his eyes suddenly heavy. "Next time around, we'll know what we're doing."

"Hmmm."

"Hmmm indeed."

"I forgot to ring the doctor, let him know."

"You can call him later. I'm sure he's figured it out by now that everything worked out just fine."

"I'm so happy," she murmured, her arm across his chest.

"Me, too." He closed his eyes, resting his cheek against the top of her head. Her hair so thick, soft.

"Walter, Jenny's had her baby. I thought you'd like to know."

"That's wonderful. A boy or a girl?"

"A girl. Walter, I have a great number of things to tell you. I'm not quite sure where to begin."

"Begin wherever you like. Just answer me one thing. Would you like Barbados or St. Lucia?"

"I don't know. Either. You'll have to decide."

He laughed. For a long time. And then he said, "I'm coming to see you."

"How on earth do you think you're going to manage that?"

"For you I could do anything. Later this afternoon. I'll be there."

Pat came in, saw the two asleep on the floor, and tip-toed through to the kitchen to set the tray down on the table. Then went silently back to the bedroom to stand looking at Jenny and the baby. Smiling, a very full feeling inside.

The children, she thought, returning to the living

room. All the children. Isn't it grand? Let them all sleep, she thought, settling in the armchair, easing off her shoes. Time enough to eat, celebrate, later on. I'll just close my eyes for a minute. It feels so good to sit down. He'll manage it, she thought, and smiled. He'll get here. She sighed, sinking a bit lower into the chair. Sleep easing its way through her.

About the Author

Charlotte Vale Allen is the author of eleven novels, among them LOVE LIFE, HIDDEN MEANINGS, MEET ME IN TIME, and RUNNING AWAY. Born in Toronto, Canada, she now lives in Darien, Connecticut, with her young daughter.

Other Bestsellers from SIGNET

☐ MISTRESS OF OAKHURST—Book II by Walter Reed Johnson. (#J8253—$1.95)

☐ OAKHURST—Book I by Walter Reed Johnson. (#J7874—$1.95)

☐ THE RAGING WINDS OF HEAVEN by June Shiplett. (#J8213—$1.95)*

☐ THE TODAY SHOW by Robert Metz. (#E8214—$2.25)

☐ HEAT by Arthur Herzog. (#J8115—$1.95)*

☐ THE SWARM by Arthur Herzog. (#E8079—$2.25)

☐ BEWARE MY HEART by Glenna Finley. (#W8217—$1.50)*

☐ I CAME TO THE HIGHLANDS by Velda Johnston. (#J8218—$1.95)*

☐ THE SERGEANT MAJOR'S DAUGHTER by Sheila Walsh. (#E8220—$1.75)

☐ BLOCKBUSTER by Stephen Barlay. (#E8111—$2.25)*

☐ BALLET! by Tom Murphy. (#E8112—$2.25)*

☐ THE LADY SERENA by Jeanne Duval. (#E8163—$2.25)*

☐ LOVING STRANGERS by Jack Mayfield. (#J8216—$1.95)*

☐ BORN TO WIN by Muriel James and Dorothy Jongeward. (#E8169—$2.50)*

☐ BORROWED PLUMES by Roseleen Milne. (#E8113—$1.75)

☐ ROGUE'S MISTRESS by Constance Gluyas. (#E8339—$2.25)

☐ SAVAGE EDEN by Constance Gluyas. (#E8338—$2.25)

☐ WOMAN OF FURY by Constance Gluyas. (#E8075—$2.25)*

☐ BEYOND THE MALE MYTH by Anthony Pietropinto, M.D., and Jacqueline Simenauer. (#E8076—$2.50)

*Price slightly higher in Canada

More SIGNET Big Bestsellers You'll Want to Read